Waterhole

3/1/12

To Jack + Diane,

I'm hoping anyone with the surname of Masterson might enjoy reading a western novel. Good luck with your book, Jack, I enjoyed reading about it in the newspaper.

Best wishes,

[signature]

Waterhole

a western saga

Kurt Adkins

abbott press®
A DIVISION OF WRITER'S DIGEST

Waterhole
a western saga

Copyright © 2011 Kurt Robert Adkins

All rights reserved. No part of this book may be used or reproduced by any means, graphic, electronic, or mechanical, including photocopying, recording, taping or by any information storage retrieval system without the written permission of the publisher except in the case of brief quotations embodied in critical articles and reviews.

Abbott Press books may be ordered through booksellers or by contacting:

Abbott Press
1663 Liberty Drive
Bloomington, IN 47403
www.abbottpress.com
Phone: 1-866-697-5310

Because of the dynamic nature of the Internet, any web addresses or links contained in this book may have changed since publication and may no longer be valid. The views expressed in this work are solely those of the author and do not necessarily reflect the views of the publisher, and the publisher hereby disclaims any responsibility for them.

Any people depicted in stock imagery provided by Thinkstock are models, and such images are being used for illustrative purposes only.

Certain stock imagery © Thinkstock.

ISBN: 978-1-4582-0047-1 (sc)
ISBN: 978-1-4582-0046-4 (e)

Library of Congress Control Number: 2011915139

Printed in the United States of America

Abbott Press rev. date: 09/13/2011

Contents

Acknowledgements vii

Part 1: *Dodge City, Kansas, 1878* 1

Part 2: *Oklahoma Territory, 1884* 21

Part 3: *Waterhole, Arizona, 1885* 51

Part 4: *Oklahoma Territory, 1885* 90

Part 5: *St. Mary's College, California, 1890* 121

Part 6: *Bar-CJ Ranch, Oklahoma Territory, 1893* 186

Part 7: *San Francisco, California, November 1896* 200

Epilogue 235

Acknowledgements

I'd like to thank my sons, Jake & Kyle, my friend and colleague, Linn Kissinger, and my in-laws, Don and Diana Miller, for reading early versions of my manuscript. The feedback they provided and the editing they did was invaluable to my being able to complete this project.

For my favorite reader, Christa

"It was a hard land, and it bred hard men to hard ways."

—Louis L'Amour

Part I

Dodge City, Kansas, 1878

"Pa, how much longer we gotta' dig this ditch?" Cole asked. "You gotta' do more than give it a lick and a promise," replied his father, Clint, to his six year old son, "or you'll be there all night long. Maybe you shoulda' got yerself some quality help, instead of that young 'slinger over there," Clint said with a smile as he nodded towards Cole's best friend, Chad Henry, who was practicing his quick draw with a short piece of a willow tree branch.

Cole Herbert and Chad Henry shared more than just the same initials. They were born just eight days apart, and their parents came to Dodge City in 1871 when the Buffalo trade was centered here. Both fathers had once been Buffalo hunters, right after the War Between the States. For as long as they could remember, they had been best friends.

Chad smiled as he pulled the stick from his belt, aiming his weapon at Clint.

"Better holster that stick, young un, or I'll show you how my pa used to use it against my backside," advised Clint, his thick, sandy-colored eyebrows raised.

"Okay, Mr. Herbert. I can't help it, I want to be a deputy for Marshall Masterson, like you and Joshua Rines and Wyatt Earp and the Marshall's brother, Sheriff Bat."

"Well, that's an honorable goal, but I'm pretty sure that Ed likes his deputies a bit older than six years old," replied Clint.

"Pa, when you gettin' back this time?" asked Cole.

"Hard to say boy, depends on the weather, partly," said Clint. "Take care of yer ma. Expect I'll see you in a few days, week at the most."

Clint walked up the path to his small, two room house on the edge of town. Most of the house was taken up by the main room, which included the kitchen, eating area and living room, with a glass window overlooking the front porch. A separate bedroom was shared by Clint and his wife, Katherine, while Cole slept in the loft above the living room, on the opposite end of the house from the bedroom. The house was clean and sparse. The Herbert's didn't want for much, nor did they have it.

"Gotta go now, Katherine," Clint told his wife, in a soft, I'll-miss-you-type of voice.

"Tell that Ed and the others to make this a quick posse, so you can get back home before that big storm hits," scolded Katherine, playfully. She lifted her chin, letting her long golden hair fall far down her back and looked up at Clint as they put their arms around each other.

"Be safe, and bring them thievin' robbers back for trial," she added with a tone of authority.

"Sure thing, Marshall," smiled Clint as he gave her a short, but firm kiss on the lips, and a quick, playful slap on her backside. "Be back in a few days, likely," he said with his back to Katherine as he walked out the front door, onto the porch that overlooked the town from the west.

Far down the dustless street, Clint could see the rest of the posse on horses, waiting to ride. Clint mounted his tall pinto he called Lula, after Katherine's mother, which she always shook her head about to express her disapproval.

"Bye, Katherine, see ya boys," sounded Clint as he rode down the street to join the posse.

Cole joined his mother at her side as they watched Clint trot down the street, away from them. It had been a while since he last rode off with a posse, but whenever Ed Masterson needed someone, he turned first to Clint and Joshua Rines for help. Both would be on the posse, along with Bat Masterson, sheriff of Dodge City, and Wyatt Earp. Wyatt had just returned to town July past, after a short stint in Deadwood of the Dakota Territory.

It was a cold January morning, as the group of five men rode out, headed south, towards the Indian Territory.

* * *

Two nights gone, Cole was asleep in his loft when Katherine woke up in a daze to a strange sound. She rolled over and turned toward the bedroom door, but before she could focus her eyes she was hit on the back of her head, rendering her unconscious.

Cole woke up early the next morning, like always, and went out to collect the chicken eggs and feed the small bay pony that Clint had brought home for him a few months earlier, which was corralled up behind the house.

When Cole returned to the house, he called out, "ma, when we gonna' eat, I wanna' go over to Chad's. We's gonna go see if we can help clean out the jail cells afore pa and the others get back."

There was no answer.

"Ma?" Cole called out again, as he walked across the room and knocked on her bedroom door. "You awake, ma?" he called out. With no answer, Cole slowly opened the door and called her name once more, while his eyes scanned from one side of the room to the other. She was not there.

Cole could not remember a time when his mother was not waiting for him, breakfast ready, once he had completed his chores. He went outside, stood on the porch and called her name again. Still no answer. Concerned, but not worried, Cole walked off towards Chad's house to see if his ma went there. Chad's ma had been ailing. His pa had been killed when Chad was four-years old by a drunken cowboy. Clint shot and killed his friend's murderer. Katherine took to looking after her. Cole knocked, and Chad answered.

"I'm lookin' for my ma, she here, Chad?" asked Cole.

"Naw, haven't seen her this mornin'. Could use her though, my ma's really ailing today," responded Chad.

Cole looked around Chad to see Mrs. Henry lying flat on a bed in a corner of the one room house the two Henrys' shared.

"Hope you're feelin' better soon, Mrs. Henry," greeted Cole, as he reached to tip his hat, realizing he had forgotten to put it on, "I'll send ma over when I find her," he finished. Mrs. Henry nodded back and gave a small smile in return.

"I can't find my ma, Chad, I ain't never known her to be gone when it's meal time," Cole fretted.

"I gotta help my ma right now," said Chad, "but if she gets to feelin' a better, I'll come help ya."

"I'm beginnin' to feel all balled up." Cole sounded worried to Chad. "I don't know where else to look. It's too early for any stores to be open for her. What should I do?"

"You're welcome to take a meal with us, but I ain't much of a cook, like your ma," offered Chad, "she makes the best bear signs I ever ate!"

"Thanks," said a somber Cole, "but I better keep on a lookin'. See ya, Chad."

"See ya, Cole."

Cole spent the rest of the morning looking for his mother, but she was nowhere to be found. Cole went over to Martha Rines' house. Her husband, Joshua, was his father's best friend. The Rines had no children of their own, and Martha had always taken a liking to Cole.

"Mrs. Rines, I can't find my ma," a now exasperated Cole cried.

"Come in, boy, come in," said Mrs. Rines. "What in tarnation are you goin' on about . . . where is your ma?"

"I don't know, ma'am. I woke up and gathered the eggs and fed the pony, then went in the house and I ain't seen her all day." Cole's voice was now shaking and tears welled in his eyes.

"Have you walked through town to look?" asked Mrs. Rines.

"No, ma'am, I ain't allowed in town by myself."

The storm that had been expected was beginning to blow into Dodge City.

"Come, boy, lets you and me go in together. We'll find her," directed Mrs. Rines.

* * *

With the rain beginning to fall, Clint Herbert and Joshua Rines walked right into the front of the camp where three holdup men were sitting and drinking. Earp and the Mastersons were waiting on the backside in case the thieves made a run for it.

As good and well earned as Wyatt Earp, and Bat and Ed Mastersons' reputations were, they all knew that Joshua Rines was the fastest gun in the bunch, faster than any of them had ever seen, including Bill Hickok and Doc Holiday. Clint had nerves of steel, could stare down those he chased, and was better than most with his gun, but Joshua was the fastest.

"Whatcha got there, boys?" Joshua spoke as he and Clint broke off in different directions upon entering the camp.

The outlaws had been drinking and their senses were not quite together. They hadn't heard Joshua and Clint approach the camp. One of the surprised men was compelled to reach for his gun, but Clint, who was standing close by quickly put the butt of his Remington New Model Army .44 across the side of the man's head. Blood began to flow as the injured outlaw grabbed his injury with his left hand and let out an expletive, directed at Clint. Another outlaw had his gun strapped to his side, and tried to draw on Joshua. His barrel never cleared its holster. Joshua drew and shot the man square in the middle of his chest, dropping him instantly. The third man threw his hands up.

As the gunfire rang out, Earp and the Mastersons entered the backside of the camp, guns drawn. But the gunplay had ended. Ed Masterson had begun directing his deputies to tie up the captured men, when they heard a rustling back where they had left their horses. Clint took off running in the direction of the noise, and as he arrived, he saw a fourth outlaw, one who had not been in camp, but out relieving himself in the trees, riding away at a full gallop atop his horse, Lula. He had scattered the other horses to give himself time to get away.

Clint retreated to the camp where the others were joined, marched straight to the man who had thrown his hands up, and threw a right cross that landed on the outlaw's chin, knocking the man to the muddy ground.

"I'm going to ask you just one time," Clint coldly stated with a dead eyed stare. "Give me the name of the man who just rode off on my horse."

"Who?" the outlaw asked with a sly smile as he rubbed his jaw.

Clint did not ask again. He stepped forward towards the man who had begun to lift himself off the ground. Clint delivered a kick to his groin, sending the man into the fetal position, rolling and groaning on the ground. After a minute, the man glanced up at Clint and as he did, Clint began moving towards him again.

"No! Wait!" the outlaw hollered. "Billy Thatcher, his name's Billy Thatcher."

A name that Clint would not forget.

It took a couple of hours before the posse could round up the rest of their horses. With Clint's horse stolen, he now rode the horse of the dead outlaw, with the dead man's body slung across the saddle horn of one of the other captured men's horses.

They were on their way back to Dodge City.

* * *

Katherine's hands were bound and her mouth covered by a rolled up handkerchief, pulled tightly so it separated her mouth and set against the back of her teeth. While she could make noise, none of it was comprehendible, and when she tried, she was smacked across the head. It had been three days now since she was captured. They traveled by night to avoid being seen. She rode in front on the horse, her captor riding behind her. There was no saddle, but an Indian blanket that rested between her and the horse they both shared. Her head still occasionally ached from where she had been hit the night she was taken from home. She was grateful that Cole was left to sleep in the house and had not also been taken. Katherine did not know if Cole was undetected up in the loft, or had purposefully been left behind. Either way, she was grateful.

Indians raids had occurred frequently in Kansas during recent years, but were beginning to die down a bit. Most raids were made by a larger band of Indians, and usually resulted in killings and scalpings. Katherine did not know why this lone Indian had taken her. He did not seem intent on killing her. Maybe, she thought, she was to be his squaw, a thought that made her feel queasy. She knew that Clint would look for her as soon as he got home. It was that thought that kept her somewhat peaceful.

* * *

A hard rain was coming down when Clint rode into Dodge City with the rest of the posse and their prey, late on the ninth day of their trip. Ed and Bat Masterson led the two surviving outlaws into the jail, while Wyatt took the dead man over to the undertaker on the horse he was strapped to, then was headed off to Texas to inquire about a job in Fort Worth. Clint and Joshua knew their jobs were done and trotted their horses towards home. Cole was at the Rines' house, taking supper as he had for each of the past seven nights when he heard the horses ride up outside. He jumped up out of his chair and ran for the door.

"Pa!" he cried out, as he ran to Clint and threw his arms around him. This was not a typical reception for Clint and he immediately sensed something was wrong.

Martha Rines had followed Cole outside and stood on the porch as she looked at Joshua and gave him a look that confirmed there was a problem. Joshua stood quietly, waiting to hear what had happened. Clint looked up at Martha, then at Joshua, then back to Cole.

"What is it, boy? Where's your ma?" pressed Clint.

"I don't know, pa, she ain't been seen for pert near a week now," answered Cole.

A puzzled expression adorned Clint's face as he looked up to the porch and asked Martha, "What's happened? Where's Katherine?"

"Don't know, Clint. Cole woke up one morning after you'd been gone a couple of days, and she warn't in the house. She ain't been seen anywhere. That kid deputy that Ed Masterson left in charge while you was gone tried looking around and outside of town, but there's no sign of her. The rain washed away any tracks that there might have been. Don't know if she was taken or went somewhere on her own," finished Martha.

"She wouldn't leave Cole home alone, Martha, you know that," said Clint.

Nothing needed to be said, but Clint, Joshua and Martha suspected Katherine's disappearance was not voluntary.

"Been any Indian sightings in the area?" asked Clint.

"None we've heard about," answered Martha.

"Any other problems with outlaws, or any strangers seen in town while we been gone?" Joshua asked Martha.

"Nope," she responded.

While he hugged Cole, Clint and Joshua held a steady gaze between them. They had known each other too long to have to talk openly about what to do. Both knew that they would begin their search for Katherine as soon as they had a chance to grab some fresh gear, swallow a quick meal, and saddle three fresh horses, one for each of them, and one for Katherine.

* * *

Where are you taking me!?" Katherine screamed at her captor.

Waterhole

The Indian looked at her with out speaking. He had made enough comments for her to know that he knew how to speak English, and he certainly understood her questions. But he did not answer. They had been traveling south, Katherine knew that by the sun always rising from their left and setting on their right. Now that they were in what she assumed to be the Indian Territory, they were traveling by day. After the Indian Territory, would come Texas, then Mexico. If she was not to be his squaw, then what?

Katherine's long blond hair was now full of dust. It had been more than a week since she had fully bathed, the night before Clint left with the posse. Her pale blue eyes were beginning to develop worry lines around them as was her forehead. Her soft white skin was becoming blistered and dirty. Her five foot, five inch frame was weltering in the daily, hot sun. They had left the storm behind by the third day of captivity. Her hourglass figure was keeping its shape, but losing pounds. She was being fed and had plenty of water, but the traveling was nonetheless physically excruciating for her.

After close to an hour of silence, the Indian said, "Texas."

Katherine looked at him and repeated, "Texas. What about Texas?"

The Indian did not respond.

* * *

"I wanna' go with you, pa!" a determined Cole Herbert stated.

"I know you do, son, and I appreciate it, as would your ma. But you need to be here in case she returns before we get back. And Mrs. Rines will need you to be the man of her house while Joshua is with me," said Clint.

"Find her, pa, please find her," pleaded Cole.

Clint gave him a smile as he sat atop his borrowed horse, one of Joshua's, then reached down and patted him on top of his brown hair. "Don't forget to care for the chickens and your pony each day," reminded Clint, "and help Mrs. Rines with her chores too."

"Okay, pa."

"It could be a long trip, Cole," said Clint, "but I'll be back when I can."

Clint and Joshua dug their heels into their horses and began to gallop off.

"Which way do we go?" asked Joshua.

Clint shook his head. "Don't know where to start, but we won't finish until we've looked everywhere. Might as well start by looking the direction we're heading, east."

* * *

Katherine was pretty sure she had been in Texas for days, but they continued to travel south. Now out of the Indian Territory, they were traveling by night again. She knew the Texas Rangers would not take kindly to an Indian traveling with a white woman, and her captor was taking great lengths to avoid them at all costs.

As near as Katherine could figure, it had been close to three weeks since her capture. There were some days they didn't travel, and they were holed up in a cave for a while, to rest and hide she suspected, so she couldn't be sure.

"Tomorrow," the Indian said.

"What about tomorrow?" Katherine answered.

He tied her up as he did every time he was to sleep. If she was to make noise, he would hear her, and he would slit her throat he had told her. Believing him, she slept quietly.

The next day they rode into the first town Katherine had seen since leaving Dodge City. She determined it was somewhere near the Mexican border, but on which side she could not be sure. It was a dirty and apparently lawless town she concluded, as she watched a man being drug by his heels, through cactus, tied to the back of a horse through town. He was dead before they untied him. A couple of young Mexican boys fought over his boots.

"Ah, my good Indian friend," greeted a stoutly built man as her captor dismounted from his horse and pulled Katherine down behind him.

"It has been a long time," the stoutly man added as his eyes were cast on Katherine. "And what do we have here?" he asked.

"Five hundred," the Indian answered.

"Five hundred!" the stoutly man answered in a booming voice.

After a few seconds pause, the stoutly man burst out in laughter.

"Of course, my Indian friend, five hundred dollars for the beautiful lady is a fair price indeed," he followed.

Katherine became aware for the first time of her fate. She had been captured and brought to Texas to be sold.

* * *

Clint Herbert and Joshua Rines had served in the War Between the States, fighting on the side of the Union. Both men had been raised in Ohio, about 50 miles apart. It wasn't until they enlisted in the 70th Ohio Infantry, however, that they met.

They had enlisted in February 1862 as young idealists, Clint at age 18, Joshua two years older. They stayed with the regiment, marching to Kentucky, Tennessee, and on through Georgia as part of General Sherman's Atlanta campaign. They fought in the Carolinas and Virginia, before finally mustering out with the regiment in Arkansas in August 1865, Clint as a sergeant, Joshua as a corporal.

Clint had grown into a broad shouldered, sandy color-haired man with blue eyes, who stood an even six feet tall, and carried 185 pounds on his strong body. Joshua had a slighter frame on a taller body. He measured a tall 6'2" and weighed 170 pounds. His hair and eyes were both brown, and he wore a thick, longish mustache.

"How long you gonna keep holstering that army pistol of yours?" Joshua asked Clint one night as they sat around a campfire about 20 miles northeast of Jefferson City, Missouri. They had been searching for Katherine for more than six weeks now.

"Still serves me well," answered Clint. He had been growing shorter on words the longer they searched for his wife.

"You know they don't even make them things any more, don't you?" Joshua teased. "Stopped about three years ago I believe."

"As long as they make caps and balls for it, I reckon I'll keep using it," surmised Clint.

While faster to the draw than his friend, Joshua always admired the calmness that Clint maintained whenever he had to draw his pistol. With the eight inch barrel on his Remington New Model Army .44, Clint was a deadlier marksman than Joshua. He always out shot him when they held their private contests, but not one to boast, few people besides Joshua were aware of how accurate a shot Clint was.

Now 34 years of age, Clint's mind was on Katherine as he and Joshua drank their coffee on that cold March evening. "You know, Josh," began Clint, "Katherine will be 28 years old next week. I've been in love with her since I first laid eyes on her during that square dance back in '68, you remember?"

Joshua remembered, and he was glad that Clint was talking. It was back in Ohio, where they settled after the war ended. Joshua had married Martha within weeks of returning in September 1865, the two of them having been childhood sweethearts. It was a July 4th dance, and Martha and Joshua practically dragged Clint with them. Reluctantly, Clint went, and after leaning against the barn wall most of the night, 18 year old Katherine Adams approached Clint when he wasn't looking, and gently grasped his hand, gave a little tug towards the dance floor, and asked him to dance. Although Clint must have stepped on Katherine's toes every third time he moved a foot, they fell in love that night, and were wed five months later. Clint and Katherine moved to Dodge City in 1871, followed a year later by Martha and Joshua.

"I don't know who's responsible for all this, Joshua, but somebody's going to die for it before its all done," warned Clint.

"Whatever it takes, Clint. However long it takes," said Joshua as he sipped from his now tepid cup of coffee.

* * *

Salvador Gregorio was a tall, stoutly built, physically strong man of 39 years. He wore quality Mexican clothes, and liked to keep a small brimmed sombrero over his balding head. He was rich, cruel and ruthless. After paying $500 for his new woman, he asked her for her name. Katherine did not answer. Gregorio smiled, then smacked her across the face. His smile never changed.

"When I ask you a question, senora, you will answer. Your name please?" Gregorio asked again.

After a slight pause, Katherine responded. "My name is Katherine," she told him.

"Katherine. A beautiful name for a beautiful lady. But I think I will call you Kate," Gregorio informed her.

"It's not Kate, it's Katherine," she scowled in response.

Gregorio slapped her again, this time hard enough to knock her to the floor of his lavishly decorated, single story casa.

"I think it will be Kate," he stated bluntly. "I do not care what your last name is, or was. From now on, you will simply be known as my Kate. And you may call me Salvador, a name I will not permit anyone else to call me. It will be just between us."

"What I call you to your face and what I call you behind your back are likely to be two different names," Katherine told him as she stood back up.

Gregorio hit her with a closed fist this time, again knocking her down and drawing blood from her mouth. He once again smiled as he turned and left the room. She heard the door lock behind him.

For the first time since being kidnapped, Katherine felt a sense of hopelessness. *Oh Clint, she thought to herself, where are you?*

* * *

Cole was a big help to Martha Rines while he stayed with her. He also spent many a day playing with Chad Henry, but Chad, even at age six, could see a difference in his friend. He was no longer happy and full of energy. He was now often sullen, and lacked his mischievousness, a quality both boys shared and which had gotten them into trouble their fair share of the time.

"When's your pa comin' back?" asked Chad one April morning while the boys sat at the shore of a nearby creek, trying to catch supper.

"Don't rightly know," Cole sighed.

"I knows he'll be alright, why your pa and Joshua Rines, there ain't nobody they couldn't catch," claimed Chad.

A proud smile crossed Cole's face, but Chad didn't see it as Cole was staring down at the ground.

"Think he'll find your ma?" inquired Chad.

"I expect so," said Cole, "but sometimes I don't know what to think."

Chad nodded his head as the boys watched their fishing poles dangle in the shallow creek bed.

* * *

Sal Gregorio was forming a small, private army in southern Texas, which he, as best Katherine could decipher, planned to take and use somewhere else for personal gain. She did not know where. Gregorio was intent on making Katherine his woman. He did not care about marriage, or any legal formality. Gregorio took what he wanted, and anyone who resisted was killed. So far, Katherine had been able to refute his advances, but she knew the time would come that she would have to comply or be killed. Gregorio had been so involved in recruiting and forming his army, that he had given little attention to her. But she knew that would soon change, as he was nearly completed with his mission.

Gregorio's top hand in Texas was a comanchero called Coyote Jim. He appeared to be part Indian and part Mexican. She had seen how the others in Gregorio's army gave way when Coyote Jim walked toward them. He stood just short of six feet tall and looked wiry strong. But it wasn't his physical strength they feared, it was his use of the Bowie knife he wore in a sheath on his right hip. Katherine overheard two men discussing Coyote Jim's claim to having killed 14 men with the Bowie knife.

About a week earlier Katherine had seen another man who seemed to be in favor with Gregorio. A 5'7" scrawny looking red-haired man with a derby hat. He carried two pistols on his belt. She saw him ride out one day and hadn't seen him since.

* * *

It was now August. Winter and spring had both come and gone, and soon, so too would summer. Clint and Joshua had been away from home for seven and a half months. They'd sent wires to Martha whenever they could, letting her know where they were and how they were getting along. The two men had covered parts or all of 12 states or territories. Not once had they learned of any information that would help them find Katherine. No one had seen or heard of her.

It was mid-August when Clint woke up one morning in the Wyoming territory. Joshua was still asleep. Clint sat on his bedroll thinking about Katherine and Cole. Joshua woke minutes later, sat up and looked over at Clint.

"What ya thinkin' about?" Joshua asked his friend.

There was silence for a long minute before Clint answered. "It's time to get home."

Clint never thought he'd hear those words come out of his mouth until he had found Katherine. But it had been nearly eight months of searching, without a clue. He didn't know whether to think if she was alive or dead. And he had Cole waiting back home, a son that needed to be raised.

"Let's go home, Josh," Clint repeated.

Without another spoken word for the next hundred miles, the two men broke camp and headed for Dodge City. Joshua led the way with Clint riding behind him, pulling the third horse. The one with the empty saddle.

* * *

Sal Gregorio's army was assembled and ready to move on his orders. It was early September, and he wanted to travel towards his destination during the coolness of autumn, but arrive well before winter set in. They would leave the next day.

That evening, Gregorio entered Katherine's room. "Good evening, Kate," he offered in a gentlemanly manner. "We will be leaving tomorrow, I will have one of my servants help you pack this evening. The journey will be long."

"Where are we going?" asked Katherine.

"To a small town in northern Arizona, near the Colorado River. A place called Waterhole. I hear they have found gold there, and are in need of . . . how should I put it . . . of civic leadership." Gregorio sounded proud as he made his statement. "But before we go, there is something we must do."

"What?" asked Katherine bluntly, afraid she already knew what the answer would be.

"It is time for you to become my woman," said Gregorio.

Katherine's heart raced and chills sped throughout her body. She had known this day would come and she had tried her best to put it out of her mind, but she now must make a choice. Refute Gregorio and she would be killed, she knew and accepted that. If she complied, she may not be able to live with herself. She knew Clint would understand whichever decision she made, but when she thought of Cole, she knew she couldn't risk never seeing him again.

Gregorio sat down at the foot of her bed. Katherine stood in a far away corner of the room. "Come sit next to me, Kate," Gregorio asked, as he patted the space on the bed next to him. Katherine found it hard to swallow as she slowly moved towards the bed. She sat down, leaving a three foot distance between them. Gregorio laughed.

"I think you will enjoy our time together, Kate," Gregorio promised, as he reached out and ripped at the dress she was wearing. His strong hand tore away the front of her dress, exposing her undergarments. Gregorio smiled. Katherine now found it hard to breathe. She was gasping as she sat frozen in fear. Gregorio moved closer to her and pulled her to him so they sat side by side.

"Tonight, my golden haired beauty," Gregorio told her, "you will make me a happy man."

* * *

Clint and Joshua arrived in Dodge City within 15 days of leaving the Wyoming territory. They had wanted to make the trip home quicker, but Clint found himself wrestling with what to tell Cole. This slowed them down as they neared the Kansas border.

It was late at night when they arrived at the Rines' house. Cole was asleep. Martha met the two men on the front porch, and gave a long hard hug to Joshua. Then she turned toward Clint and gave him an equally hard and long hug. She took them both by the hand, and stood between them on the porch, too choked up to speak, as she alternated glances from one to the other. So as not to wake Cole, they sat out on the porch. Martha brought them some coffee and biscuits.

After a while, Martha opened the discussion. "I'm sorry, Clint."

Clint just nodded, head hung down between his shoulders.

Joshua asked, "any news to report since we've been gone?"

"I guess you haven't heard," Martha started, "Ed Masterson was killed back in April. Terrible thing. Wyatt came back and was named Assistant Marshall in Dodge. He's talking about goin' to the Arizona territory to do some law work, but he ain't gone yet. Bat is taking over for Ed, along with their brother, Jim."

"Ed was a good man," Joshua stated.

"Oh, and Clint, I'm sorry to have to tell you that Chad Henry's ma passed on in June. His mother's sister came out from Boston to take him back to live with her. Losing Chad has been extra hard on Cole, with Katherine gone, and you . . ." Martha did not know how to finish.

"It's gonna be hard to face the boy in the mornin'," Clint muttered, "I've failed him, I couldn't find his ma for him."

"You stop that talk right now, Clint Herbert," scolded Martha. "You did everything you could have, and more than most men would've even 'tempted to do."

Clint sat stone silent as he listened to Martha. She was a good friend.

"'Bout time I sleep next to someone who doesn't snore, partner," Joshua chided Clint, "and in a feather bed, too."

Martha gave a smile to her husband, then poked him with her elbow.

"How 'bout you, Clint, you want to sleep inside tonight?" asked Joshua.

"Naw, I think I'll set up a spell. I got some explainin' to do in the morning and I want to think on it some more. You both go on to bed. I'll head home in a little while and be back before Cole wakes up in the mornin'," Clint finished.

Joshua put his arm around Martha and they proceeded quietly back inside their house, closing the door softly so as not to wake Cole.

Clint sat silently for a long time. "I'm sorry, Katherine," Clint eventually said, looking up to the night sky. As he did so, tears ran down his stubbled face.

* * *

Sal Gregorio's army was small, smaller than Katherine had imagined it would be. It totaled 12 men, along with three servants and Katherine. Having found comfort in Katherine's company almost nightly since they left Texas three weeks ago, Gregorio was at ease with her, and spoke openly of his plans.

Katherine, however, felt as though she had become another person, one who was detached from her soul. She feared getting pregnant by the sick bastard, Gregorio, and tried not to think of anything but Clint and Cole whenever she could. She continued to hope that Clint would one day find her and take her home.

Gregorio and his men were headed to a small town in northern Arizona called Waterhole. It was a new town, just sprung up due to a gold strike nearby. It had a town-appointed lawman, but Gregorio had sent two men on ahead to help remedy that situation. One man was the red-haired Irishman she saw in Texas, Archie, they called him. She didn't know who the other man was, but they were to entice the sheriff into a fight, and kill him. When Gregorio arrived, he would offer his assistance in forming a new town council to replace the dead sheriff. Gregorio's plan included running the town and appointing his own sheriff. Then he would slowly gain control of all of the business in Waterhole. In a mining town, that promised to be a lucrative operation. Gregorio looked forward to having an out of the way town where no law could touch him. That, and a good woman to serve him.

* * *

Spring of 1879 came early. Katherine had been gone for 14 months now. It had been a hard winter for Clint and Cole. Both had kept their distance from other folk, even the Rines, and it had been that way ever since Cole woke up to Clint's return last September, and discovered that his ma had not been found. Cole felt a tremendous pain all winter in his stomach. Clint carried a tremendous burden of guilt for having failed to find Katherine.

After weeks of discussion, Clint and Cole decided to leave Dodge City and get a new start elsewhere. Emotionally, it was too hard to remain in Katherine's house without her there.

In mid-March, Clint packed the wagon. He said his goodbyes to Wyatt and Bat before stopping in front of Joshua and Martha's house. Clint couldn't climb down. He just sat up in the buckboard, reigns in hand, looking at his feet. Cole ran to the door to announce their departure.

Joshua and Martha stepped out on the front porch. Clint continued to sit motionless.

"Where ya headin'?" asked Martha.

"Oklahoma territory, I reckon'," answered Clint. "I thought I'd try my hand at ranchin'. Sold the house to the bank. Gave me a fair price, enough to get us started."

Joshua stood by Martha, but had not joined in the conversation. After many years of friendship, especially the seven and a half months looking for Katherine, there wasn't much to be said.

"Gotta go," Clint announced.

Joshua stepped off the porch and walked over to where Clint was sitting atop the wagon. He reached up with his right hand. Clint reached down and grasped it firmly. They held their handshake for what seemed like forever to an observant Cole. Clint nodded, as did Joshua, as they broke their grasp.

"Take care, Clint," Joshua said, "take care of your pa, Cole," he added.

"You too," said Clint. "Goodbye Martha."

Martha waved and broke into tears as Clint and Cole started down the street in their wagon. Both Clint's new horse and Cole's pony were tied behind the wagon.

They would begin a new life elsewhere. One without Katherine.

Part II

Oklahoma Territory, 1884

"I never could figure out why you named that bay "Slinger," a puzzled Clint asked his son, Cole. The two Herberts were sitting on the porch of their ranch, following an evening supper. Clint in his big, hand made rocker, Cole on the top step of the porch.

"Doncha 'member, pa, that's what you used to call Chad Henry when he'd practice his quick draw with a stick from a bush or a tree," responded Cole. "The name reminds me of good times; a good friend and a good place."

Clint took in a big sigh, then let it out as he maintained a slow but steady rocking motion with his chair. He nodded his head. "Good times, good memories," he added.

It had been six years since the Herbert men moved to the Oklahoma territory. Cole was now 12 years old and beginning to grow like a weed. Clint had taken to homestead a 160 acre ranch for a ten dollar fee. Most of the good land was taken up back in 1862 when the Homestead Act was passed by the federal government, but being so close to the Indian Territory, Clint found this site available and acceptable. And with no neighbors to homestead near them, Clint and Cole had thousands of adjoining acres to use as free range for their cattle to graze. This was where he and Cole started a small herd of cattle. They'd drive their herd to Kansas every couple of years, and stop in to visit with the Rines. Joshua, still a part time deputy, spent most of his time as a fix-it man around town. He specialized as a gunsmith. Martha was aging quickly. She was now 42 years of age, same as Joshua, but it showed more on her.

"When we goin' to Kansas again, pa?" Cole asked.

"No plans in the near future, son. Herd won't be big enough for more than another year."

"We ain't seen Joshua in near four years, since he was gone deputyin' the last time we was through," reminded Cole.

"Yep, but we did get to see Martha, and taste some of that delicious homemade apple pie of hers, didn't we?" Clint said.

Cole smiled in response.

"Pa," Cole began to speak. Clint could see he had something on his mind, which usually meant questions about Katherine.

"Yeah, son?" he inquired.

"How often do you think about ma?" Cole could not look at Clint when he spoke of his mother. It was an uneasy subject for both of them.

"Same as when you asked me last, son, every day."

"Ya ever think we might find her someday?" wondered Cole.

"I hope so, son, but I've learned that thinking that way will drive a man crazy. We do what we can do," said Clint.

Cole pondered what his father had said. He didn't quite understand it, but somehow it comforted him nonetheless.

* * *

Waterhole, Arizona had become a booming mining town. Since Sal Gregorio arrived six years earlier, he had slowly taken control of all key business ventures; the general store, the hotel and saloon, the land & deed office, and most importantly, the sheriff's office. And once he had control, he did not allow for any competition. Waterhole was a monopoly for Gregorio.

Taking control turned out to be a simple matter. Gregorio's two henchmen arrived in town in late October 1878, just weeks before Gregorio arrived with his army. After taking inventory of the town, Gregorio's men killed the sheriff one crisp, fall night. Shot eight times while he slept in his bed. There were no witnesses, including the dance hall girl found dead in his bed also. She had been shot twice, once through each eye.

Since there was no town council at the time, residents were in a quandary over what to do about replacing the sheriff. When Gregorio arrived, he called a meeting of the town's citizens. Without wasting time, once they were assembled in the town hall, Gregorio stood and nominated his man to be the new sheriff of Waterhole. He had been one of the two who had killed the former sheriff. Gregorio's small army of 14 men had been fanned out around the town hall, and posed a menacing and intimidating site to the town folk. Gregorio had Katherine seated next to him.

"Do I hear a second to my nomination?" asked Gregorio loudly. Nobody moved.

"I second the nomination," laughed red-haired Archie, as he swigged on a whiskey bottle following the slurring of his second.

"Do we have any discussion?" Gregorio proposed, though he was hardly asking a question.

"Yeah," said a small, scrappy looking miner leaning against a side wall of the town hall, "I have something to say. I don't know who you are mister, nor your group of thugs you brought with you, but I say we need to offer up more candidates for sheriff for us to consider. Someone we know and can trust."

Gregorio looked over to the comanchero, Coyote Jim, who drew his Bowie knife and threw it through the crowded room, striking the miner in his right shoulder with such force that it pinned him against the wall. The room was full of gasps and shrieks, followed by silence, as Coyote Jim walked slowly and deliberately towards the old miner, maintaining eye contact with him the whole way. The miner was in a state of shock when Coyote Jim reached him. He placed his left hand on the wall behind the miner's head, and with his right hand, he pulled the knife out of the miner's shoulder. The man let out a terrifying scream as the knife vacated his shoulder. Coyote Jim wiped the blood from his knife blade across the miner's pants leg, then in an upward motion, drove the Bowie knife up through the miner's stomach. The force of the blow lifted the miner into the air. He was dead before his feet hit the ground. Coyote Jim again withdrew the knife, and wiped it on the dress of a frightened young lady, frozen by fear, standing next to where the miner fell.

Without missing a beat, Gregorio mockingly asked, "do we have any more discussion? Okay then, all in favor of my man here as your new sheriff, say, 'aye.'"

There was a scattering of 'ayes' throughout the town hall.

"All opposed?" asked Gregorio. The room remained deathly silent.

"Ah, good, a unanimous decision!" sounded a pleased Gregorio. "Please join me in congratulating your new town sheriff, Billy Thatcher!"

* * *

"Now exhale and squeeze," Clint instructed Cole.

The shot from Clint's pistol rang out but missed its mark, a bottle sitting on a fallen tree log, 25 feet away. "Try again, Cole, but remember to squeeze, don't jerk the trigger," Clint said. Cole's next shot hit its mark, shattering the bottle.

"Finally," Cole exclaimed, "It only took about 12 shots for me to hit something."

"Actually, you hit something every time," Clint said smiling, "just not what you were aiming at."

"You try, pa, show me how."

Clint loaded the pistol, and raised the barrel. "See that broken tree branch out yonder on that big oak?" asked Clint.

"Yes sir, I see it," Cole replied.

The pistol fired, surprising Cole that it was shot so quickly. Though he blinked, Cole found the target in time to see the tree branch fall to the ground.

"Wow, pa, that was a great shot!" hollered Cole.

"A gun's just another tool, Cole," Clint warned, "learn to use it and treat it with respect and it can be good to you when you need it."

"How come you only got the one gun, pa? I know that the Masterson's and others have a lot of them, including rifles," Cole asked.

"When I was your age," Clint began, "my pa didn't believe in guns being anything but a killer. He blamed the weapon, not the man who used it. He'd seen his brother shot by accident and killed when he was a boy, and he never had use for them after that. He passed his thoughts on to me when I was growing up."

"How'd you get so good at shootin'?" asked Cole.

"When I enlisted in the war, they gave me this gun, and I figured I'd better know how to use it," answered Clint. "So I practiced every day after we stopped marching. It seemed to be one of those things I had a knack for learning quickly, like you and shoveling manure," Clint finished, explaining with a smile.

Cole had been listening so intently, it took him a minute to realize that Clint was teasing him. He looked at his father and smiled.

Clint rarely wore his army pistol anymore. Since he gave up deputying, he only wore it when traveling away from home, but never on the ranch. It was a part of his life he left behind, along with Katherine.

As Clint and Cole walked back towards the ranch house, Clint asked, "Cole, I never asked you about the day your ma went missing. Is there anything you remember about that day that seemed different?"

"No, pa, I've tried hard to 'member if I saw somethin' or heard somethin', but I don't. I'm sorry, pa. I hope it warn't my fault that she left or got taken."

"Nothin' for you to be sorry about, son, and rest assured, your ma would never have left on her own, not with you in the house. She loved you somethin' fierce. I don't know what happened, but I do know she wouldn't have left you."

This was the longest conversation they'd shared about Katherine since they arrived in the Oklahoma territory six years earlier. Finally, their pain was subsiding enough for them to be able to talk about her.

* * *

Billy Thatcher had been the sheriff of Waterhole for going on six years. The position, in reality, was to be Sal Gregorio's hired gun. Thatcher took his orders directly from Gregorio. During his six years as sheriff, he had killed five men, and run another dozen out of town on trumped up charges so Gregorio could confiscate their land or mining claims.

The 28 year old Thatcher was small in stature, about 5'8" and weighed 145 pounds. He wore his dark, scraggly hair shoulder length. He was left handed, and very quick on the draw. Thatcher was not going to intimidate anyone physically, but his gun scared people into submission. Few had chosen to defy Gregorio or Thatcher.

Thatcher had joined Gregorio's army in March of 1878, when he rode into that Texas border town on Clint's horse, Lula. The horse had been ridden so hard that when Thatcher arrived in the small Texas town, he dismounted, pulled his pistol, and shot Lula through the head, right there on the street. Gregorio had witnessed the incident, and when he asked Thatcher why he shot the horse, Thatcher replied, "so no one could steal it from me." Gregorio didn't understand the logic, but his instincts told him that this man was wanted by the law, and had a mean streak that could serve well in his army.

Two days later, Thatcher drew on two men who had accused him of cheating in a poker game. He fired twice and left the two men dead. Again Gregorio witnessed the occurrence, and he asked Thatcher if indeed he was cheating. Thatcher's one word response was accompanied with a smile. "Yeah," he said. Gregorio hired Thatcher on that evening, with the promise to make him a sheriff.

Promise fulfilled.

Waterhole

* * *

Katherine had now been Gregorio's woman for half of Cole's lifetime. As the years passed, Gregorio began to tire of her, and he added other, younger women into his stable. Katherine had become nothing more than window dressing by 1884. She was grateful to have avoided becoming pregnant, but her involuntary involvement with Gregorio over the years had taken a tremendous emotional toll on her. As part of his mining operation, Gregorio had brought Chinese miners to Waterhole, with promises to make them rich. They became his slave labor. As Waterhole continued to grow, other Chinese arrived and established opium dens. After hearing of the effects of the opium, Katherine began to visit them to help her forget her situation. She had given up hope of ever being rescued by Clint. It had been so many years now. The opium became her solace. She had become addicted. Her addiction showed by making her unable to communicate for long periods, and helped her envision dreams that were surreal. Though she was 34 years of age now, she looked more than ten years older. Because Gregorio had her painted up most of the time, Katherine could somewhat hide the effects of the opium. Gregorio knew about Katherine's addiction, but he didn't concern himself with it. She was still in his control, and that was all that mattered to him.

* * *

Cole continued to practice shooting his father's pistol, not regularly, as ammunition cost money, but often enough to be comfortable with the weapon. He had also grown proficient as a rider. Helping Clint with the cattle daily had made him quite the horseman. Cole felt as comfortable atop Slinger as he did walking on his own two feet.

It was a bright, chilly late October morning. Clint was mending a broken board in the corral, and Cole was handling his *specialty*, as his pa called it, shoveling manure. The Herbert's were about finished with their chores and were ready for some lunch when they heard the sound of horses coming up the road. Clint removed his handkerchief from his back pocket, took off his hat and wiped his sweaty brow. He glanced in the direction of the noise down the road. Cole walked around the corral over near his father and they both viewed the small wagon approaching, a single driver sitting up top, being pulled by a pair of weary looking horses. It took a few more minutes for the wagon to reach the ranch house, where Clint and Cole walked up and welcomed the elderly man handling the reigns.

"Howdy," greeted the man.

"Howdy," returned Clint, "name's Clint Herbert, this here's my son, Cole."

"Mornin'," Cole said as he tipped his hat.

"Looks like you've traveled a ways," noticed Clint.

"Yep, been on the road for a couple of months. Don't make time like I did when I was younger. Been out Arizona way doing some mining," told the visitor.

"Any luck," asked Clint.

"Might have found a small vein, but I was quickly encouraged to leave it behind by the sheriff. Told me to move on," said the visitor.

"That don't sound right," commented Cole.

"No, son, it ain't, but in Waterhole, you do what the sheriff says, which is the same thing as what Sal Gregorio says, or you don't live long enough for it to matter much," finished the visitor.

"You look beat, mister," said Clint, "care to sit a spell and take a meal with us? You're welcome to."

"Sounds like a good idea to me," the visitor replied. "By the way, name's Leroy McAlister."

"Welcome, Mr. McAlister," said a smiling Cole, "I'll take care of your horses for you while you sit a spell."

"Thank you, Cole," a grateful Leroy told him.

Clint and Leroy McAlister walked up on towards the house where, on the way Clint grabbed a bucketful of water from the well for McAlister to wash up in.

"Sure feels good to get this trail dust off of my dry, wrinkled skin," McAlister told Clint as the two men proceeded to sit on the front porch, Clint in his rocker, McAlister in a sittin' chair Clint had built the week prior.

"We aren't much for fancy meals around here, Mr. McAlister," Clint told him.

"Please, call me Leroy, and I'll call you Clint. I'm too old to pay much attention to formalities," Leroy offered. "And food is food, doesn't have to be pretty to fill your belly."

Cole had watered McAlister's horses, and given them some grain and hay. As he approached the house, Clint asked him to slice off some of the beef they had in the house for them to chew on.

"Where you headed, Leroy?" asked Clint.

"Don't rightly know," answered Leroy. "I'd done some ranchin' before I set out to gold minin'. Don't have no family, so I'm just movin' along until I find someplace to set for a spell. Have a little money saved up. Enough to keep me goin' 'til I find a place to settle."

"You're welcome to stay here long as you need," Clint told McAlister. "Don't have room inside, but the barn has a nice soft hayloft that'll keep you warm."

"Appreciate the hospitality," thanked McAlister, "I reckon I'll stay tonight and see what tomorrow brings."

* * *

Red-haired Archie was the kind of person that few tolerated and even fewer liked. He was an Irishman who paraded around in his derby hat and always wore his two pistols, worn cross-over style on his belt. He had made a reputation as a heavy drinker and a backshooter. Nobody had ever seen him face up to anyone in a fight, but he was credited with having shot eight men, in the back, to settle quarrels he had had with them. His last name was unknown, but due to his propensity for heavy alcohol consumption, he was always on a bender. Bender became identified as his last name. He proudly carried a folded up wanted poster of him from the state of Arkansas, offering a $2,500 reward for the capture of Irishman Archie Bender.

He wasn't a big man. Maybe 5'7", and a thin 138 pounds. Not being willing and able to physically match up to his loudmouth made him easily unlikable, even by those he worked with. One of Gregorio's men got into an argument with him one evening over a girl in the saloon. The man nearly beat Bender senseless. The man was found dead the next morning, backshot, with a note pinned to his back with a knife. The note said, *I think she'll choose me now.*

Bender liked to claim that he was a member of the infamous Kansas family of serial killers known as the Bloody Benders. They had been credited with murdering around two dozen people before fleeing Kansas in the early 1870's. Most people didn't believe the connection, but it added to the mystery about his real identity.

Even Gregorio despised Bender as a person. He was loud mouthed, a result of always being drunk, but he served a purpose, and he had no sense of morality or fair play, which came in handy at times for Gregorio's purpose. Gregorio couldn't trust him like he did Thatcher, or Coyote Jim. Those two sold out to the highest bidder, who was Gregorio. Due to his state of drunkenness, Gregorio couldn't always be sure where Archie Bender's loyalties laid.

As frightened as the citizens of Waterhole were of Billy Thatcher and Coyote Jim, Archie Bender made them restless in a different way. Once the sun set, Billy Thatcher and Coyote Jim's duties were usually done for the day. With Archie Bender, however, Gregorio would send him around at night if he wanted a task addressed without much visible attention given to it by witnesses. Since his arrival in Waterhole, three citizens, all of whom had something Gregorio wanted, had been found backshot early in the morning. It had become such an epidemic that nobody dared to walk the streets at night, preferring to remain behind the locked doors of their homes. Miners slept with their guns loaded and handy. Many had gotten dogs to serve as alarms of unwanted strangers.

Despite the control that Gregorio had over the town, the news of gold in Waterhole continued to bring fortune seekers coming, which in turn, made Gregorio even richer.

* * *

Clint woke early the next morning, like always about the same time as the sun did. After buckling his pants and pulling on his boots, he heard a chopping sound from outside. He opened the front door and walked out onto the porch. Off to his left, about halfway between the house and the barn, Leroy McAlister was chopping wood.

"Mornin'!" Clint hollered.

Leroy McAlister slowly stood and straightened out his back, letting the axe drop to his side, one hand still on the handle.

"And I thought I was an early starter," Clint called out.

"Well," a half out of breath McAlister answered, "I figure a man's got to work for his supper. Saw this pile of wood and figured I'd help out."

"Appreciate it," Clint told him. "Soon as Cole takes care of the animals, he'll fry us up some ham and eggs. You hungry?"

"Hungry enough to eat a whole hog if it's set before me," called out McAlister.

Clint smiled, turned around and walked back inside the ranch house. It was a cold fall morning. Winter appeared to be on its way early this year. Clint lit a fire in the fireplace, then stood and watched as it caught on. As he stood, he looked at the picture sitting on top of the fireplace. It was a picture of Katherine, taken on their wedding day. Clint sighed heavily, and felt his heart jump a little, like it did each time he thought about his wife. He missed her terribly.

Cole had risen when Clint did, and was now through with milking the cows, collecting eggs and feeding the horses. The cattle took care of themselves on the range.

"Ham 'n eggs, Pa?" Cole asked

"Sure," he replied softly, still looking at Katherine's picture.

The door opened again, and McAlister walked in. He was carrying a stack of freshly split firewood. "This'll keep us warm for a while," he said.

Clint motioned in the direction of the wood holder for McAlister to place the wood down. After unloading his arms, McAlister stood next to Clint and looked at Katherine's picture.

"Pretty lady," he said. "Mind if I ask who she is?"

"Her name's Katherine, she's my wife, Cole's ma," answered Clint.

"She pass on?" asked McAlister.

Clint took a deep breath and held it slightly before letting it out.

"Don't rightly know where she is," Clint told a confused McAlister.

An inquisitive and perplexed look shown on McAlister's face, but he did not know how to respond to what Clint had said.

"I was on a posse around seven years ago come January. Katherine and Cole were home. Cole woke up one morning and she was gone. We ain't never seen her since," Clint explained.

"Pa looked for her with Joshua Rines for near eight months, but found 'nary a clue 'bout where she was," Cole added.

McAlister saw how much hurt there was in the Herbert's, so he didn't ask if maybe she'd run off.

"Happen here, her missing and all?" he did ask.

"Nah, back in Kansas. Dodge City," Clint said. "We settled here about six years ago to get a fresh start."

McAlister studied the picture as he stood next to Clint. "Yes, sir," he spoke randomly, "very pretty indeed."

* * *

"How you feeling today, Martha?" asked Joshua Rines.

"'Bout like yesterday, Joshua," she answered, "I don't think I'm gonna get better."

Joshua knelt beside her as she laid in bed, holding her hand and burying his chin in his chest so Martha could not see his worried face. She did not need to see it, she knew.

"Doc says he'll stop by later today to check in on you," Joshua offered encouragingly. Martha smiled. It had become increasingly harder to talk over the past two months. She knew she had what they called cancer. The doctor had told Martha that he was not good enough to operate on it, and it might not do any good even to try. He could give her laudanum to dull the pain, but that was all he could offer.

Joshua stood up and went to look out the window. Winter had come and gone, and spring was just arriving. It was a balmy March morning of 1885.

"Looks like it'll be a nice day, Martha. Maybe we could go for a buggy ride later today, if you're feeling up to it." Joshua waited for Martha's response. It did not come. Joshua turned around and looked at his wife. She was gone.

* * *

It had been going on six months since Leroy McAlister made his way to the Herbert's ranch. Late one evening after Cole had turned in for the night, as Clint and Leroy sat on the porch with their coffee, Leroy made a comment that caused Clint deep concern.

"Clint, I've seen how often you look at your wife's picture and I know how much it hurts you not to have known what happened to her, so I've held my tongue," McAlister began. "But back in Waterhole, Arizona, I saw a lady who sure looked a lot like your Katherine. I can't be sure and I don't want to stir up any ill feelings, but I've gotten to know you well enough over these past number of months that I thought I could say right out what I was thinkin'."

Clint was stunned. He didn't know how to respond. They each sat in silence for a long couple of minutes.

"What makes you think it could be Katherine?" Clint asked carefully.

"Well, the picture has a strikingly similar resemblance. The gal in Waterhole is a bit older now, but they sure look an awful lot alike. And they called the gal in Waterhole, Kate. She was the woman of a very bad man who runs the town, a man called Sal Gregorio."

Clint sat in silence between their question and answer period. He could not have planned to find out this kind of information this way. He didn't know what to do, which was an uncomfortable feeling for Clint Herbert. He always knew what to do.

"Let me ask you, Leroy," Clint continued. "Were there any distinguishing marks on this gal you saw in Arizona?"

"I never got too close of a look, and she was usually painted up, if you know what I mean. But this one time I did see her early in the morning, without any face paint on. She was comin' out of . . ." Leroy stopped.

"Comin' out of where, Leroy?" Clint asked, disturbed that Leroy would cut himself off during his story.

"This'll be hard to hear, Clint, but she was comin' out of one of them Chinese opium dens," finished Leroy.

"What's that? What's an opium den?" asked Clint.

"It's a shady place where people go, usually not wanting to be detected, to ease themselves of various pains. Some physical, some other types of pain. Makes people act funny, kind of like laudanum in that it numbs a person's senses" Leroy told him.

"Why was she there?" Clint wanted to know.

"Don't know for sure, but rumor had it that Kate was a regular visitor to that place." Leroy said.

Clint sat speechless. "What about any marks on her?" he finally asked again.

"Seems to me she had a small scar under her right eye," Leroy said.

Clint instantly froze on the inside.

Shortly after they had been married, Katherine was kicked by a horse. It left a permanent scar under her right eye.

* * *

A United States Marshall arrived in Waterhole, Arizona on the first Tuesday of March, 1885. He had received complaints from a couple of folks who had left Waterhole that illegal shenanigans were happening, causing good town folk to leave town, often times without their rightful belongings. They had been confiscated for the good of community service, whatever that meant.

The Marshall sat in the office of Sheriff Billy Thatcher, who was standing next to the door. Sitting across the desk from the Marshall, in the sheriff's chair, was Sal Gregorio, self appointed head of the Town Council. On the wall behind the Marshall stood Archie Bender and Coyote Jim.

"Good of you to come, Marshall," began Sal Gregorio, "I too have heard of some unfortunate events here in Waterhole, and I would like your assistance in seeing that they are stopped," sounded Gregorio, in a sincere tone of voice. "Our sheriff here has been unable to determine who is behind some of the unlawfulness that folks have been subjected to," he concluded.

"According to the complaints I've received, Mr. Gregorio, . . ."

"Please, Marshall," Gregorio interrupted, "it's Councilman Gregorio, if you please." Gregorio smiled proudly.

"Very well. Councilman Gregorio, I hear it that most of the unfortunate events, as you put it, have been caused by you and your men. Any thoughts about that?" asked the Marshall.

"Sheriff Thatcher, have you anything to say in defense of the complaints lobbied by our good United States Marshall?" Gregorio asked.

As the Marshall turned a quarter turn to his right to look at Billy Thatcher, Thatcher drew his pistol and shot the Marshall right through his forehead.

"I object," Thatcher stated coldly, as Archie Bender broke into a howling laugh.

"Better send a telegram to the U.S. Marshall's headquarters," Gregorio instructed Thatcher. "Have it read, '*Everything fine in Waterhole. No cause for alarm. Be back in a few days.*' Sign the Marshall's name to it."

"What do we do in a couple of days when he don't show up at headquarters?" asked Thatcher.

"The Marshall will become the unfortunate victim of a band of Indians, and will be senselessly killed by them," thought Gregorio. "In a few days, we'll send a follow up telegram informing his office of such."

* * *

Clint and Cole were out riding on the far side of their 160 acre ranch. There was no real reason for them to be out here that Cole could see, but his pa had asked him to take a ride with him. They stopped under a grove of oak trees. Clint dismounted. Cole followed.

"What's on your mind, pa," asked Cole, sensing that there was some reason for their ride.

"Cole," Clint started, "Leroy told me something last night that got me to thinkin' real hard. It's about your ma. Leroy has been reluctant to say anything so as to not upset us if he was wrong, but he knows us well enough by now to speak openly."

"What is it, pa, what did he say?" asked a confused Cole.

"When Leroy was in Waterhole, Arizona, he saw a woman who he believes could be your ma." There, he had said it. Clint didn't know how the words were going to come out, nor how Cole would take them in.

Cole was quiet as he looked deeply at his pa's face.

"Pa, whadah' think?"

"Son, I don't rightly know what to think. I guess part of me had given up hope of ever finding your ma. But now . . . well, this is the first clue we've ever had. I decided I gotta go to Waterhole and see if it's her."

Without hesitation, Cole boldly claimed, "I'm goin' with ya, pa."

Clint had not considered that Cole, now age 12, would be old enough to go with him. As he looked at Cole to consider his statement, Clint saw the determination in Cole's face. All of the sudden, he looked older, more capable.

Clint continued to look at Cole, as Cole anxiously waited to hear what his pa had to say. Clint simply nodded. Cole smiled.

"We'll leave in two days," Clint told his son.

The next morning, Clint sat down with Leroy McAlister.

"Leroy," Clint began, "you've been with us for a while now, and we've come to trust you like family. Cole and I have decided to leave the Oklahoma territory and head west to Waterhole. We've got to find out if this Kate you saw really is Katherine."

Leroy listened intently, not knowing where this conversation was heading.

"I'd like you to stay on here at the ranch and take it on in a partnership while we're gone. If we don't come back, it's yours. If we return, the partnership stays intact," Clint offered. "What do you say?"

"That's a right generous offer, Clint," Leroy told him. "I'd be proud to stay on as your partner. The ranch will be in good hands while you're gone."

"Thanks, I know it will," Clint said. "If you need any help, there is a ranch about ten miles to the east. They've got a couple of sons who have helped out during roundup season before. Tell them I sent you."

Leroy nodded.

Clint had thought hard about another difficult decision he had to make. He'd like to ask Joshua Rines to join him on the trip to Arizona, but did not feel good about taking him away from Martha again. He decided to send Joshua a wire, and let him and

Martha decide. He knew Martha would want Joshua to help find Katherine.

Clint rode into the nearest town with a telegraph wire, about 15 miles north. When he arrived at the telegraph office, he wrote out the telegraph and asked it to be sent to Dodge City, Kansas.

The telegraph operator looked at the name, Clint Herbert, and said, "Well, I'll be, I got a telegraph here for you yesterday. I was going to have a boy ride it out to you later this week." Clint took the telegraph, opened it and began to read. When he was done reading, he gently folded it up and put it in his pocket. He then asked the telegraph operator to return his telegram. He was not going to send it. The telegram he received had been from Joshua. It said that Martha had died of cancer. Knowing what it felt like to lose your wife, Clint decided not to send his wire asking for Joshua's help. He knew that Joshua needed his time to grieve. Clint and Cole would make the trip alone.

It was a beautiful spring morning in mid-March, although a light spring shower was beginning to fall. Clint and Cole were saddled up, with Clint pulling a mule to pack their extras. If they found Katherine, Clint would buy a horse on the other end of the trip for her.

"Be careful," warned Leroy as he shook hands with Clint, then Cole. "Sal Gregorio is a very dangerous man, and he has some mighty ruthless men backing him up."

"Thanks, Leroy," acknowledged Clint. "We'll be careful. You take care of yerself and the ranch. We'll hope to be back before the end of summer."

"We got a long ride ahead of us, son, best we get started," Clint told Cole, and they began their way towards Waterhole, Arizona.

* * *

Clint and Cole had been two weeks out on their journey. They had entered the New Mexico Territory. As they passed through the Indian Territory a few days back, they had been watched by a handful of Apache braves, but Clint and Cole moved quickly, and were not bothered by the Indians.

They made camp one night about 25 miles east of Santa Fe.

"Pa," Cole began as they sat around the campfire. Cole had had his first taste of coffee earlier on the trip. He had not yet acquired a taste for it, but drinking it made him feel more adult-like. "What's going to happen if it is ma in Waterhole?"

"Well, I reckon we'll bring her home, son."

"But what if she doesn't want to come. She's been gone so long, maybe she doesn't want to be with us anymore," Cole fretted.

"First off, we don't know if it's her. Second, if it is your ma, whether to come home or not will be up to her. But I can't believe she wouldn't want to be with us. From what Leroy said, I don't think she's in Waterhole of her own free will. There's a lot we don't know, and won't 'til we get to Waterhole."

"And maybe not even then, if it's not her," added Cole.

Clint sipped his coffee, but did not respond.

The following morning, Clint and Cole woke early to get a start on the warming temperatures. "Traveling early will allow us to get more out of the day," Clint told Cole. As Santa Fe was at a high elevation, the nights and early mornings were cold, even in the spring. Clint hoped to make it to Santa Fe by nightfall for supplies and treat Cole to a good meal and a bed for the evening.

It was mid-morning when Clint noticed a trail of blood on the ground beneath them. Cole had not seen it, but Clint slowed the pace a bit to be able to use his eyes and ears in case there was trouble. He gently reached down to feel for his army pistol. He had kept in on his right hip and loaded since they left home.

Cole noticed the slowing of the pace and his father keeping a keen, watchful eye all around him, more so than usual. "What's wrong, Pa?" he asked.

"Don't rightly know, son," he told him without changing the pattern of his eyes and ears keeping watch. "We came upon a blood trail just a bit ago, and it's still under us."

Cole looked down and saw the blood. It would appear every few feet, sometimes in drops, other times it almost looked like a puddle.

"Ya think it's trouble, pa?"

"Don't know. Could be animal, could be human. Either way, looks like a lot of blood has been lost."

A few minutes later, Clint saw the source of the blood. A Comanche brave lay face down on the ground, blood covering his clothing, and ripped nearly off his body. Cole was immediately frightened by what he saw.

"Stay on your horse, son," Clint told him, as he scanned the area before dismounting himself. He handed the reigns of the mule to Cole.

Clint drew his pistol and cautiously made his way over to the fallen Indian. Clint had learned enough about Indians during his years in Kansas to recognize the injured brave as a Comanche. He had never known one to be friendly. Clint reached down and placed his left hand on the back of the bleeding Indian. He groaned softly, but he did not move.

"He's still alive," Clint told Cole. "Bring me some water and a blanket. Then get a clean shirt from my bed roll, and rip into pieces, about this long and this wide." Clint showed Cole with his hands how big to make them.

Clint laid the blanket down beside the Indian. He took the canteen full of water and, using one of the strips of his shirt, he dabbed the Indian's wounds, trying to clean them. There were so many of them, Clint was surprised the Indian had survived. From what he could surmise, the Indian had been mauled by a bear. Clint knew that most would not survive such an attack. Clint noticed the empty knife sheath on the Indian's belt, and guessed it must be stuck somewhere in a bear. No other explanation for why the bear would quit.

"I know we only got started this mornin', Cole, but we can't go off and leave this here fella to die. We'll take some time to help him, and when he's strong enough, we'll move on."

"How long will that take, pa?"

"Hard to say," Clint answered, "but it's the right thing to do."

"But what about, ma?"

"If that's her in Waterhole, she'll still be there even if we're a day or two behind."

* * *

"Good morning, Kate!" A cheerful Sal Gregorio sounded as he pulled open the blinds covering her bedroom window. Katherine barely heard him and did not move in her bed.

"It's a beautiful morning, my dear, time to start the day," laughed Gregorio.

He knew that she had visited the opium den the night before and had only returned and fallen into bed a couple of hours prior. He also knew that she was growing more dependant on her opium each day, and was incoherent more than not. She had lost nearly 25 pounds during her time with Gregorio, most of it in the past two years as her dependence on opium grew rapidly, and was a waif like 85 pounds. As her condition had deteriorated, Gregorio had ceased to show any interest in her as his woman.

"Kate, I'm afraid I have to tell you that I will need your room for a new girl who has been recruited to join our establishment. I'll give you until the end of the week to pack your things and get out of the hotel. Should you need a horse to leave town, I'll gladly sell you one at a fair price."

Gregorio was letting Katherine go, but she was not able to comprehend any of the one-sided conversation between them. She continued to lie on her bed in a stupor.

"I'll be back in a few days to see how your packing is going. It's been fun, Kate."

* * *

Clint and Cole nursed the Comanche for a little more than a week. After nine days, his wounds were scaring over, even the deep ones, and there didn't seem to be any signs of infection. He was eating a little more each day. Clint was cautious around him and never let Cole get near him by himself. The Comanche did speak some English, enough to let Clint know his name was Running Wolf, and that he had been attacked by a bear. As bad as Running Wolf looked, the bear looked worse, he told Clint, smiling.

Cole had found Running Wolf's horse a couple of days after the attack. He also found the bear that had attacked Running Wolf. It was dead. Cole slowly approached the bear, feeling mostly afraid. He pulled Running Wolf's knife from the bear. It was stuck in deep, and he had trouble pulling it out at first. He wiped the blood off onto the bear's hide, climbed back on his horse and headed for camp, less than a half a mile away. Cole felt as though it was the bravest thing he had ever done, even though the bear was already dead.

When he was ready to ride, Clint told Running Wolf, he was welcome to join them on the trail until he felt strong enough to go on his own. Running Wolf agreed, and the next morning, they all headed towards Santa Fe.

Due to the lost time, Clint chose just to replenish their supplies, and did not take a meal or a hotel in Santa Fe. They had spent no more than 30 minutes in town, in part due to the unwelcome looks that Running Wolf was getting from townsfolk.

After clearing through the west side of town, Clint stopped and asked Running Wolf what his plans were. Running Wolf felt an indebtedness towards Clint, and knowing that they could run into Indian trouble between Santa Fe and Waterhole, Arizona, Running Wolf chose to stay with the Herbert's to help give them safe passage.

Clint was still a little uneasy, but respected Running Wolf's offer enough to accept it.

Based on information obtained in Santa Fe, Clint felt that with early starts and long days, they could reach Waterhole in about a week.

* * *

Sal Gregorio returned to Katherine's room six days later, this time, accompanied by Archie Bender.

"Kate, my dear, you have not begun to pack, why the delay?" asked Gregorio.

"What are you talking about?" Katherine asked without opening her eyes. She was coherent now, but still lying in bed, wearing the same clothes she had on the last time he saw her.

"Kate, Kate, Kate," Gregorio announced, "as I told you days ago, I need this room for another one of the ladies. I'm afraid you'll be leaving us tonight."

Katherine was confused. She had been a prisoner for seven years, and now Gregorio was letting her go free? She did not know what to think. Was this some kind of a trick? Gregorio never let anyone in his employ, voluntary or otherwise, go free.

In all the years she had been with him, Katherine never once called Gregorio by name. She sat up in her bed and opened her eyes to look at Gregorio.

"Why now?" she asked, "Why after all these years am I able to walk out of here?"

"Kate, I was once very fond of you, but quite simply, you have grown old and with your addiction, you are no longer an interest of mine. You haven't been for some time, but some part of me felt as though I owed you something for all these years of service," Gregorio informed her. "Just call me a nice guy," he said smiling.

"I don't understand," Katherine went on, "you mean I can just walk out of Waterhole?"

"Yes, that is what I mean. You never told me Kate, if you had a family, but maybe there is someone to return to." said Gregorio.

Katherine had never told Gregorio anything about her family, for fear that he would be on the lookout for Clint. She wanted him to be caught off-guard if Clint ever did find her. She no longer had those delusions.

"Whatever you can pack in the next 15 minutes, you are welcome to take," Gregorio told her. "My new girl would like to see her new room, and I'd like to make it available to show it to her personally."

Gregorio and Archie Bender left the room. When they reached the hallway, Bender anxiously asked Gregorio if he could have Katherine.

"She's old and a drug addict, why would you want her?" asked Gregorio.

"Because none of your saloon girls will have anythin' to do with me," Bender said almost pityingly.

"Alright, Archie, if you really want her, I suppose so. But wait until you are out of town before you take her. In your case, I don't think the style of accommodations will make much of a difference to you," Gregorio told him.

"You mean I can do whatever I want with her?" Bender asked in an excitedly, sick manner.

"I don't want her to suffer, Archie, no more than being with you will cause her suffering, you understand?" said Gregorio.

With an uncontrollable smile, Bender agreed to the terms. Katherine was now his.

* * *

On the sixth night since leaving Santa Fe, Clint estimated they would reach Waterhole by noon the following day. As Clint and Cole sat around their campfire, Running Wolf tended to the horses and the mule.

"You trust him, pa?" Cole asked Clint regarding Running Wolf.

"A little more each day, son." Clint responded. "Guess he could have given us trouble by now if he wanted to."

"How do you know he ain't out there planning to steal our horses?" Cole asked.

"I guess I don't rightly know," Clint answered, "sometimes you just gotta trust a man based on how he treats ya. Running Wolf has been trustworthy in the short time we've been together. I think he feels as though he owes us for helping him when he was hurtin' from that bear attack."

"Ya think he woulda died, pa, if we hadn't come along?"

"I reckon he woulda, Cole, but supposin' is a difficult thing to do, and somethin' I don't put much time into."

After tending to the horses, Running Wolf went down to the creek to get water for the coffee, about a quarter mile from the camp. The Comanche was just out of sight when Clint hushed Cole, putting his hand up to signal him to be quiet. Clint had his army pistol still holstered on his belt. He listened intently, moving his eyes from one side of camp to the other without moving his head. Clint continued to keep his hand up so Cole knew to keep quiet. Cole was frightened, not knowing what his pa was doing. He didn't hear anything, nor see anything. Clint made a signaling motion with his hand for Cole to move over to his left, behind a rock on the edge of camp. Cole obliged.

"Evenin' in the camp," a voice called out from the darkness beyond the circle of trees surrounding their campsite.

"Who are ya, whadah ya want?" Clint called out, pistol already in hand, hidden beneath a blanket across his lap. Cole never saw him draw it from its holster. He continued to keep his eyes moving across the outskirts of the camp, though he knew where the voice came from.

"Deputies from Waterhole, we're comin' in the camp," the voice answered.

Three men walked into camp, all spread out with 10 feet or more between them.

"What can we do for ya?" asked Clint.

"Well, actually, we're a special delegation of tax collectors," the one with the voice continued.

"A bit far from your taxable boundary, aren't ya fellas?" Clint asked, smiling. "What are we being taxed for?"

"Anyone who spends time within the jurisdiction of Waterhole, must pay for the privilege," said the voice of the deputies.

"And just what is that jurisdiction?" asked Clint.

"Kinda changes from day to day. I guess it happens to be wherever we happens to be?" the deputy laughed.

The deputy off to Clint's right, drew his pistol. Clint raised his pistol from under the blanket and dropped the deputy with one shot. As he did, the middle deputy, the one doing the speaking drew his pistol and aimed it at Clint. The third deputy had his pistol leveled against Cole's head.

"Looky here, mister," the deputy said. "If you don't want this boy of yours killed, you'll hand over your traveling money. Do it now," he said in a somber voice.

Clint was in a stand off with the deputy right in front of him, but he couldn't see a way of putting both of the remaining deputies down without risking Cole's life.

"Looks like you're carrying a single shot revolver. I don't think you're good enough to be able to pull that hammer back twice and get both of us before you and the boy are dead," the deputy from Waterhole reasoned.

"Don't have to be," Clint told him, "just need to be good enough to get you. My friend will take care of your partner."

A look of confused panic appeared in the deputy's eyes. He had not seen anyone but the two Herbert's. Within seconds, Running Wolf slipped up behind the deputy near Cole, and from behind, reached around and slit his throat. The deputy stood bleeding for a moment, in shock, then dropped his gun and followed it to the ground shortly after. Almost simultaneously, Clint shot the mouthy deputy in his gun shoulder. The deputy dropped his gun and fell to his knees.

"Kinda hurts being shot with a .44 caliber, don't it?" Clint asked the deputy mockingly. "First time in my life I ever shot my weapon at a man without trying to kill him," he told Cole. "He was close enough for me to be a little picky where I shot him, and I'd kinda like to know a little more about Waterhole from someone on the inside."

Cole was visibly shaken as Running Wolf stepped over the deputy he had felled, and joined Clint.

"Thanks," Clint nodded at Running Wolf.

"Pa," Cole began, but he did not know what he wanted to say.

"It'll be okay now, son," Clint told him. "Running Wolf saved me from a difficult spot."

"What would you have done if he had not been here?" Cole wondered.

"I knew he'd have heard the first shot, and figured he was already on his way back anyways," said Clint. "I figured I needed to buy enough time for him to get back and surmise the situation. One thing, Cole, is you never give up your gun. I don't know if I could have gotten both of them, but without trying, they would have killed us both."

"Who would you have shot first?" he asked his pa.

"The one closest to you. Dropping him would have given you time to clear out, as the other would have been targeting me."

"Running Wolf saved our lives, pa, didn't he?"

"Made it a lot easier to get out of that predicament, surely," Clint told him.

"Thank you, Running Wolf," Cole said as he extended his hand to his friend.

Running Wolf took his hand and gave a firm, single shake. He nodded at Cole.

"So, Mr. Tax Collector, lets talk a little about Waterhole," Clint suggested as he put his left foot against the wounded man's right shoulder, causing him to let out a howling scream.

"You son of a bitch," the tax collector said, "you may as well let me die, I ain't tellin' you nothin'," he brazenly spoke.

"Well," Clint pondered, "I suppose I could do that. Running Wolf, I'd like to break camp and get a move on to Waterhole. Think you could scalp him quickly so we can git. Might not be able to wait 'til he dies first. You okay to skin him alive?" Clint asked.

Running Wolf pulled his knife from its sheath and approached the deputy. He grabbed him hard by his dirty long hair, and tugged it back.

"Wait!" screamed the deputy as he looked at Running Wolf's knife blade. "Whadah ya wanna know? I can always find a new town, but not if I'm dead."

"Running Wolf, see if you can round up their horses, while I talk with this here tax collector." Running Wolf nodded and set out to find them.

"Tell me about Sal Gregorio," Clint asked once Running Wolf was out of the camp.

"Gregorio runs Waterhole. Everything and everyone in it. He started out with about 14 men, but he's down a few with these two gone, and after I high tail it out of here. He can recruit more if he wants, but he is very protective of his ownings," said the deputy.

"Any top hands?" asked Clint.

"Three mainly," the deputy named, "Archie Bender, he's a backshooter without any morals. Hell, none of them have any morals, but Bender enjoys killing. Got a comanchero named Coyote Jim. Deadliest man with a knife I ever seen. And the town sheriff is Gregorio's top man. Fast with a gun. Name's Billy Thatcher."

Clint stopped his movements for a moment to think about that last name.

"Billy Thatcher," Clint repeated. "I know that name. Stole my horse years back when I was on a posse that caught a pack of bank robbers. I'll look forward to making his acquaintance. Any others?" Clint asked.

"No, those three do all his dirty work in and around town," said the deputy. "Some of the rest of us git a little extra by collecting taxes from travelers we see."

"Know anything about a woman named, Kate?" Clint asked nervously, while Cole leaned forward from where he was sitting, to listen.

"Yeah, Kate was once Gregorio's main woman, but he just cut her loose from the herd," the deputy smiled. Clint jabbed the deputy in the nose with the butt of his pistol, hard enough to draw blood.

"Just tell me about her," Clint warned.

Waterhole

With his eyes watering, and his nose and shoulder bleeding, the deputy began, "Gregorio brought Kate with him seven years ago when he first came to Waterhole. She was a real looker back then, but she never connected with Gregorio. You could tell she didn't want to be there. After a while, she began visiting the Chinese opium dens, and became hooked on their drugs. Gregorio eventually replaced her, just last week. She was set to leave town tomorrow with Archie Bender."

"Why Bender?" Clint asked.

"I heard tell that Gregorio gave her to Bender. I wouldn't wish my own ugly sister on Bender, he's plain mean," said the deputy. "That's all I know. What are you going to do with me now?" he asked.

Clint thought about the question.

"I'll leave you your horse about five miles down the road. Give you time to think about where to ride out to once you reach it, if the bears don't smell the blood and find you first," Clint told him. "If I see you in Waterhole, I'll kill you."

"Between you and Gregorio, I ain't got no more reason to make time in Waterhole, mister, you won't see me again," the deputy promised.

Running Wolf returned with three horses. Clint told him of the plan. They packed, broke camp, and headed out towards Waterhole.

* * *

Everything Katherine was able to pack was contained in a single satchel. She wanted little as possible to remind her of Waterhole, so she only packed her essentials, a few changes of clothes, and ladies things. She had one canteen full of water, a blanket and a bedroll. She also had a bottle of laudanum. Gregorio decided to give her a horse to ride. As she reached her already saddled horse, she tied her satchel to it, and climbed into the saddle. Archie Bender rode up and pulled his horse next to hers.

"What's he doing here?" Katherine asked Gregorio, as he leaned against a hitching post outside his saloon.

"Well, Kate, Archie here has taken a liking to you. I've given him my blessings," Gregorio smiled as he told Katherine.

Katherine had no response. She guided the reins of her horse to the left and began to trot out of town. Archie Bender pulled up alongside and smiled at her. As they rode together towards the east end of town, three riders approached, heading into town. A man, a boy, and an Indian.

Part III

Waterhole, Arizona, 1885

Waterhole, Arizona was a small town. It was not much to look at. A single main street, with storefronts and businesses lining each side made up the majority of the town. The main street was about 300 feet long. Mining camps surrounded the town, with more than three dozen within a 10 mile radius. This did not include many single miners who moved around frequently. Any business owned directly by Sal Gregorio was profitable, if not aesthetically pleasing. Gregorio was concerned with the bottom dollar, and would only stay in control of Waterhole as long as there was money to be made. Once it dried up, so would his presence. As a result, he did not see value in putting his money into the upkeep of the town's buildings, at least beyond working functionally.

* * *

Katherine rode past the three riders who were coming into town. She gave a long glance at the one closest to her when they passed. In doing so she fainted, slumping in her saddle, before falling to the ground a few feet later, in front of the blacksmith shop. Bender had not paid attention to the three riders, as he had his smiling eyes on Katherine. As she began to fall, he reached for her, but was unable to prevent her from falling. Bender dismounted and knelt next to Katherine.

Gregorio had been standing in front of his saloon, watching his former woman and Bender ride away. He, too, saw her fall from her horse. After watching Bender kneel over her for a minute, he slowly exhaled and began a slow walk towards the two, as he debated whether it was worth his effort to move in the hot weather. His curiosity got the best of him, and he decided to see what had happened.

Clint heard the woman fall from her horse and lay motionless in the street. He stopped to look back, before turning his horse around to offer help. Cole and Running Wolf also stopped, but remained in their saddles, watching. Clint stood over Katherine, who was face down, and looked at Archie Bender. Bender glanced up, scowling.

"What ya lookin' at, tinhorn?" Bender growled.

"Just wanted to see if the lady was alright," Clint replied.

"Ain't none of yer business if she is or she ain't, now you best git!" demanded Bender.

Clint stared hard at Bender. Bender looked back up at him as Gregorio arrived at the fallen Katherine.

"Howdy stranger, welcome to Waterhole," said Gregorio. "My name is Sal Gregorio, I'm head of the local Town Council, pleased to make your acquaintance."

Upon hearing Gregorio's name, Clint flinched, but caught himself, not knowing whether to pull his pistol or physically grab Gregorio. He felt his muscles tighten all over. Clint did not respond, but kept his stare on Gregorio now.

"Time to git, Hayseed," Bender repeated as he now stood next to Gregorio, with Katherine still unconscious on the ground.

Without taking his eyes off of Gregorio, Clint reached out, pulled Bender towards him, and landed a hard fist on Bender's jaw. He went down immediately, groggy, but conscience.

"I understand you know a woman named, Kate," Clint said deadpanned, eyes still on Gregorio.

"Well my new friend, it just so happens I do," Gregorio told him, "how is it you know her?"

"Don't know if I do, just heard about her," Clint said. "Thought I'd take a look."

Bender began to get up, his knees still wobbly. Clint hit him again, harder this time and put him down for good.

"That's a good man of mine you've hit. He won't take kindly to your actions once he wakes up," Gregorio told Clint.

"He's got a big mouth and a mean disposition for a guy his size," Clint informed Gregorio. "Can he back it up?"

Gregorio laughed, "yes, he does at that, and he does his backing up in a different manner. You asked about my Kate," Gregorio continued, "as it happens, that is her lying on the ground."

Gregorio's eyes did not leave Clint as he pointed to the fallen woman on the ground, not more than 10 feet away. Gregorio had taken notice of Clint's ability to handle himself, and decided to remain an interested, but inactive bystander until he could determine Clint's interest.

Clint stood still. Though he had been waiting for the time when he would see Katherine again, he was not emotionally prepared for the moment. He did not know for sure that the woman lying on the ground was his wife.

Gregorio eyed Cole and Running Wolf, but did not say anything.

Clint slowly moved over towards Katherine. Cole had been far enough away on his horse that he did not hear Gregorio tell his pa that the fallen woman was the Kate they were looking for.

Clint looked at Cole, but did not say anything. Cole recognized the strange look on his father's face, but remained on top of Slinger.

Clint knelt down and slowly turned the woman over. He looked hard for a moment. She was not the same, attractive looking Katherine of seven years ago. Her time away from home during those years had aged her terribly, and she looked physically weak, having lost so much weight. But it was Katherine. She was still unconscious as Clint lifted her upper body off the ground and hugged it against his. Gregorio just watched.

Cole jumped off his horse and ran to Clint, sliding to a stop on his knees. He couldn't speak. Clint looked at his son. "It's your ma," Clint smiled weakly, "it's her."

Cole broke into tears, but could not move. He sobbed as he sat on his knees, two feet from his mother.

Running Wolf took Clint's and Cole's horses down the street to hitch them to a post in front of the hotel.

Clint realized his surroundings, and immediately knew he was not in friendly territory. He slowly reached Katherine over and placed her upper body in Cole's arms.

"Hold her, son," Clint told him.

Clint stood back up and looked at Gregorio.

"It seems you know this woman," Gregorio noticed.

Clint nodded. "I'll be taking her over to the hotel with me," Clint told Gregorio.

"Well," Gregorio began, "our friend here," he said nodding towards Archie Bender, "will be disappointed when he wakes up."

Clint didn't say anything in response. He walked over, picked Katherine up off of the ground, and began walking towards the hotel. Cole followed.

As Clint carried Katherine towards the hotel, Bender began to wake up. He shook his head, but continued to look at the ground as he sat on his backside in the dirt. He slowly collected his senses and realized what had happened. Bender looked around and saw Clint carrying Katherine down the street. He blinked his eyes a few times to finish clearing his head. Then he smiled as he stood and reached for one of his pistols, worn cross-over style in his holster. Bender muttered to himself, "she's mine, Gregorio gave her to me," as he pulled a pistol and began to take aim.

Running Wolf had hitched the horses and looked in Clint's direction when he noticed Bender had risen off the ground, pistol in hand. Running Wolf hollered and pointed behind Clint, who turned and looked, Katherine still in his arms. Bender was startled as he was not used to facing his prey, but he kept his pistol held steadfastly on Clint, who could not reach his gun with Katherine is his arms. Bender laughed as he cocked the hammer on his revolver.

"Nawt t'day, missah Archie," said a voice from the blacksmith shop.

Bender, Gregorio and Clint looked towards the direction of the voice. Standing in the doorway of the blacksmith shop was a large, black man, holding a shotgun aimed at Bender.

"Now, Blacky," Gregorio began, "this is between these two fine gentlemen. No need to interfere."

"Ah sees it a little differently, missah Gregorio," the black man responded. "Appears tat missah Archie set on shootin' tis fella in the back. I sez not t'day."

"Unless you want a visit from me tonight, Blacky, best you go back inside and mind yerself," Bender said.

The black man stood about 30 feet from where Bender was standing, but covered the ground between them in just a few seconds, keeping his shotgun leveled on Bender the whole time. He stopped when he had the shotgun poking into Bender's ribs. Bender stood frightened.

"G'back ta sleep, missah Archie," the black man said as he quickly swung the stock of the shotgun against the side of Bender's head. Bender laid on the ground, unconscious again. "Go ahead, missah," the black man said to Clint, as he stood over Bender and next to Gregorio. "You'll have safe passage now."

Clint smiled and nodded at the black man, turned and continued with Katherine, toward the hotel. Cole stared at the black man for a minute, before following in behind his pa. Gregorio watched them until they cleared the threshold of the hotel lobby and were no longer in sight. Gregorio turned his head and looked at the black man. The black man smiled. Gregorio returned the smile then headed back towards his saloon.

* * *

Gregorio had taken in all of what had occurred in the street earlier that afternoon. He recognized that Clint knew 'his Kate' from somewhere, but chose not to ask questions. He wanted to be in a position of force when he made his inquiries, and with Billy Thatcher and Coyote Jim out of town, and with Bender unconscious most of the time, he would wait. Waterhole was his town. He would find out whatever he needed to know from whomever he needed to know from. Including a former acquaintance he saw during the afternoon.

* * *

Clint had no trouble getting a hotel room, even in Gregorio's hotel. The man at the desk knew Katherine, and saw that Clint meant business when he asked for a room. Cole signed for the room, and took the key from the man. As they headed up the stairs, Katherine in Clint's arms still, Clint told the man at the desk to summon some water in a pitcher and some towels right away. The man knew not to dally.

Their room was on the second floor, overlooking the street they had come in on. Clint laid Katherine down on the bed.

"Cole," he summoned, "you recognize her?"

Cole shook his head slowly, "not really pa. She looks mighty sickly and different from what I remember."

Clint sat on the bed beside Katherine and stroked her head. A knock at the door startled him as he stood quickly, skinning his pistol from its holster by the time his knees were straightened. Clint aimed it at the door as he motioned with his head for Cole to answer it. The hotel man had arrived with Clint's order. He sat them down on the bureau and left immediately, not a word spoken. Clint settled his pistol back in its holster.

"Don't know what caused your ma to faint, son," Clint told Cole. "She may not know us when she wakes up, so you got to be prepared for it."

"Why wouldn't she know her own husband and son?" Cole asked.

"Son, it looks like she's been treated somethin' terrible. She don't look like herself, and the years haven't been good to her. Though I suspect somethin' else has contributed to her lookin' this way," Clint explained.

"What do we do when she wakes up, pa?"

""We'll need to give her space. Time to recognize us and see how she feels about us," Clint told Cole.

It had been nearly three hours since her fall. Clint had dabbed her forehead with damp cloths, while Cole sat by closely, trying to recognize her.

As Katherine moaned, Clint took the cloth away from her head, stood up and moved away towards the window. Katherine moaned again and reached for her head with both hands. She continued to moan a few more times, before opening her eyes. She lay still in the bed as she collected her thoughts and got her surroundings. She first saw Cole standing by the door to the room.

"Who are you?" she asked.

Cole smiled, "it's me, ma," he said quietly.

A confused look appeared on Katherine's face. Then she noticed the shadow over to her left. She turned her head and saw the man standing in front of the window. She recognized him, but it took some thought to remember.

"Clint," she smiled, and extended her left hand towards him.

A shot rang out from the street, followed by shattering glass. Clint's eyes widened as he stood momentarily, then he stepped towards the bed, and fell face down over Katherine's legs. He had a bloody hole in his back.

"Pa!" Cole shouted and raced for his father.

"Clint?" a stunned Katherine said.

As they both reached for Clint, a high pitched laugh came up from the street.

"Oops," the laughing voice said, "here I come, Kate!"

It was Archie Bender. From the street below, he had shot Clint in the back as he stood in the window of his hotel room.

Bender continued to laugh, all the way to the Herbert's hotel room door.

"Knock, knock," he howled, as he opened the door and stepped inside. The smiling Bender suddenly lost his sense of humor. Clint was sitting up in the bed with his .44 caliber army pistol pointed at Bender's chest. Clint fired two times, both shots hitting within the size of a silver dollar. Bender fell backwards into the hallway. He would not laugh again.

"Close the door," Clint told Cole who had been waiting out of sight, with his mother. Then Clint slumped over in the bed and dropped his pistol to the floor.

* * *

Gregorio sat around the circular poker table in his saloon with three other men. Around the table with him were Billy Thatcher and Coyote Jim, back from a tax collecting visit to local miners. The fourth member of the party was Running Wolf.

"Gentlemen," Gregorio said, "we have a small problem that needs attending to. The former Mr. Bender attempted to clean it up on his own, but foolishly miscalculated his opponent. There is a man up in the room with Kate, whom I have been informed by my old friend, Running Wolf, is Kate's husband. Shame on me for not knowing. Their son is with them, but it is my understanding that the husband has been wounded. At least Bender wasn't a completely inept fool. Sheriff Thatcher and I will visit their room and see what accommodations we need to make in order to remove them."

* * *

"Ma, what are we going to do?" a frightened Cole asked.

"Your pa is hurt bad. We need to get him a doctor," she replied.

"Is there one in town?" Cole asked.

"Yes, son." It was the first time she said that and it brought a smile to her face. "But he's one of Gregorio's men. I don't know if

Gregorio will allow him to help us." She smiled again, but it was short lived. "Cole," she continued, "how come your pa never came to get me?"

"Ma, pa and Joshua Rines looked for you for near seven months, but they never found a clue. Ain't a day goes by that he don't think of you. Me too. What happened to you?"

Katherine felt chills go up her back, as she remembered why she had fainted. When on her horse, she saw the three riders coming into town, but only recognized one of them right off. The Indian. Running Wolf had been the Indian that had captured her and sold her to Gregorio. Cole clenched his fists as he thought about Running Wolf taking his ma. Confusion soon followed as he thought about how Clint had helped save his life, and in return, he had saved Cole's from Gregorio's bandits in their camp. It was too much for him to think about right now. His attention needed to be directed to his father.

* * *

The door to the hotel room opened and in walked Billy Thatcher, followed by Sal Gregorio.

"Kate, my dear," Gregorio welcomed.

"She ain't your dear, she's my ma," Cole sternly told him.

Thatcher back-handed him, sending Cole backpedaling against the wall, blood oozing from his mouth.

"Stop it!" Katherine shouted. "Salvador," she begged. It was the first time she had ever used his name. "My husband needs a doctor, please."

"Kate, I never knew you had a husband. It's too bad we couldn't have met under better circumstances. However, be that as it may, I'm afraid I will not be able to allow the doctor to visit your husband. Oh, and he looks hurt bad, too," Gregorio explained.

"You bastard," Kate said through clenched teeth. "He'll die without help."

"Kate, here is what I will do. I will not kill him immediately. Consider that favor number one. Secondly, I will allow you and your boy to stay in the room, with your husband, for as long as he lives. Once he dies, however, you will leave town at once. I guess I have a soft spot for you, Kate. No one else would get the same generosity from me," Gregorio told her.

Gregorio turned and left the room. Thatcher winked at Kate, smiled at Cole, then followed his boss out the door.

* * *

Four hours had passed since Gregorio and Thatcher had left their room. Katherine and Cole had not eaten, nor had they gotten any food for Clint. Gregorio had seen to it that no one would serve them. They had stopped his bleeding, but they feared the bullet wound between his shoulder blades was deep. Clint had not regained consciousness.

It had been dark for an hour when they heard a knock at the door. Cole had been holding Clint's pistol. He pointed it towards the door, and then called out, "who's there?"

"It's me, Blacky," the voice called back, softly.

"Open the door," Katherine directed Cole. Cole followed his mother's instructions.

Standing in the doorway was the large black man who had helped Clint earlier in the day, when Archie Bender tried to backshoot him. He was holding a bag.

"Howdy, Miss Kate," the black man said, as he removed his hat.

"Hello, Bertram," Katherine greeted the visitor.

Bertram Smith was a giant of a man. Six foot, four inches tall, and a solid 250 pounds. He was the one man in town not afraid of Gregorio and his men. He had stayed out of their way, and never caused or received any trouble, until today. He was the town blacksmith. Due to his occupation and his last name, along with his race, the name 'Blacky' became the name he was known by. By everyone except Katherine. She had always called him by his given name, Bertram.

"Bertram, I'd like you to meet my son, Cole," a proud Katherine said.

"Howdy, son, why yous looks ta be 'tween hay and grass," greeted Bertram.

Cole grinned. "But I'm still growing, Mr. Smith," he said.

"Be pleased ta haves ya call me Bertram, or Blacky," the blacksmith told him.

"Okay," Cole said, "I'll make it Bertram, like my ma."

"Bertram," Katherine continued, "please call me Katherine. "I was Kate only to Gregorio. To my family and friends, I'm Katherine."

"Be mah pleasure, Miss Katherine," Bertram responded.

"How's yah husband doin'?" asked Bertram.

"Not too good, I'm afraid," replied a concerned Katherine. "Gregorio won't let the doctor see him. Clint's a strong man, but I don't know how long he can hold out without a doctor."

"Ah done some doctorin' back home," said Bertram. "If yaw'd likes, Ah can takes a look at him."

"Please, Bertram. I'm afraid the bullet is deep," Katherine said.

Cole and Katherine helped Bertram to roll Clint over on his side. Bertram examined the wound. Katherine had removed Clint's shirt and had bandaged the wound, making it easier to clean frequently.

"You's right, Miss Katherine," informed Bertram, "dat bullet looks deep. Be best if it come out," he told her.

"Ah kin try, ma'am," Bertram told her, "but Ah ain't fah sure Ah can git it out. Bein' how it's dark now, be best to wait 'til da morning so Ah'll have good light."

"Okay," Katherine said, "okay, I suppose you're right. We'll wait until tomorrow," she sighed.

"Bertram," Cole asked, "can you stay with my ma 'til I get back?"

"Where are you going?" a worried Katherine asked.

"There's somethin' I got to do, ma. I'll be careful and be back shortly. Bertram?" Cole asked again.

"Miss Katherine be okay wit me," Bertram told Cole.

Cole was confident in Bertram's ability to protect his mother and father. He quietly left the room, went down the stairs, and exited the hotel lobby without being seen.

The noise across the street was loud and vociferous. It was coming from the saloon. Not having to cross the street, Cole made his way to the end of the block, moved quickly across an alley and up on the planks of the next block. About halfway down, he had reached his destination. He tried to open the door, but it was locked. Cole knocked on the window in the door. No answer. He knocked again, a little louder this time. Shortly after, a light went on in the back room of the building. A man came to the door, peered out and saw the boy standing just outside.

"I need some help," Cole feigned a hurt leg as he hobbled on one apparently good limb.

The man inside shook his head. "Go find the doctor," he told Cole.

"He ain't in town," Cole began to cry. "It's been hurtin' all day and I can't go any further on it."

The man stood for a minute, thinking about his options. He shook his head again, a bit less so this time, then unlocked his door, and stepped aside for Cole's entry.

"How can I help you, boy, I ain't no doctor," the man told him.

Cole straightened up quickly, leg healed, and pulled his father's Remington New Model Army .44 caliber pistol from under his coat. He pointed it at the man. In an instant, Cole absorbed all the lessons of manhood his father had taught him over the years. Clint had told him. *If you deal honestly with folks and work hard, there'll be a place for you in this world.* Cole was being true to his folks with his actions, and he knew the work he was embarking upon would be hard, but Cole felt it had to be done.

"I need to send a telegraph," Cole told the man.

"Telegraph office is closed for the night, and besides, I can't send any telegraphs without Mr. Gregorio approving them," the man told Cole.

Cole pulled back the hammer on the pistol and said, "I think you'll be sending this one."

"But Mr. Gregorio will have me killed if I send one without his knowing," the frightened telegraph operator said.

"I don't know what Gregorio might do to you later. But I promise you, I'll kill you right now if you don't send this telegram," a suddenly adult-like Cole told the man as he stepped closer to him, putting the barrel of his pistol against the tip of the man's nose.

Shaking, the man agreed to send the telegram and he sat down at his desk, ready to send Cole's message.

"Where is it going to?" asked the telegraph operator.

"Dodge City, Kansas," Cole told him, "to the attention of Joshua Rines."

* * *

Gregorio and Thatcher returned to the saloon. It was getting on to about midnight, but the activity in the saloon was at a peak. The poker tables were full, as was the line of drinking cowboys and miners at the bar. Gregorio had a dozen working women in the saloon who were up and down the stairs all evening.

Gregorio and Thatcher made their way to the back table in the saloon. Already seated were Coyote Jim and Running Wolf. They had remained there while Gregorio and Thatcher visited the Herbert's room in the hotel.

"Kate's husband does not look good," began Gregorio. "Without a doctor, he will surely die. We will wait and allow nature to take its course of events. Once the man dies, we will encourage Kate and the boy to leave immediately."

"What about Blacky," asked Thatcher. "You told me he interfered with Bender this morning. We can't have citizens taking the law into their own hands?" Thatcher smiled.

Gregorio looked at Running Wolf. "Where do you stand in all of this, my old Indian friend? Do your loyalties lie in my camp, or with your traveling partners?"

Running Wolf remained silent momentarily. Then he spoke, "I will not kill them. The boy and his father saved my life."

"Once they find out that you were the one who stole Kate and sold her to me, I think they'll be after your hide with more tenacity than they will mine," Gregorio told him.

Running Wolf sat again in his own quietness.

"Blacky, what do we do about Blacky?" Thatcher repeated.

"We'll keep an eye on him. If his involvement was an isolated incident, we'll deal with him later. If he gets involved, we'll eliminate him sooner," was Gregorio's explanation.

* * *

Cole woke up the next morning to find his mother sitting on the side of the bed beside his father. When Cole had returned to the room from the telegraph office the night before, the two had been lying side by side in the bed, his mother asleep, his father unconscious. Bertram had been sleeping lightly in the chair next to the door. He heard Cole come in, and showed him the place on the floor that had been made up for him by his mother. Once Cole was inside, Bertram moved the chair against the door, and slept there.

"Ma," asked Cole, "how's pa doin' this mornin'?"

"I don't know, son, he seems to be the same, but it's hard to tell without him waking up."

Cole looked around the room and saw that Bertram was gone.

"Where's Bertram?" Cole wanted to know.

"He went to his blacksmith shop to get some instruments he'll need to try and get your pa's bullet out this morning. He's going to get us some food, too," she told Cole.

Bertram entered the room a short while later. He carried a small black satchel and a larger cloth bag. He also brought his shotgun. As Bertram placed the cloth bag just inside the door, and the satchel on the table near the bed, he told Katherine of a conversation he had had with the doctor.

"Ah went ta sees da doctah, but he ain't comin' ta helps us. He knows missah Gregorio would kills him if he tries ta help, but he give me his old doctah's bag and told me what ta do ta git the bullet out, or try ta." Bertram said. A look of concern came over Bertram's face, and he looked downward.

"What's the matter, Bertram," asked Katherine.

"Miss Katherine, when Ah tole da doctah about yah husband's condition, he sez yah husband has ta be stronger 'n ordah ta have a chance ta survive da operation. He thinks we needs ta wait."

"How long?" Katherine asked.

"Well, doctah sez missah Clint haz ta get food 'n him ta replace da blood he's lost and build up his strength. But 'til he wakes up, it be hard ta git food inta him," Bertram said. "Don't knows how long dat'll take."

Katherine looked at Clint. "Oh, Clint, wake up, please wake up," she pleaded quietly, as she slowly tipped a small cup full of water to get it down her husband's throat.

Cole sat watching the room and those in it. He was surprised that he was not more fearful of the situation. Clint badly wounded, Katherine out of his life for seven years until yesterday, and trusting a black man he'd never met until last night. On top of that, a man who could try and kill them or remove them from town at any moment. He could no longer be afforded the luxury of being just 12 years old anymore.

* * *

It had been four days since Clint and Cole rode into town with Running Wolf. Clint had maintained a steady heartbeat, no better, no worse. On the fourth day since entering Waterhole, Clint woke up in midday. Katherine was asleep next to him. Bertram and Cole were playing a card game in a far corner of the room. Clint looked around without speaking. No one had noticed he was awake. He looked at Cole, and the black man sitting with him. Clint recognized the black man as the one who had helped him in the street. Clint had never seen a black man so big, and figured there weren't two of them. Clint turned his head and saw Katherine lying next to him. He reached out, placed his hand on hers and gently squeezed. Katherine woke up slowly, then realized what she was feeling. Startled, she looked at Clint, broke into a big smile and leaned over to hug him gently. Clint smiled at his wife.

"How ya doin', Marshall?" he asked jokingly in a weak voice.

Katherine couldn't speak. She was having a hard enough time controlling her tears. She placed her face against his and kissed him lightly on the lips.

"Welcome back," she told him.

Cole heard his mother speak and looked over to see his father awake.

"Pa!" he shouted, running over to his bedside. Bertram stayed where he was and smiled at the family reunion.

"How long I been out?" Clint wanted to know.

"Been four days," Katherine told him.

"I don't recall all of what happened," Clint said.

"Archie Bender shot you in the back, through the window. Though you blacked out for a minute, by the time Bender reached the room, you were awake, lying on the bed with your pistol ready for him. You killed him as he entered the room," Cole explained.

Clint looked over at the black man.

"You helped me in the street," Clint said.

Bertram stood. "Yessah, Ah did," he replied.

"Our new friend's name is Bertram Smith. Some folks in town call him Blacky 'cause he's the town blacksmith, and, well, I reckon you can figure out the rest," Cole said.

"I'm beholdin' to you, Bertram," said Clint. "I guess you're not a follower of Gregorio."

"Ah's bin in Waterhole for more dan two years. Ah's seen some mighty bad things done by missah Gregorio and his men. Ah stays out of his way, and he and his men stays outta mine. Don't knows why Ah ain't left. Been a lot of places. Guess Ah just got nowhere else ta go," Bertram explained.

Waterhole

"Well, Bertram, I'm mighty glad you chose to stay," smiled Clint.

A worried look came over Katherine's face, as she contemplated Gregorio.

"Gregorio didn't expect you to live. Once he finds out you're alive, he'll likely try and kill you," she feared.

"No reason we can't keep it our little secret," Clint mentioned. Everyone else smiled at the idea.

* * *

"Been almost two weeks," said Coyote Jim as he sat in the saloon taking breakfast on the 13th day since Clint arrived in town. The rest of the foursome was also there, Sal Gregorio, Billy Thatcher and Running Wolf. Coyote Jim was slicing his beefsteak with his shiny, sharpened Bowie knife.

"You know Blacky has continued to help them folks," Thatcher said, stating the obvious.

Gregorio sighed. "So many problems. I think it's time to eliminate some of them. I don't know why that cowboy is still alive. Bender doesn't usually miss."

Gregorio looked at Running Wolf. "My Indian friend, you can join us, or die where you sit. Your choice, of course."

Running Wolf just nodded his head.

"Sheriff Thatcher, I'd like you to go over to the hotel. Take these two deputies with you," Gregorio said as he looked at Coyote Jim and Running Wolf, "and arrest Mr . . . . Kate's husband, for vagrancy. He hasn't been gainfully employed since he arrived in Waterhole. We can't have vagrants in our town, it sets a bad example for the other fine citizens."

"What are you going to do?" Thatcher asked.

"I'm going to finish my breakfast," Gregorio answered without looking up from his plate.

* * *

"I think its time to git that bullet out of my back," Clint told Katherine on the 13th morning in Waterhole. "I'm feeling strong. Expect I'm gonna to be okay."

Bertram looked at Clint and asked him, "Missah Clint, ya think yous' strong 'nough ta travel and find a doctor ta git it out?"

"How far to the next town?" Clint asked.

"Couple days ride," answered Bertram.

Before Clint answered, someone turned the doorknob, but the chair Bertram had wedged against the door prevented it from opening.

"Sheriff Thatcher here. Open the door."

Clint pulled the pistol from under the covers, and nodded for Bertram to get his shotgun.

"Stand in that corner," Clint whispered to Katherine and Cole as he pointed with his pistol.

Clint looked at Bertram and nodded towards the door. Bertram quietly removed the chair from the door and stepped back. "Door's open," Bertram called out.

Thatcher opened the door, but remained in the hallway. He looked straight in on Clint.

"Mornin'," Clint said.

Thatcher was startled to see Clint awake. Coyote Jim and Running Wolf stayed out of sight, standing in the hall, off to the side of the doorway.

"I expect you're not alone," Clint told Thatcher. "By the way," Clint began, "whatever happened to that pinto you stole back in Kansas?"

"That's where I know you from," said a smiling Thatcher, "you was with that posse that chased me clear out of Kansas. Well, truth be told, I shot that horse when I was done with it."

Clint stared at Thatcher. His stare caused Thatcher to remove the smile from his face.

"Come to collect taxes?" asked Clint.

"Come to arrest you for vagrancy," Thatcher replied.

"Vagrancy!" Clint hollered, then laughed.

Thatcher had been embarrassed to even say the charges against Clint. Thatcher didn't take kindly to being embarrassed, much less laughed at.

"You be in the street in 10 minutes," Thatcher told Clint, "or I'll be back up here, and people will die, and I won't be alone." Thatcher reached inside the room, grabbed the doorknob and closed the door. Clint heard the footsteps head down the hallway. He knew there was more than one, but he couldn't make out how many.

Bertram quickly wedged the chair back up against the door. Clint slumped in his bed, and frowned. Katherine and Cole ran to him. It had taken a lot of Clint's energy, nearly all he had, to present a strong figure to Thatcher.

"Clint, you can't face Thatcher. He's really fast on the draw, and he won't be alone," a worried Katherine informed him.

"If I meet them in the street, they'll likely leave you alone. You and Cole can slip out the back way. Bertram, you get them my horses and point them out of town when I get downstairs," Clint instructed.

"I won't go without you," Katherine told him.

"Me neither," echoed Cole.

"If we stay holed up in this room, it's likely they'll kill us all," Clint told them. "Our best bet is to let me get them out in the open."

After feeling like a man for a few days, Cole suddenly felt like a young boy again. He didn't know what to do. He had always minded his pa.

"Clint, I lost you for seven years. I'm not gong to run off and lose you again," Katherine told him. "I won't."

Clint smiled at his wife. Her coloring had already improved since he had first seen her two weeks ago. She'd even begun to gain back some of the weight she'd lost.

"I can't do this unless I know the two of you are alright," Clint told his wife and son. "I can't afford to be worrying about you, it'll distract me."

"Clint, you can't even git yourself down the stairs, likely," Katherine continued to plead.

"I'm strong enough to give you a ten minute head start while I call on them in the street," he told her.

Bertram had remained quiet during the family conversation.

"Bertram," Clint said, "time to get them horses for Katherine and Cole."

"Yessa, Missah Clint," he replied, and quickly left the room.

"Give me five minutes to git downstairs, then follow me down, and go out the back door. I saw one when I carried you upstairs," Clint directed Katherine. "Cole, take care of yer ma, don't let nothin' happen to her."

Katherine moved swiftly towards Clint and hugged him, while at the same time sobbed against his shirt.

"Careful," Clint said smiling, "you'll mess up this here shirt of Bertram's that I'm wearing."

Katherine began to cry harder. Cole walked over and hugged his father, too.

"Alright you two, time to get started," Clint said. He kissed Katherine on the lips, and Cole on the forehead. He opened the door to the room, turned and looked at his family. "Five minutes," he said. As he closed the door, he gave a smile and a wink.

When he reached the hotel lobby, he was met by Bertram.

"Missah Thatcher gots dat Indian ya come to town wit, and Coyote Jim. Looks like Gregorio has 'bout five or six others out der, too."

Clint didn't know why Running Wolf would side with Gregorio's men. That was not a conversation he had been privy to, about how it had been Running Wolf that had stolen Katherine seven years ago, and sold her to Gregorio.

"Tawt ya could use a second gun," Bertram said as Clint spied the shotgun and the rifle he was carrying.

"You sure?" Clint asked.

"Ah is tired of seeing missah Gregorio kills people 'round here, or runs dem off ta suit his fancy," said Bertram. "Either Ah lives ta see it end or Ah don't, but no mo."

Clint leaned against the wall of the lobby as he spoke with Bertram. He was already winded. Bertram noticed.

Thatcher was in the street with the rest of Gregorio's men.

"Time's up!" he yelled into the direction of the hotel lobby.

Clint and Bertram stepped out onto the wood planks in front of the hotel. As they reached the outside of the building, Clint stepped five feet to his left, and motioned for Bertram to move some to his right. Clint didn't want to make a single target by having them stand too close together.

The outside wooden planks were covered by an eight foot wood overhang, which not only provided shade in the daytime, but also provided some cover, as Clint suspected Thatcher has some men stationed in the upstairs windows across the street. By staying where they were, Clint and Bertram could not be seen clearly by those shooters.

"Kind of surprised I didn't have to come and git you," Thatcher claimed.

"I try not to be too hard to find for cowardly horse shooters," responded Clint.

Thatcher frowned at being called cowardly. He slowly reached down and unhooked the thin leather strap holding his gun in its holster. Clint's eyes scanned the street. Coyote Jim was off to his left, at about ten10 o'clock. Running Wolf was over on the right, standing at three o'clock. Clint was startled to see Running Wolf siding with Thatcher. There was something about their relationship that he didn't know, but now was not the time to learn about it. Two other men sandwiched Thatcher, each with about four to six feet between them. Across the street, standing outside the saloon were three more men with holstered guns. That counted eight in all, but Clint suspected there were more up top, across the street.

"Step out into the street, and let's git this over with," Thatcher proclaimed. "I got a breakfast to finish."

With the eight inch barrel on Clint's army pistol, he was better off keeping some distance in a handgun fight. His aim would be better than those shorter guns he saw holstered on Thatcher and his men.

"This distance here suits me just fine," Clint said.

Clint had decided that Thatcher was the gunhand. The others were hired guns, but not equal to Thatcher. He'd have to be the first one Clint went for when the shooting started. If he could drop Thatcher first, the others, he thought, may scatter, except for Coyote Jim and Running Wolf. They were not likely to be scared off.

Clint wasn't expecting this to be an honorable fight. As soon as Thatcher thought he had an advantage, he was likely to start things. Could be he was waiting for a window shooter across the street to start up, but Clint's lack of cooperation in moving out to the street was spoiling that plan.

The north south direction the combatants were facing removed any advantage of the sun being favorable to one side. As Clint looked in the southerly direction, keeping his eyes on Thatcher, Bertram rotated his head back and forth between Coyote Jim and Running Wolf. It was beginning to warm up and Clint could see Thatcher beginning to sweat. Feeling uncomfortable in the heat was likely to cause him to act sooner rather than later.

The street had been empty except for Thatcher's men. As Thatcher began to move forward, Clint let his hand slowly slide down to the handle of his pistol. Thatcher had not moved more than two steps when both he and Clint heard a horse trotting down the street from the east side of town. Clint didn't want to look away from Thatcher, who reacted in a similar manner, not losing eye contact with Clint. Thatcher stopped his forward progress and waited. The horse continued to move up the street, now at a slow pace. The rider stopped twenty feet east of where Thatcher and Clint faced each other.

"Afternoon, gents," the rider said.

Clint immediately recognized the voice and smiled. Joshua Rines was in Waterhole.

* * *

"Howdy, Joshua," Clint said.

"Howdy, Clint. Got me a telegram from Cole couple weeks back, said you might like my assistance," said Joshua.

"Thatcher," said Clint, "meet Joshua Rines."

Thatcher's brow ruffled. He had heard of Joshua Rines. And what he'd heard was that Rines was fast with his gun. Real fast. Thatcher turned his head away from Clint for the first time, now eyeballing Joshua.

"Best you leave town now, while you can," Thatcher told Joshua.

"Whether I leave now or later, it'll be on my own account, and I just ain't ready yet. Haven't seen my good friend, Clint, for a long spell. Guess we got some catchin' up to do," Joshua told Thatcher.

Thatcher surveyed the situation. He was nervous and was sweating more by the minute. Trying to save his reputation, Thatcher told Clint, "today's not the day. But it'll come soon. Might be that with Bender gone, I'd like to spend some time with Kate when this is all done."

Clint didn't take the bait.

"Come on in, Joshua," Clint told him.

Joshua got off his horse slowly, knowing where Thatcher, and Coyote Jim were at all times. Joshua Rines could assess a situation better than anyone Clint ever rode with. He knew who the dangerous ones were. He tied his horse to the hitching rail out front of the hotel.

"Careful, Joshua," Clint told him, "the sheriff here likes to shoot horses."

Thatcher turned and headed back towards the saloon. Coyote Jim calmly stayed where he was for a minute or more after Thatcher entered the saloon, before he followed. Running Wolf, then the rest of the street emptied into the saloon. Within minutes, the street was empty except for Joshua. He stepped up on the porch of the hotel.

"Good to see you," Clint smiled.

"Been a long time, too long," said Joshua.

The two men smiled at each other as they held onto their handshake.

* * *

Sal Gregorio was still sitting at his table in the saloon when Thatcher, Coyote Jim, Running Wolf and the rest of his men came back inside. He glanced up briefly, then back down at his game of solitaire.

"From the looks on your faces, I don't think your mission was successful," Gregorio deadpanned.

"Our problem just got a little bigger. Wanted time to plan a little more," Thatcher told his boss. "Ever hear of Joshua Rines?" Thatcher asked.

"Can't say that I have," answered Gregorio.

"Well I have," said Thatcher. "He's good with his gun."

"How good?" asked Gregorio.

"Word up Kansas way was that he was the best. Better than Wyatt Earp, Bill Hickok, the Mastersons, all of them," Thatcher told Gregorio. "And Kate's husband, I think he's Clint Herbert. Use to deputy with Rines, and them other lawmen. We bit off a bit more than usual with them."

"Are you telling me, Sheriff Thatcher, that you can't handle these two men, with all the backup you have?" Gregorio asked.

"These aren't any two men. And besides, Blacky seems to be thrown in the pot with them," Thatcher reasoned.

"What do you suggest we do, Sheriff?" Gregorio asked.

"We might be able to handle them with what we've got, but I'd feel certain if we added a couple of guns to our side," Thatcher said.

"You have anybody in mind?" asked Gregorio.

"I know a couple of brothers up in the Indian Territory. Might be that they'd be willing to help for a price," Thatcher suggested.

"Won't they be afraid, like you?" chided Gregorio.

"They ain't afraid of nobody, especially when the price is right," said Thatcher.

"Send Coyote Jim to get them. He knows the Indian Territory and can be persuasive if necessary," Gregorio told Thatcher.

"I'll take care of it," said Thatcher, "they should be back in two or three days."

* * *

Clint, Joshua and Bertram entered the lobby of the hotel, and there stood Katherine and Cole. They had not left. Katherine ran to Clint and hugged him like she wouldn't let go. Joshua smiled at the reunion. He looked at Cole.

"My, boy, yer just about as tall as a big old willow tree," kidded Joshua.

Cole walked over and gave Joshua a hug.

"I knew you'd come," Cole said with a sigh of relief.

"You know somethin' about this?" Clint asked Cole regarding Joshua's arrival.

"I sent a telegram a couple of weeks ago, right after you got shot," Cole told his father.

"Well I'll be," smiled Clint.

Katherine walked over and hugged Joshua.

"It sure is good to see you Josh," she told him. "I hear you helped Clint to look for me for a long time," she said thankfully.

"Joshua just smiled and hugged her a little tighter.

"How's Martha?" asked Katherine.

Clint didn't say anything. He had not told Katherine that Martha had passed on.

"Died of cancer a few months back," Joshua told her.

"Oh, Joshua, I'm so sorry. I loved her like a sister," Katherine told him.

"I know that, and so did she. She was torn up somethin' awful when we couldn't find you," he said.

Turning to Clint, Joshua began, "I know you've been shot, you've found Katherine, and you just about got yourself killed outside. But I think there's still lot I don't know. Care to fill me in?"

"Just as soon as I get back to our room. I'm still trying to get my legs and wind back," Clint offered.

As Clint laid on his bed, he spent the next half hour telling Joshua about Leroy McAlister coming to their Oklahoma ranch, and about how he had seen a woman who looked like Katherine in Waterhole. He told him about Sal Gregorio, about coming across Running Wolf, and Katherine informed them both that he was the one who had taken her. Clint then went on about Archie Bender, and the rest of the Waterhole experience, including Katherine's experience in hell. Clint introduced Joshua to Bertram Smith and explained how Bertram had saved his life, and continued to offer his help.

Joshua just shook his head. "Terrible thing," he said. "Well, I reckon it's time we get out of Waterhole, don't you? asked Joshua.

"Gregorio will not let us leave," Katherine told Joshua. "He's got a lot of men. They backed down once, but they'll regroup and make a plan. Sure enough, though, he won't let us leave peacefully."

"Well then, I reckon we'll have to come up with a plan of our own," Joshua informed the group.

Clint smiled and nodded in return.

* * *

The next morning, Thatcher dragged the telegraph operator into the street, just below the window of Clint's room. Running Wolf was with him.

"Here's what happens to those in Waterhole who don't follow directions." hollered Thatcher.

Clint and Joshua moved toward the window, keeping their bodies off to the side. Katherine and Cole were shooed into a far corner where Bertram stood in front of them. As they peered down to the street, Thatcher saw their heads peeking out of the window. Once he had their attention, he turned and nodded to Running Wolf. The Comanche stepped behind the telegraph operator, reached around with his left hand and grabbed the man by his hair, then with his right hand he pulled his long knife out of it's sheath and with one quick swipe, he slit the telegraph operator's throat. He held on to the man's hair until he was dead, then he let him drop to the ground. Without a word, Thatcher and Running Wolf turned and walked back to the saloon.

Coyote Jim returned in less than two days. Two men rode in with him.

"Looks like someone knows how to get a job done, Sheriff," Gregorio said to Thatcher, as Coyote Jim brought the newcomers into the saloon.

Thatcher did not look pleased at Gregorio mocking him.

The newcomers to Waterhole were Pete and Jim Talbot. They had ridden with Quantrill's raiders for a while after the War Between the States. Being from Missouri, they were known in Kansas as well. The Talbot brothers were known to be fearless, better than average with a gun, without scruples, and would kill for a dollar. They spent most of their time hiding out in the Indian Territory when they weren't reeking havoc on towns and stages.

"Welcome, boys, said a smiling Gregorio, "Sheriff Thatcher tells me that you two would make fine additions to our deputy force here in Waterhole."

Neither Talbot responded. They continued to stand in front of Gregorio's table.

"What's the pay?" Pete Talbot said, more of a statement than a question.

"I believe you will find me to be a fair man," Gregorio responded. "How does ten dollars a day sound, with a hundred dollar bonus each for Joshua Rines and Clint Herbert, doesn't matter who kills them. And I'll throw in another fifty dollars for Blacky, just for the sport of it."

"We didn't know it was Rines and Herbert we was gunnin' for," said Jim Talbot. The Talbot brothers had stayed out of Kansas, due to the presence of Joshua, Clint, Earp and the Masterson's.

"I had heard that the Talbot brothers were not afraid of anyone," Gregorio said.

"You heard right," said Pete Talbot, "but for Rines and Herbert, it'll cost you fifteen dollars a day and two hundred when they is killed, no matter who does it."

"I was not told that you were shrewd businessmen, Mr. Talbot, but I accept your terms," concluded Gregorio. "Sheriff Thatcher, please arrange for our guest's accommodations. We'll take supper this evening and discuss our plans for ridding Waterhole of our undesirable friends. Until this evening, gentlemen," said Gregorio as he adjourned to his lavish room upstairs over the saloon. The girl who had taken over in Katherine's room followed him upstairs.

* * *

It had been three days since the standoff in the street. Clint was feeling a bit stronger each day, but he was still far from recovered. The bullet remained inside of him. Clint had become more concerned with the safety of Katherine and Cole. Everyone agreed that it was not likely that Gregorio would let anyone leave uncontested, woman and child included.

Joshua had been watching out the window of their hotel room. It had been cramped quarters, but Bertram had confiscated a second and third feather mattress from other rooms on the second floor of the hotel. Since the trouble began, no one else had registered at the hotel, so the second story belonged to the Herbert party. Even still, they decided it was best to keep together rather than fan out across different rooms.

"It appears some old friends of ours have come into town, Clint," Joshua informed him.

"Friendly?" asked Clint.

Waterhole

"Nope," responded Joshua, "not unless you're doin' the paying. Looks like the Talbot brothers."

An uneasy feeling moved through Clint's stomach as he heard the news. Clint, like Joshua, was not afraid of anyone, but he was worried for Katherine and Cole. The Talbot's were going to make their departure from Waterhole that much more difficult.

"Are they good?" asked Katherine.

"More fearless than good," answered Clint, "but sometimes those kind are more dangerous."

"Whatda' ya say, Clint?" Joshua began.

"I think we need to make our way out of town tonight. I'm as strong as I'm going to be," Clint fibbed. "Besides, we're running out of the food Bertram brought us. If we travel under darkness, we'll be forcing them to respond in the darkness. That should work to our advantage."

"I've been watching the moon. It's been getting smaller each night. Should be almost no moon tonight. That'll help," Joshua added. "So what do you have in mind?"

* * *

Joshua Rines was not the only one who was aware of the waning moon. After their initial meeting upon the Talbot's arrival in town, Gregorio and his men had been meeting each night to finalize their plans. Thatcher had wanted to go bust in and start shooting the day the Talbot's arrived, but Gregorio, though he knew he had the numerical advantage, likened his planning to a chess game. He wanted to thoughtfully create and execute a plan that would be a thing of beauty.

As Gregorio hosted dinner for his hired guns, Thatcher, Coyote Jim, Running Wolf, and the Talbot brothers sat around the table, enjoying their feast.

"Tonight, gentlemen," Gregorio informed the table, "tonight we will rid Waterhole of Kate and her crew."

"What about Kate and the boy?" asked Thatcher.

"Tonight, everyone dies. Kate, the boy, everyone," Gregorio stated matter of factly. "The longer Kate has remained, the more out of favor she has fallen. She should have left when she had the opportunity. The rest mean nothing but trouble to me."

* * *

"Pa," Cole began to speak as they sat together in a corner of their hotel room. Katherine and Joshua were in another part of the room, discussing Martha, while Bertram kept watch out the window. The door remained shut with a chair wedged tightly against it.

"I don't get it. Why'd Running Wolf take ma? And why didn't he try and kill us once he was healed from the bear attack? And now, he's helpin' them other men try and kill us?" Cole kept asking.

"I don't rightly know, son," Clint answered, "I guess he took your ma to be able to sell her. Times was tough for the Comanche. They were losing their land, and having to constantly fight for their survival. I surely don't side with what he did, and when I get the chance, I plan to kill him. But I somehow understand what he done."

"Are all Indians like him?" asked Cole

"No, son, you can't judge a man by the way he looks. Folks are different. Indians, white folk and black folk, we may look different, but it's a mans character that you need to judge. Sometimes that can be hard to do. I reckon its best not to sit in judgment until you've had a chance to get to know someone," Clint reasoned with Cole.

"How long did it take you to get a fix on Joshua?" Cole asked.

Clint smiled as he looked across the room at his best friend.

"First night we shared a campfire during the war. Didn't take long with him. I could tell right off he was a good man. Didn't realize how good of a friend he'd become. Sometimes it's circumstances that determine that. I suppose that's what happened with us," Clint summarized.

"Think it's time to leave Waterhole," Clint told everyone in the hotel room at 10:00 that night. Their few belongings were packed. Mostly only what they were wearing, including Bertram who was walking away from many years worth of belongings at his blacksmith shop.

It began to drizzle on that late-April evening, a spring shower. It had been nearly two months now since Clint and Cole had left Leroy McAlister to handle the ranch, and head west. As he prepared for leaving, Clint realized for the first time since finding Katherine, that his family was back together, intact. It had been all he had wanted ever since the day he rode back into Dodge City and found that Katherine was missing. He immediately felt whole again. It gave him confidence.

"I figure Gregorio's got twelve or thirteen men with him," Clint told Joshua as they checked their pistols and extra cartridges.

"Most are probably average at best with their guns," said Joshua. "If we can take out Thatcher and the Talbot's, and the Indians, the rest will likely run."

"Good chance they're scattered anyways, not together until they plan to make a move. That should help," reasoned Clint.

The plan had been discussed. It was not much different than their last plan, except Bertram would remain with Katherine and Cole to ensure they leave town. Bertram had his rifle and shotgun, and he had confiscated a pistol from the hotel desk clerk for Cole.

Clint and Joshua would head straight for the saloon and eliminate as many of Gregorio's men as possible by surprise, duck out of the saloon into the alley next door and reload while Gregorio's men, those that may be left, began to retaliate.

"Time to go," Clint said.

He walked over slowly to Katherine, and put his arms around her. "Be back before you know it," he told her. Clint pulled her tightly to him and held her for a moment. Then he leaned her slightly away from him and bent over to kiss her. "I'll see you outside of town, soon," he told his wife.

Cole moved swiftly to his father and gave him a long hug. Clint patted him on top of his head.

"Pretty soon, I'll have to reach up to do that," Clint smiled as he spoke to his son.

Cole smiled back.

"Bertram, you ready?" Clint wanted to know from the man he entrusted with his family.

"Yessa, Missah Clint," Bertram acknowledged, "dey'll be safe wit me."

Clint nodded at Bertram, then at Joshua.

"Well, partner," Clint began, "time to go rid this town of some bad men."

Clint and Joshua went down the stairs first. They tied up the hotel clerk, who was the only one in the lobby. Bertram brought down Katherine and Cole. The three of them made their way for the back door. As they did, Clint and Joshua stepped out through the front door, onto the wooden planks and down to the street level. They began their descent towards the saloon.

* * *

Clint pushed open the saloon's swinging door on the right and immediately shot two of Gregorio's tax collectors. Joshua passed through the left door and put another two men down. Four shots had been fired in less than six seconds, and Gregorio was down four men. In the far corner of the saloon, Thatcher and the Talbot's were caught by surprise. They had planned on an attack of their own later in the night, but had been beaten to the punch. Jim Talbot stood and fired a shot towards Clint, but missed. Pete Talbot flipped over the table he was sitting at to use as cover while he pulled his revolver from its holster. Clint fired once at Jim, missing, but getting him to take cover. He then directed his pistol at Pete, and fired three rounds through the table. His .44 caliber was enough to pass through the turned over table top. Pete Talbot stood and attempted to fire, but the three bullet holes in him were enough to send him tumbling over the table, dead. Another shot from upstairs hit Clint in his left shoulder. Clint winced, then dropped to one knee and fired in the direction from where the shot had come. Another of Gregorio's men dropped from the second story railing, hit the ground and never moved again. As he fired, Clint was hit again by Jim Talbot's shot, this time in the left thigh. Clint dropped behind the bar and took a handkerchief from his pocket to wrap around his leg wound. With his adrenaline flowing, though the shots hurt, they did not incapacitate him.

Meanwhile, Joshua had taken in the direction of Billy Thatcher.

"Always wondered how fast you were," said a half drunk Thatcher. Though Gregorio had ordered him to watch his alcohol intake, he was just afraid enough of Clint and Joshua to think that he needed the reassurance found in a bottle.

Thatcher lifted his gun from its holster. Joshua did the same. Both men fired. From his position on the floor at the end of the bar, Clint looked over at Joshua, eyes wide open. His eyes then passed on to Thatcher. Both men stood frozen. A split second later, Thatcher dropped to his knees, gun still pointed at Joshua. Joshua emptied the rest of his rounds into the body of the kneeling Thatcher, nearly tearing him in half, as he fell to the ground.

Clint pulled himself up to the bar, and fired towards Jim Talbot, who was ducking behind the far side of the 20 foot long bar. Clint had emptied his gun, but before he could use the bar as cover to reload, Jim Talbot rose and fired. His shot struck Clint in the chest, dropping him to the ground. Almost simultaneously, Joshua had reloaded his revolver and fired at Jim Talbot, striking him three times in his chest and once in the head. He dropped his pistol and slumped over the bar, before sliding to the floor. Joshua looked around the saloon. There was no sign of any more of Gregorio's men.

* * *

As Bertram, Katherine and Cole heard the first shots fired in the saloon, they headed out the back door for the blacksmith shop. Bertram had saddled five horses earlier that evening, including those ridden into town by Clint, Cole and Joshua. They were waiting behind his shop.

As they exited the backdoor, Bertram was hit across the back of his head. Katherine screamed, and Cole lost his breath. Standing before them were Coyote Jim, who had hit Bertram, and Running Wolf. Not wanting to wait for the rest of Gregorio's men, the two Indians had decided to begin their attack on their own, and were as equally surprised by the exiting visitors as Katherine, Cole and Bertram were to encounter them.

Coyote Jim lifted the Bowie knife from his belt and began to thrust it towards Bertram, who had gathered his senses and stood back up. The big man lifted his left hand up to catch the forearm of Coyote Jim, but his hand missed its mark. Instead, the knife struck him in the palm of his left hand. Coyote Jim's strength drove it all the way through his hand, exiting on its backside. Bertram let out a loud yell, but did not stop. He grabbed Coyote Jim around the neck with his right arm and began to squeeze as hard as he could. Coyote Jim struggled, but was no match for the physically stronger blacksmith. Bertram squeezed Coyote Jim around the neck for minutes, well after he had stopped squirming. When he let go, Coyote Jim slumped to the ground. Bertram had strangled his attacker to death.

Shortly after Bertram had grabbed Coyote Jim, Cole pulled from under his coat the pistol he was carrying. He aimed it at Running Wolf, who did not move. Cole cocked back the hammer of the pistol and kept it leveled at Running Wolf. After a minute or so, Running Wolf sensed that Cole would not be able to pull the trigger, and he began to move towards the boy.

Katherine reached to the ground, where Bertram had dropped his rifle when hit over the head. She lifted it up to her shoulder, and as Running Wolf reached out for Cole, Katherine fired. She cocked the rifle and fired again. And again. Each shot hit her mark, the last one after Running Wolf had fallen.

"You took seven years from my life, you bastard," she said shaking. She shot him again as he lay on the ground, already dead.

Cole reached over and slowly pulled the gun barrel down and took it from his mother.

"Cole," Bertram summoned, "Ah is gonna ta need ya ta pull dis here knife from mah hand."

Cole and Katherine looked over and got a good look for the first time at the large knife that went in one side of Bertram's hand and out the other. Cole looked pale as he contemplated Bertram's request.

"Gots ta do it, Cole," Bertram said. The pain was beginning to mount as his adrenaline ceased.

Bertram knelt on the ground, Katherine standing over him, holding her hands firmly on his shoulders. Cole reached down, gripped the knife and pulled as hard as he could. Bertram let out a muffled scream. His head dropped, as he remained on his knees. Katherine quickly ripped off a part of her skirt and wrapped Bertram's hand. The wrap stopped some of the bleeding, but not much.

"We's gotta git ta mah blacksmith shop 'fore leavin' town," Bertram said. "We's gotta cauterize dis here wound. No udder ways ta fix it."

Within minutes, the three of them were in the blacksmith shop. Bertram's assistant, who had continued his allegiance to Gregorio, had a fire going for working on his anvil. As Bertram entered with Katherine and Cole, Bertram pointed his shotgun at the assistant, with one arm. The assistant turned and ran from the blacksmith shop as fast as his legs could carry him.

Bertram found a piece of iron and set it in the fire. "Once dis iron gets hot, you's gotta have ta hold it 'ginst mah hand ta stop da bleeding. Both sides. If'n Ah pass out, you still gotta do both sides, den git outta town. Yah knows where ta meet your pa and Missah Joshua. Leaves me and get yerselves there," Bertram directed.

After a few minutes, Bertram reached in the fire, and grabbed the hot iron. He was wearing a leather glove and had directed Cole to do the same. He handed the iron rod to Cole.

"Do it quick boy," a sweating Bertram instructed.

Cole grabbed onto the iron rod with his leather gloved hand.

"Do dah palm of mah hand first, den dah backside," said Bertram. "Hold it on fer a count of three 'fore ya takes it off."

Cole obliged and placed the iron rod against Bertram's left palm. Bertram let out a yell, scaring Cole, but he managed to keep the rod in place. When he pulled it away, Bertram was still conscience.

"Now dah backside!" Bertram hollered.

Cole quickly placed the rod on the back of Bertram's hand. Doing so was not unlike branding cattle, which Cole had helped his father with on their Oklahoma ranch. At the three count, Cole pulled the iron off of Bertram's hand. He was still awake. Cole had never seen a stronger man than Bertram Smith. Any less of a man would have crumbled and passed out. The smell of burning flesh was nauseating to Cole and Katherine.

"Let's git," Bertram managed to say before standing. "Heps meh up."

Katherine and Cole helped to lift Bertram from his knees. As much as any two their size could help lift a man of Bertram's stature. Katherine wrapped lightly Bertram's hand, then placed a leather glove over it. She finished by finding some cloth in the blacksmith shop, and made a sling out of it for him to use. The three made their way to the horses out back. They left two tied up for Clint and Joshua to find, climbed into the saddles of the other three, and lit out of town to wait for Clint and Joshua.

* * *

Clint sat up, with his back against the end of the bar he had been using to shield himself. The only other living person in the bar was Joshua. Everyone else who had been in the bar ten minutes earlier was either dead or had left as soon as the shooting had started. Clint had three bullet wounds, to go along with the bullet still inside from Archie Bender's gun, weeks earlier. He was losing a lot of blood. The shoulder wound was not a concern, but the thigh was bleeding badly, and the chest wound was serious.

Joshua holstered his pistol and knelt next to Clint.

"Most people try to get out of the way of bullets," Joshua kidded, knowing the wounds were serious.

"Well, hell, Josh, I had to draw some fire away from you, otherwise you'd never let me hear the end of it," responded Clint, weak in voice.

Clint could no longer hold his pistol. It rested next to him on the floor.

"I've got to find the doctor," Joshua told Clint. "You okay until I get back?" he asked.

"I'll hold on. Got me a wife to get back to, and she's a might prettier than you," Clint joked.

Joshua smiled as he stood up and looked at Clint.

"Be back soon," he told his fallen friend.

As Clint and Joshua shared a look of mutual respect and friendship, a shot rang out. The smile was erased from Joshua's face. He fell over, face down on the saloon floor. Standing in the doorway with a shotgun was Sal Gregorio. He had backshot Joshua. Clint reached for his gun. Gregorio had emptied both barrels, not realizing that Clint was still alive. As he saw Clint reach for his pistol, Gregorio dropped the shotgun and ran. He climbed on his horse, tied up outside at the saloon's hitching post. He turned and headed west, out of town. Gregorio never returned to Waterhole.

Clint crawled over to where Joshua lay on the floor. He used what little strength he had to roll Joshua over on his back. Clint placed his hand on his friend's chest. He held it there for a while before he sadly concluded that Joshua Rines was dead.

* * *

Bertram, Katherine and Cole were waiting about a mile southeast of Waterhole, in an old mining camp that Bertram knew about. Clint had seen it on the way into Waterhole, so he and Joshua would not have trouble finding it, they decided. The three kept a cold camp, not wanting to draw any unwanted attention to their presence. They stayed out of sight, camping on the edge of the tree line that surrounded the old mining camp. They had heard the shots from the saloon as they had turned their horses and galloped out of town. They had been in camp about an hour and a half when they heard what sounded like a single horse riding in slowly from the west.

Bertram had his shotgun loaded and in his good hand. Katherine held the rifle and Cole manned the pistol. The horse continued slowly into the camp. Its rider was slumped in the saddle, and the horse continued as if on its own. Bertram jumped out from the edge of the tree line and ran to the horse. He grabbed the reins and saw that it was Clint in the saddle, badly wounded.

"Miss Katherine! Comes quick, it's Missah Clint! He's hurt somethin' awful!" cried Bertram.

Katherine and Cole ran from their hiding place as Bertram helped bring Clint out of the saddle and laid him gently on the ground. His clothes were soaked with blood. The doctor had left town as soon as the shooting started, so there had been no one to tend to Clint's wounds. Bertram quickly examined Clint and found the three bullet wounds. He was most concerned about the one in his chest.

Clint lay unconscious as Bertram tried to get him to swallow some water. Within a few minutes, Clint was awake. Katherine had knelt down and placed his head upon her thighs, softly stroking his hair. Cole sat next to his father's side, opposite of Bertram.

"Bout time I got here, huh?" Clint nearly gagged as he tried to talk.

With tears making her eyesight blurry, Katherine smiled and continued to stroke his hair.

"Don't talk," she told him, "you've got to save your strength."

"No, I've got to tell you," he responded. "Gregorio shot Joshua in the back. Killed him, then ran like the coward he is. We got the rest of them, so don't worry about being followed." Each sentence was becoming harder for Clint to speak. "Cole, you take your ma back to the ranch, and take care of her. Honor the partnership with Leroy. Take Bertram with you, if he'd like. He's earned the right to be part of the ranch." Clint began to cough up blood. "Katherine, looks like we'll have to postpone a second honeymoon. Having found you has made me whole again." Clint reached out for Katherine's hand. She saw his and grasped it tightly. He could barely make a grip. "You're the prettiest Marshall I ever did see," he said smiling. "I love you."

Clint's eyes rolled back in his head, then closed. His breathing stopped.

Katherine and Cole wept as they held on to Clint. Bertram backed away to let the family have their time, and he went over to tend to the horses. Before they left camp, Katherine and Cole had decided to take Clint's body back home for burial. Joshua's too. Bertram bravely rode back into Waterhole the next morning and found Joshua's body where it had fallen on the saloon floor. All the dead bodies still lay where they fell.

Bertram brought Joshua back in a wagon, wrapped up tightly. He brought enough cloth for Clint to be wrapped up in also. The following morning, Katherine, Cole and Bertram began the long journey back to Oklahoma.

Part IV
Oklahoma Territory, 1885

Fall had arrived early in the Oklahoma Territory when the wagon carrying the bodies of Clint and Joshua rolled into the ranch in mid-September. It had been a hot trip, and the bodies of the two men were ripe. It had been difficult to be close to them for the past two weeks. Leroy McAlister heard the wagon coming up the trail. He looked down the dirt road and immediately recognized Cole, riding his horse, Slinger, alongside the wagon. As the wagon got closer, he recognized Bertram. Though they had never met, Leroy had seen Bertram in Waterhole months back. It was hard to forget a man of Bertram's stature. Leroy did not recognize the woman. Katherine's appearance had changed since Leroy had last seen her in Waterhole. Immediately, Leroy noticed that Clint was not riding in with the rest.

"Howdy, Cole," Leroy called out as the wagon neared the ranch house.

"Hi, Mr. McAlister," Cole answered.

Leroy sensed that this was a somber and tired traveling party. He chose to hold his words until he had a better idea of the situation.

"Mr. McAlister, this here is my ma," said Cole as he stood Slinger next to where his mother sat on the wagon, his hand on her shoulder.

"Nice to meet you, ma'am," a polite Leroy welcomed with a slight tip of his hat.

Waterhole

"And this here is Mr. Bertram Smith," continued Cole with the introductions.

"Hello, sir," said Leroy, "I recognize you from Waterhole."

Bertram smiled and nodded his head, but did not say anything.

"Mr. McAlister," began Katherine, "my husband was killed back in Waterhole, along with our friend, Joshua Rines. They are in the back of the wagon. I'd be grateful if you and Bertram could help us plan for their burial."

After not seeing Clint ride up with the rest, it was what Leroy McAlister had feared.

"Yes, ma'am, I'll see right to it. I'm very sorry. Your husband was an honorable and decent man. None better," responded Leroy.

Leroy and Cole helped Katherine climb out of the wagon, while Bertram, with only one good hand, attended to the team of horses. Even though she was home, it was a place that was new to her. As she entered the house, Katherine stood inside the doorway and looked around. Her eyes were immediately drawn to the picture of her on the mantel over the fireplace. Leroy noticed her gaze.

"Clint used to stare at that picture every night that I knew him," Leroy told her.

Katherine smiled.

"Here, ma, take this seat. Pa made it himself, and it was his favorite," Cole directed as he led his mother by the elbow over to Clint's chair.

She sat down, and slowly began to rock. Within minutes, her eyes closed. The rocking stopped. Katherine was fast asleep.

Cole covered his mother with a blanket, then he and Leroy stepped outside.

Bertram had finished with the horses, and the three of them sat in chairs on the front porch. Leroy expected there was a long story to tell, but he would hear it when the others were ready to tell it. The first conversation had to do with where to bury Clint and Joshua. Though the land was mostly flat, Cole decided on a small knoll, with a pair of willow trees on it, about a quarter mile from the house. You could see the trees from the front porch of the house. He'd want to get his ma's approval, but he knew the ranch better than she did. There was no better place.

Leroy had some cut lumber that was to be used for the completion of the bunkhouse he had been building. He and Bertram went off to use some of the boards to build a pair of coffins.

By the time Katherine woke, it was early evening, and Leroy and Bertram had finished one coffin and were halfway through the other. Cole was sitting on the porch when his mother appeared. He told her about the location he had picked out for the gravesite. Katherine asked Cole to walk her to it so she could see for herself. She put her arm through his and the two of them made the short walk north.

Katherine agreed that it was a lovely place for Clint and Joshua to lie, and she was pleased to be able to see it from the porch. With the coffins built, Bertram used a large pick with his one good hand to soften the dirt for Leroy to dig the holes in the ground the following morning. That afternoon, as the sun began to set, creating a colorful red and orange sunset, Clint Herbert and Joshua Rines were laid to rest.

* * *

It had been a couple of weeks since Clint and Joshua were buried. Katherine was beginning to make herself feel at home, while Cole helped Leroy and Bertram work on the bunkhouse. There had not been much conversation during the weeks past. Everyone seemed comfortable with the silence, but Katherine knew that she would have to gather everyone and discuss the future of the ranch. "No time like the present," she thought to herself late one afternoon in early October.

That evening, she called all the men into the house for supper as usual.

"Cole, Leroy, Bertram," she began, "I'm aware of Clint's wishes for this ranch, and I feel it's time to talk about it. But before I do,

I have become aware that Clint never gave a name to this place. With your permission, I'd like to call it the "Bar-CJ," after Clint and Joshua." She looked around the table. "What do you think, Cole?" asked Katherine.

"I think it's a great idea, ma," he said smiling.

"Okay then, the Bar-CJ it is!" she exclaimed, in the happiest tone of voice anyone had heard from her since arriving at the ranch. "Now, the next topic is the partnership in the ranch. Leroy, I know Clint made you a full partner when he and Cole left to find me. That agreement stands." She turned to look at Bertram. "And Bertram, I know how Clint felt about you're helping us in Waterhole, and what you gave up in doing so. Before he died, he asked me to make you a part of this ranch also. I'd like for you to have an equal share in the ranch as well, giving all of us one-fourth share in the Bar-CJ. What do you say?"

Tears began to run from Bertram's eyes. He had never owned any property before, and never dreamed that he would. He was so choked up, he couldn't speak. He just smiled and nodded his head as he kept his gaze upon his feet.

"I'll be a pig-toed mule," hollered Leroy, "I ain't never seen a grizzly bear cry before," he teased Bertram. Bertram just smiled even more broadly.

* * *

A year had passed since Clint and Joshua were buried. Leroy and Bertram had finished the bunkhouse. Even though they were partners in the ranch, they felt it improper to share the main house with Katherine and Cole. They slept in the barn until the bunkhouse was completed.

During that year, Leroy learned about what had happened in Waterhole. How Clint and Joshua eliminated Sal Gregorio's stronghold on the town, but in doing so, were killed themselves.

The fall of 1886 brought Cole's 14th birthday. He was continuing to fill out and grow taller. He now stood about 5'10" and weighed 165 pounds. His birthday had been overlooked by everyone, including Cole, the previous fall when they returned home from Waterhole. Katherine felt bad about forgetting, but was determined not to let it happen this year.

Though it took most of a day for a wheeled vehicle to get to the nearest town, Katherine declared that for Cole's birthday, everyone was to dress up in their Sunday best, and they would all go in to town and celebrate with the best steak dinner the town had to offer.

On September 22nd, Cole's birthday, Katherine and Cole climbed into the back of their carriage, while Leroy sat up front to handle the pair of horses. Bertram sat beside Leroy.

"Alright, birthday boy, let's go have us a celebration!" howled Leroy, as he gave a light snap to the reins and the horses led the foursome away from the ranch.

With the Bar-CJ situated in the panhandle of the Oklahoma Territory, the nearest town was a small town just across the Colorado border.

It was nearly a four hour ride to reach the hotel and restaurant. Cole had worked up an appetite just anticipating his steak dinner. As Leroy hitched the carriage in a side alley to keep the street clear, Katherine led the rest of the party inside. Their plans were to stay in the hotel for the night, following dinner, then make the long trip home the next day.

"May I help you?" asked a tall, light-skinned man with a dark, narrow mustache and thinning hair. The proprietor was dressed in a well-tailored dark suit.

"We'd like three rooms for the evening, and your best table in the dining hall for our supper," answered Katherine.

"You and the boy are welcome, ma'am, but the darkie is not permitted in the dining hall, nor in one of our rooms," the proprietor stated.

"Is that a fact?" asked Katherine sarcastically. "And why is that?"

"Well, ma'am, patrons of our establishment don't care to share a meal with darkies. Don't matter much to me, but I am a businessman, and I must listen to my public," acknowledged the proprietor.

"Any law against my friend eating and sleeping here?" asked Katherine.

"Well, not an actual law, ma'am . . ." continued the proprietor.

"Good," interrupted Katherine, "then this will be a learning experience for your regular patrons. Come on Cole, Bertram, I see a nice table over there by the window." Leroy had joined the party at this point, and followed them inside the dining hall.

The dining hall was half full as Katherine and the rest sat down to eat. Their waiter approached sheepishly, eyeballing the proprietor for directions. The proprietor nodded his approval. The waiter asked to take their orders. Without hesitation, Katherine ordered the three biggest steaks they could find, and a smaller one for her.

Every eye in the dining hall was focused in the direction of Bertram. He was not only the single black patron, but certainly the largest as well. Bertram leaned over towards Katherine and asked her, "ya sure 'bout dis, Miss Katherine?"

"As sure as I am that we've got a good steak on the way," she smiled back at him. The rest of the evening was uneventful.

The steaks arrived and were every bit as good as Katherine and the three men were hungry. After dinner, they received their rooms, one each for Katherine and Cole. Bertram and Leroy agreed to share a room. Leroy had said that he wouldn't be able to sleep unless he had Bertram's snoring close by to sooth him.

The following morning, as the Bar-CJ party was loading the carriage to head for home, three men approached Bertram in the lobby of the hotel.

"Well lookie here, boys, seems as though the hotel became a barn overnight. Why else would this darkie be sleeping in here?" chided the leader of the trio, a man named Bart Jackson, a self-claimed distant relative of Stonewall Jackson, and the son of a South Carolina plantation owner. Jackson was a scrappy six feet tall, 43 years old, and owner of a large ranch outside of town. His ranch was just a three hour ride from the Bar-CJ, though neither owner was aware of the other.

Bertram just continued on his way without looking at the three men.

"Hold on there, boy," Jackson ordered. "I don't know why you slept inside last night, but it'll cost you double what the white people paid." Jackson placed his hand out, palm up, to collect from Bertram. Again Bertram avoided eye contact, and moved past the three men, out onto the porch of the hotel. Jackson was riled that he didn't scare Bertram.

Jackson and his men followed Bertram outside. Jackson reached for Bertram from behind, grabbed his arm, and swung him around. The act caught Bertram's attention, as he cast a mean scowl in Jackson's direction. All at once, Bertram recognized Jackson. He was the son of the plantation owner who kept Bertram's parents as slaves until the Emancipation Proclamation of 1863. Bertram had been born on the South Carolina plantation in 1851. He lived there as a slave child until he left with his parents when he was 12 years old, but not before he witnessed the cruelty his parents suffered at the hands of the Jackson patriarch. Bart Jackson had been taught by his father to treat the slaves with hostility and contempt, and he too had taken to flogging slaves before they were freed, including Bertram's father. It was all coming back. As a ten year old boy, Bertram was witness to an 18 year old Bart Jackson whipping his father.

Bart Jackson did not recognize Bertram, as he was only a child when they last exchanged glances.

It took all the patience that Bertram had not to throttle Bart Jackson. As the two men continued to exchange stares, Leroy came out of the hotel, followed closely by Katherine and Cole.

"Excuse me, gents," Leroy said politely as he squeezed between Bertram and the other men with a handful of supplies to be taken back to the Bar-CJ. He suspected this was not a cordial meeting, but acted to the contrary.

Waterhole

Katherine, too, saw that Bertram was acting unusually hostile in his demeanor. She broke the mutual silence between the two parties by asking Bertram to help load the supplies into the carriage.

"Sorry to be impolite, but it's time we get on our way home," Katherine told the three men on the porch.

Bertram took his glare off of Jackson, and took the four steps down from the porch to the street level, then boarded the front of the carriage. Leroy was already in his seat, and Cole had helped his mother into hers. As he put one boot into the carriage, Leroy gave a sharp snapping action on the reins and they were off.

Jackson watched the carriage head down the street until it was out of sight, then he and his men walked back inside the hotel.

"Where did that darkie come from?" he asked the proprietor.

Knowing not to get on the bad side of Bart Jackson, the proprietor responded.

"They registered as the Herbert party from the Bar-CJ ranch in the Oklahoma Territory. It's somewhere in the panhandle, I think," he informed Jackson.

Jackson nodded his head and smiled. "Always wanted to see the Oklahoma Territory."

* * *

On the way home, Bertram told the rest of the Bar-CJ party about Bart Jackson. Bertram had not disclosed his background, born into slavery, before. Both of his parents left the plantation in 1863, but not in good health, especially Bertram's father. He was partially crippled from a leg injury, and the floggings he had been subjected to had left him with such scar tissue that he had trouble standing up straight. Bertram's parents both died of natural causes within four years of receiving their freedom, much too early, due to their lifetime in slavery.

"How'd you end up in a place like Waterhole?" Cole asked Bertram after hearing his story.

"Tried many places, 'cept da more civilized de was, da more hatred der was fer mah kind. Ah was 16 when mah parents died, but Ah was big 'nough ta take care of mahself. Ah thought de north would be 'ceptin', but it warn't too good. So Ah kept wanderin'. Ne'er spent more dan a couple years in any one place, so Ah kept headin' west. Wern't til Ah gots ta Waterhole dat Ah felt less violated cause of mah color. People der leaves mah alone. Dey didn't so much 'cept mah, but dey did'n goes out of da way ta make things hard. Even with missah Gregorio runnin' da town, I was left alone ta runs mah blacksmith shop."

"You've got a home now, Bertram, and will always be accepted by us," Katherine said as she reached forward and placed a hand on his shoulder. She felt his shoulder give, as if melting. It was a soothing touch, one very much appreciated by Bertram. Once again, his eyes began to well up. Leroy had been silent throughout the ride home, but sensing Bertram feeling a bit emotional, he tried to lighten the mood by hollering, "don't get the big fella goin' again!" Cole and Katherine chuckled. Bertram tucked his chin and smiled.

* * *

Early November rolled in with a cold, biting climate. Cole and Bertram had retired for the evening, while Katherine and Leroy sat outside on the porch of the main house, bundled up, but enjoying the freshness that an early winter air brought.

"Leroy, I bet that you and Clint sat out here many a night and never spoke a word," Katherine challenged.

"You'd be right about that, Katherine, many a night," Leroy acknowledged.

"I think it is something that men can do, not having to know too much about another person's background. Clint dealt with people as he saw them. I expect many a men are the same," she surmised. "But a woman has to know things. I finally got to learn a little about Bertram on the way back from Colorado. Now I'd like to hear about you," Katherine requested.

Waterhole

"Well, I don't know that there's all that much to tell. I was born in Boston in 1829. My father taught at Harvard University, and my ma raised eight children, all but two lived into adulthood. I was working in a Boston bank when I heard about the gold strike out west, in California. It got my traveling juices flowing, and in 1850, I headed west by wagon train. Had me a nice little claim for a couple of years, down around Calaveras, but had it taken from me by some Mexican bandits. They were led by a fella called Joaquin Murrieta. They came through my claim, killed my partner, and thought they had killed me, but I was just wounded in the shoulder. Hurt like a son of a gun, though. They took almost $3,000 in gold dust from us. Decided to find a new living after that. It was too dangerous in the mining camps in those days.

A Ranger named Captain Love eventually caught up with Murrieta, and cut off his head. I saw it displayed in Stockton some time later. After mining, I spent most of my time working for folks in big cities. When I heard about the gold in Arizona, I decided to take another turn at it while I still could. Made a little money in my claim, but Sal Gregorio saw to it that I best leave or be buried there. I wandered east, and found my way here. That's about all there is to tell."

"You never married?" asked Katherine.

"Nope, never inclined to settle down. Couldn't do so myself, so I couldn't see asking another person to," explained Leroy.

"You ever do any teaching, like your father?" Katherine asked.

"Nothing formal. Did help some young uns while I was in San Francisco for a time," he acknowledged.

"I'd like for Cole to get some schoolin', Leroy. Do you suppose you could teach him? I'd like for him to go to college when he's of the age. I'm not sure he's cut out for being a rancher his whole life." Katherine offered.

"Be glad to give it a try. You think Cole's willin' to learn?" asked Leroy.

"We'll find out when we start tomorrow," Katherine responded with a smile.

As they sat on the porch, now silent, they looked out at the knoll where Clint and Joshua were buried. The moon was low in the sky and it backlit the headstones that had been made and rested atop the graves.

"How often you think of him, Katherine," asked Leroy, knowing what she was thinking.

"Every day, Leroy, every day," she answered.

* * *

Cole sat in his saddle like a man at 14 years of age. Though Slinger was getting on in age, he still used her around the ranch. With a small herd of cattle, there wasn't much need for line riders at the Bar-CJ, but Cole liked to take an early morning ride to different parts of their 160 spread and beyond, depending on how far out the cattle were grazing in the free range, just to make sure everything looked as it should. It also gave him a chance to delay beginning his daily schooling that Katherine and Leroy had started up with him a few weeks prior.

With the winter weather expected anytime, the cattle didn't wander too far from the ranch house, as most of the grazing pastures were wet from the fall rains, and would soon be blanketed in snow. At the farthest part of the Bar-CJ property away from the ranch house, the land crested on a gentle hill that overlooked a big valley. It faced to the northwest, towards Colorado. It was Cole's favorite part of the ranch to ride to and sit, just to think.

On this particular day, as he arrived on Slinger to look over the valley, Cole noticed four riders about a half mile away, with three cattle in tow. Cole had never seen any riders off in that direction before, much less any cattle. They were heading away from the Bar-CJ.

Cole returned home and spent his daily ninety minutes with Leroy, this time learning about mathematics. After his afternoon chores, he, along with everyone else, washed up and was prepared for Katherine's delicious dinner. Katherine took great pride in feeding the men of the Bar-CJ very well. As Bertram sat down, he commented that when counting the herd earlier in the afternoon, he was about five head short.

"Mawt be off searchin' fer grazin' pasture. Ah'll ga looks t'marra," he told Katherine and the rest.

Cole was still thinking about his mathematics lesson from earlier in the day, and didn't make a connection between Bertram's cattle count and the riders he saw that morning.

Cole had given a lot of thought to his mother's wish that he go to college when he was of age. The more he thought about it, the more he liked it. That made his schooling from Leroy more bearable. He hadn't really thought what it would be like to leave the ranch, but he did have a wish to see other parts of the country.

The following morning, Bertram rode out to find the missing cattle. About a half hour out, well beyond the Bar-CJ property line, and just out of sight of the chimney smoke coming from the house, he found tracks. Both from horses and from cattle. It appeared to be three or four riders, and the tracks were fresh. He glanced up in the direction that they were heading, but he didn't see anyone or anything. Bertram reached down and behind him to feel for his rifle. It was in its stock. He had a bad feeling about the missing cattle and strange hoof prints from horses not belonging to the Bar-CJ. He gently dug his heels into his horse and began following the tracks.

Bertram rode for only half a mile when he saw Cole riding Slinger, headed in the same direction as the tracks.

"Hey, Bertram, what brings you out here, I thought you were looking for the cattle?" inquired Cole as he trotted Slinger up to where Bertram stopped to meet him.

"Howdy, Cole," replied Bertram, "Ah's lookin' fer da cattle. Found some tracks a ways back. Dey was both horses 'n cattle. Ah knows de ain't ours, so Ah'm followin' dem ta see where de lead. Got a bad feelin' bout dem, Cole. Could be someon stealin' our livestock."

Cole immediately remembered that he had seen riders with cattle heading away from the ranch the day before. He told Bertram about what he saw.

"It didn't dawn on me that the cattle might be ours. We ain't never had any rustling' goin' on around these parts. The Indians leave us alone. Ain't nobody else that close, or so I thought," Cole explained.

"Dese ain't Indian ponies," Bertram explained, "dese horses are wearin' shoes. I knows of a ranch a few hours from here, 'cross da border into Colorado. Spoke ta one of deir line riders a few months back, 'fore we went ta celebrate ya birthday."

"You think they're the ones takin' our stock?" asked Cole.

"Don't know, but Ah think Ah'll foller dese tracks fer awhile, see where de lead," said Bertram.

"I'll go with you," said Cole.

"Best Ah go alone," Bertram told him, "be easier fer me ta git close without being seen if Ah needs to. B'sides, yer ma would skin mah alive if'n Ah get ya inta a ruckus." Bertram tried to downplay a possible confrontation, and he also realized that Cole wasn't carrying a firearm, and Bertram only carried his rifle. Though his hand had healed from the knife wound he received from Coyote Jim back in Waterhole, the scars remained and it still troubled him enough that a rifle was a more practical weapon for him than a handgun.

Cole had inherited Clint's Remington New Model Army .44, but Katherine still had enough influence over him not to allow him to wear it. Cole kept it wrapped in a cloth, stored in a dresser drawer, along with the holster.

"Ya ride back ta da ranch 'n tell yer ma 'n Leroy dat Ah'll foller dese tracks fer a while. Ah 'xpect Ah'll be home 'bout supper time," Bertram directed.

"Okay, Bertram, but you be careful," Cole warned.

Bertram nodded, then with a sharp whistle, broke into a gallop right away. Cole watched him go for a few minutes, then turned and began to gallop Slinger back to the ranch.

The day grew shorter, and Bertram had not returned. Supper time came and went, and Katherine did her best to disguise her worry by saying that Bertram must have traveled a might further than he expected. She didn't fool anyone. Both Leroy and Cole knew she was worried, and so were they. It was close to midnight when Katherine and Leroy heard a horse trotting up the road towards the ranch. Cole, who had already gone to sleep, heard it too, and came out onto the porch to join his mother and Leroy.

It didn't take long to recognize the size of the rider, as the moonlight allowed for a good silhouette. Bertram was home.

"Where in tarnation have you been?!" asked Katherine.

Leroy stepped off the porch and took Bertram's horse to tend to it for him.

"Go get some food, Bertram," Leroy suggested.

Bertram climbed down and nodded his thanks at Leroy. He was tired and saddle worn. It had been a long day. Bertram followed Katherine into the house, where she still had a supper plate waiting for him next to the fire. Cole followed the two of them into the house. Bertram sat down and began to eat. He finished his plate while Katherine and Cole anxiously waited to hear about his search. About the time he finished his dinner, Leroy came back inside, having tended to Bertram's horse.

Katherine asked him again, "Where have you been?"

"Ah follered da tracks fer a long ways," Bertram began, "all da ways inta Colorado. Der was three riders, with six cattle. Couldn't be sure de was ours, so Ah waited 'til da riders was all inside fer der supper. Ah sneaked on down ta da corral de put da cattle in, and sure 'nough, de wore Bar-CJ brands. Ah counted 'leven of ours'n all."

"You know who they are?" asked Leroy.

Bertram looked around the table at each of the other three owners of the Bar-CJ, his face looking more serious as it moved clockwise. When his eyes were cast on the face farthest to his right, Katherine's, he clenched his teeth as he said the name, "Missah Bart Jackson."

* * *

Bart Jackson had over 10,000 acres on his Colorado ranch. It was easily big enough to hide cattle if need be. And because the Oklahoma Territory was without any formal lawmen, it would be difficult to prevail if Katherine were to bring the cattle thievery to the courts.

Katherine sat at the head of the table, as always, in the ranch house. Cole, Leroy and Bertram joined her as they discussed their options in dealing with the cattle thieves from Bart Jackson's ranch. Bertram suspected that Jackson knew who he was stealing from. He considered it too coincidental that Jackson would begin stealing their cattle so soon after the confrontation Bertram had with him during the Bar-CJ's trip into town to celebrate Cole's birthday.

Jackson had the power; more men and weapons than the Bar-CJ. With no law to protect them, Katherine felt their options were limited.

"We'll have to bring the herd in close to the ranch," she told the others, "and not let them wander as far as usual. Maybe we'll need to hire some men to help keep a watch on them around the clock."

"That'd cost money," Leroy reasoned, "money we don't have. It might also provoke Jackson into a range war over the cattle and maybe even the land."

"But we've got the title on this land," Cole reminded, "how can he just take it from us?"

"Ah's sure dis mess is 'cause of me," Bertram stated. "Maybe Ah ought ta go over der and settle dis 'tween me and him."

"He's got too many men, Bertram," Katherine countered, "and if it was just you he was after, seems like he'd have come for ya."

"If'n he knews who Ah was, he'd come," said Bertram.

"Maybe we could send for some of pa's old friends. Maybe Wyatt Earp and Bat Masterson'd come help?" an excited Cole mentioned.

"Not likely, Cole, particularly since we don't even know where they are anymore," Katherine told him.

"They'd come," muttered Cole.

"Could be we offer to sell the herd," thought Leroy. "Not the best time of year for it, but it'd take care of the cattle rustling problem."

It was a novel idea. Not one Katherine or anyone else had considered. She asked around the table for everyone's feelings. Selling the herd was the consensus. They would keep the money from the sale until a time later when they could buy back the cattle, or other livestock. Katherine and Leroy had been concerned for sometime that the free range land their cattle had used for grazing over the years would soon be gone with other settlers moving west. The problem would be finding a buyer. In the meantime, it was agreed to bring the cattle in close to the ranch, corral what they could and feed them out of the barn. Cole, Leroy and Bertram would add a larger corral, made out of barbed wire, to keep the rest of the cattle close to home.

It only took a couple of days to build the hastily made corral. Katherine and Leroy headed south the following morning for Texas, in hopes of finding a buyer for a quick sale. Katherine was uneasy about leaving Cole and Bertram home without any other protection. They were under strict instructions not to be heroes if Jackson's men came to steal their cattle. Though they were all equal partners, Katherine was still the boss.

Cole didn't sleep very well the next few nights. Every sound he heard caused him to get up and look outside. Bertram stayed in the bunkhouse, as it was closer to the cattle, and he was a light sleeper, regardless of what Leroy claimed about his snoring.

On the fourth night following Katherine and Leroy's trip into Texas, Cole awoke to a gunshot. He jumped out of bed, threw on his pants, and grabbed his father's pistol. Without thinking, he threw open the front door, immediately drawing a shot that missed him by a foot and lodged in the door. Startled, he withdrew inside the house and shut the door as quickly as he had opened it. He moved over to the window and peeked outside toward the corral. He could see Bertram behind a hay bale, rifle in hand, and one man down just on the other side of the corral. Cole could see two others after a minute due to the light from their muzzles when they fired their pistols. He didn't know which one fired in his direction.

"Stay'n da house, Cole!" hollered Bertram.

Cole didn't answer, maybe out of fear, but he kept his eyes peeled.

Bertram and the two men exchanged shots again, more to make them aware of each other's presence than anything else. None were going to be hit from where they were hiding.

Cole could hear the two men talking, but couldn't make out what they were saying. A minute or so later, the one closest to Bertram began to fire repeatedly at Bertram, causing him to take cover. At the same time, the other rustler began making his way around behind Bertram. Cole called out to Bertram, but his voice was lost over the sound of the gunfire. Since Cole had not fired, the rustler's believed that he was not armed. The one making his way behind Bertram, threw a shot towards Cole, hitting the side of the house far from where Cole was stationed. The rustler's path was taking him closer to the house. He was within 30 feet of the front porch. Cole could see that the rustler would have Bertram in his sights within seconds. Without giving any thought to his actions, Cole cocked the hammer on what was now his pistol, and aimed out the window, just the way Clint had taught him to aim. He fired once. The rustler staggered two more steps, then fell to the ground . . . dead. His partner, having seen the result of Cole's action, fired once more towards Bertram, then turned and ran back to his horse in the dark. Though Cole and Bertram could not see him, they heard the horse take off in a full gallop.

Bertram rose slowly from his spot near the corral. He kept his gun pointed at the first man who had gone down, the one Bertram killed before Cole got to the door. He kicked his gun away, then kicked the rustler hard in the stomach, to see if he was dead. The man did not respond. Bertram proceeded over to the rustler Cole had shot. As he approached the fallen man, Cole came out of the house with his pistol still in hand, but pointed down towards the ground. Both he and Bertram were clothed only with their pants. Bertram kneeled down to examine the rustler, seeing he too was dead. Bertram looked up at Cole. Cole had a steely glaze over his eyes. One that Bertram might expect from someone who had killed before, but not from Cole.

Bertram stood and placed a hand on Cole's shoulder. After what seemed like forever, they exchanged glances. Bertram nodded at Cole, who returned the gesture.

The next morning came early. Bertram and Cole had both slept in the bunkhouse to be closer to the herd in case there was a return of the rustlers. There was not.

They loaded the two dead bodies into the wagon, and hauled them off to the east. It was the closest border of the ranch. They dug one large grave, and buried both men in it. They left the grave unmarked.

Bertram and Cole sat atop the wagon during their return home. Both were carrying firearms, Bertram his rifle and Cole his pistol, this time worn in its holster. Cole had never worn his father's holster before. It made him feel older than his 14 years.

Cole broke the silence after an hour on the return trip to the ranch house.

"I ain't never killed no one before, Bertram," Cole said as he stared straight ahead, feeling the slightest winter breeze on his face.

"Ah knows dat," Bertram responded.

"I don't feel nothing," Cole continued, "I thought that if I ever killed someone, I would feel something."

"Ah 'spect ya will. Could be that it'll be a short time comin, but Ah 'spect ya will," Bertram told him.

"How old were you when you killed your first man?" asked Cole

Bertram did not immediately answer. He kept his focus on the road ahead as he delayed in answering Cole.

"Ah was 35 years old," Bertram finally spoke.

Cole looked at him with a strange glance, knowing that Bertram was now just 36.

"Dat Indian'n Waterhole, the comanchero, he was de first man Ah ever killed. Last night made da second," Bertram told Cole.

Cole was surprised. Didn't know why he should be, but somehow he'd expected a different answer.

"Folks don't tek kindly ta a black man killin' a white man," Bertram explained. "No matta how bad Ah was treated, Ah a'ways kept my nose clean, and jest moved on."

"That rustler last night, he was white," realized Cole.

Bertram just shook his head, half in acknowledgement of Cole's statement and half in the realization that this might not be the end of it.

"There ain't no law to arrest you, or us," Cole thought. "Besides, it was self defense."

"Not havin' no law might make it worse," said Bertram. "No tellin' what missah Bart Jackson might do when he finds out. An' Ah 'spect his rider has returned, da one dat got away last night. We's know soon enough."

As Bertram and Cole arrived back at the ranch house, they saw Katherine and Leroy outside of the bunkhouse. When Katherine heard the wagon coming up the road, she ran to meet it. Bertram pulled back on the reins when Katherine got close, about 100 feet short of the house. She had a desperate look about her. She was perspiring profusely, and wore a look of relief and concern at the same time.

"What happened here?" she wanted to know.

"Three of Jackson's men came last night, trying to steal more cattle," Cole began to explain to his mother, "Bertram heard them, and shot one of them. About that time, I heard the shot, and grabbed my pistol and ran to the door."

Katherine noticed that Cole was holstering Clint's old pistol.

"I kept out of sight until I saw one sneaking up on Bertram," Cole continued. "I had to shoot him. The other one got away."

Waterhole

Katherine didn't respond. She looked at Bertram who nodded in agreement with Cole's version of last night's events. Without saying anything, she reached up and patted Cole on the knee.

* * *

Katherine and Leroy had been successful in selling the rest of their herd to a rancher in Texas. In exchange for not getting a price they were hoping for, the rancher agreed to send up his own men to drive the cattle south. They were expected to arrive within two weeks. That meant that the Bar-CJ would have to put in a lot of round the clock hours watching the herd until the Texas cattlemen came. In light of what happened while she was gone, Katherine expected it would be a long two weeks.

* * *

"What the hell happened!" Bart Jackson shouted at the ranch hand who had escaped with his life from the Bar-CJ the night before. They were standing outside the bunkhouse with a handful of other men watching.

"One of them heard Johnny," the ranch hand responded, trying to cast blame on his now dead former friend. "We was ambushed by them, in a crossfire between the main house and the bunkhouse," he continued to build his lie in his defense.

"You lying son of a bitch!" Jackson growled at the ranch hand, "we saw the woman and the old man ride out days ago. That only left the boy and the darkie." Pacing back and forth, from five feet away, Jackson stopped, pulled out his pistol and shot the ranch hand in the stomach.

"Try making up more lies while you're gut shot," snarled Jackson.

As one of the other men reached to help the gut shot ranch hand, Jackson hollered at the man, "touch him and you're dead too!"

The rest of the men retreated inside the bunkhouse, while Jackson returned to his house. Within an hour, the gut-shot ranch hand was dead.

"It appears they know what's happening to their cattle. Don't know if they figured out whose taking them, but we can't take any chances that they do. We'll go get the rest tomorrow, and kill anyone who gets in our way," Jackson instructed the eight men surrounding the chow table in the bunkhouse later that afternoon.

"Don't mean any disrespect, Mr. Jackson," began one of the ranch hands, "but why do we need to risk stealing cattle. They ain't but a pinch compared to what you have?"

"That darkie disrespected me. Nobody does that to me, especially someone like him. Why my father would have whipped him dead if it had happened to him. That's the problem with the anti-slavery laws, it allows them kind to get uppity to white folks, with no law against it," explained Jackson. "While there ain't no laws against it, there also ain't no law to protect them out here. We'll ride at first light."

Bart Jackson and six men were saddled and ready to ride at 6:30 the following morning. Jackson left two men behind to tend to the ranch.

"You think we got enough fire power to go in there in daylight?" asked one of the rustlers.

"They've got a woman, a boy, an old man and a darkie," stated Jackson. "Shouldn't take but a couple of us to overrun their place. Seven of us should have no problem."

Jackson turned his horse headed in the southeast direction. The rest of his men followed. They wasted no time in getting into a gallop. The Bar-CJ was only three hours away.

* * *

"Mighty fine, breakfast, Katherine," Leroy complimented.
"Thank you, sir," she responded.

Cole and Bertram had already finished their breakfast and were back outside. Cole had insisted on taking his turn watching the cattle during the night. It was his first time, and Katherine tried to put up an argument, but she saw the determination in her son's face, and reluctantly agreed. Cole seemed to have grown up overnight. Katherine was worried.

"Leroy," she began once they were alone in the house, "what's your take on Cole?"

"What do you mean?" he responded.

"I don't know. He seems different since we got back from Texas. For heavens sakes, he's just 14 years of age, and he's killed a man!" she exclaimed.

"Bertram says Cole saved his life. He expects he would have been killed if Cole hadn't stepped in and helped," replied Leroy.

"I know," Katherine said shaking her head, "I just wish he didn't have to experience such violence at his age. Times are getting more civilized elsewhere, but civilization is taking its own sweet time reaching the Oklahoma Territory. That's one reason I want him to go off to college when he's of the age. I didn't want him to grow up in a violent world. Bad enough he had to see Clint killed like he did. And now he's killed a man."

Katherine understood and could justify what Cole did to save Bertram, she just felt helpless in trying to spare her son from such an experience.

"What do you suppose Bart Jackson will do?" asked Katherine as she and Leroy cleaned up after breakfast.

"With no law around, he has a free hand and the manpower to pretty much do as he pleases," Leroy concluded. "Wouldn't surprise me if tries to form a vigilante committee from his ranch hands, and call it a lawful posse. I saw how vigilantes worked in the California gold country. It's an ugly sight. Men getting liquored up and hanging accused men before they even know if they were guilty."

"Then we'll need to be ready for them," Katherine informed him.

The next couple of hours were spent doing just that.

* * *

As Jackson's men neared the Bar-CJ, he put up his right hand to signal for everyone to stop. They were about 20 minutes away. Jackson passed around a bottle of tequila. It was the fourth bottle they had shared since they left Colorado, just a couple of hours ago.

"Don't expect they'll be ready to see us ride in early morning," Jackson told his men. "I want the old man and the boy put down. I'll personally take care of the darkie. If the woman don't get in the way, leave her alone. If she does, kill her too," Jackson directed. "Let's ride!"

* * *

Leroy directed the rest of the Bar-CJ about where to place weapons and themselves should Jackson arrive.

"Stay close to the house," he told them, "I don't figure on Bart Jackson to be a smart man. He'll likely be sitting on his brains as he rides. I expect he'll get here as soon as he can once he knows about his men's failure here night before last. Probably will try and use his muscle, not what brains he may have to drive us out. Stay alert," Leroy cautioned everyone. "He likely won't have a calculated plan, so we'll have to be sure we use our smarts to our advantage."

As Leroy concluded with his plan, Cole spotted a cloud of dust approaching from the north. "Here they come!" he said as he pointed towards the dust cloud.

"Let's go everyone," Leroy directed, "and remember, we will not give them a chance to gain an advantage. Shoot on my first shot."

With those last reminders, Leroy climbed up into the loft of the barn. Katherine took to the house with two rifles. Bertram planted himself behind the hay bales, just outside of the barn, and Cole was at a window on the ground floor of the barn.

It was less than five minutes later that Jackson and his men were within eyesight, riding hard and fast. Cole felt his pulse begin to quicken, and his palms were sweating. He cocked his pistol.

As Jackson's gang rode around the corral and were within the triangle that the barn, the main house and the bunkhouse made, Leroy fired from the loft, dropping one of Jackson's men. Quickly, Bertram, Cole and Katherine did the same, before any of the rustlers had a chance to fire a shot. Two more men dropped, including Bart Jackson. The four men remaining in their saddles turned and rode out harder than they had arrived. The invasion was over before it started.

There was a stillness as the echoing of the gunfire faded away. Leroy made his way down from the loft, and Bertram emerged from behind the hay bales. He hollered for Katherine to stay put. Cole came out third, gun in hand. Jackson had been hit, but was not dead. Bertram heard him groaning as he approached the lead rustler. Leroy confirmed that the other two men were dead.

As Bertram arrived at the spot where Jackson had fallen, he saw the son of his former slave master roll over onto his back. He had been shot in his right shoulder. Jackson groaned louder, but was alert to his surroundings. Bertram strode up to Jackson and stuck his shotgun in Jackson's nose, with force enough to cause it to bleed.

"You broke my damn nose, you damn darkie!" Jackson shouted as he grabbed at his nose with his left hand.

Bertram poked his shotgun into the wounded area of Jackson's shoulder.

"Aaawwwggg!" Jackson cried out in pain.

Bertram stood over Jackson, wanting to pull the trigger and blow him away. As he contemplated the thought, Leroy and Cole arrived.

"Ya don't 'member me, does ya missah Jackson?" Bertram asked.

"Yea, I do, you're the one from town that slept in the hotel," Jackson responded.

Bertram smiled.

"Ah knews ya a long time 'fore that," Bertram reminded him.

A puzzled look came over Jackson's face, and his head shook slightly as he tried to recollect.

"Da name's Smith, Bertram Smith. Mah folks were slaves of yer father's in South Carolina. Ah was born there. Ah saws ya whip mah pa 'fore we was set free," Bertram told Jackson.

"We had a lot of slaves, I don't remember one from another," Jackson griped, still clutching his nose.

Bertram stared at Jackson for a while, before turning and heading for the barn. It was at this time that Katherine came out of the house and walked over to where the rest were standing.

"Well, Mr. Jackson, it appears that justice has been served," Katherine told him.

Jackson spit in her direction, and Cole kicked Jackson in the ribs.

"Not again," Cole warned him.

Bertram returned with a whip.

"Maybe ya don't 'member me 'n mine," Bertram told Jackson, showing him the whip, "but yaw'll 'member how ya and yer pa treated us."

"No!" cried Jackson, "don't let that darkie whip me, it's unlawful!"

"If'n Ah had mah way, you'd hang," Bertram told him.

Katherine, and Leroy looked at each other, not sure whether to interfere or not. They did not want Bertram turning the incident in to an act of vigilantism.

Bertram reached down and grabbed Jackson by his collar. He dragged him by one hand for thirty feet, to the nearest tree. He lowered his whip and reached down to grab Jackson with both hands. As he did, Jackson reached into his boot and pulled out a knife. When Bertram stood Jackson up against the tree, Jackson stuck the knife into Bertram's side. Bertram winced. His hands released Jackson and he dropped to the ground. Leroy came running over and put another bullet into Jackson with his

Waterhole

Winchester, this one into his chest. Jackson dropped to the ground next to Bertram. Katherine and Cole ran to where Bertram had fallen. His wound was deep, but appeared to have caught nothing but the fleshy part of his side. He was bleeding profusely, but the wound was not fatal.

Bertram stood slowly, with the help of Katherine and Cole. He looked at Jackson, who realized that he would die soon.

"At least I wasn't done in by no darkie," Jackson said, choking on his own blood.

"When I was in the gold country, out in California," Leroy began, "they use to cut off an ear, sometimes both, of thieves, to identify them. He pulled out his large Bowie knife and held it over Jackson.

"Wouldn't do no good to do it when he was dead," Leroy said aloud for Jackson to hear. "Would you like to do the honors, Bertram?" Leroy handed Bertram the knife.

Not knowing what he would do next, Bertram knelt down next to Jackson and grabbed his ear.

"No, nooo!" Jackson coughed.

Before Bertram could decide his next move, Jackson was dead.

About an hour later, Leroy and Cole loaded the three dead rustlers into the wagon and rode out to where the other two Jackson men had been buried, for this group to join them.

A week later, the cattlemen of the Texas ranch made their way to the Bar-CJ. Though the reason for having to sell the cattle had been resolved, Katherine knew that a deal was a deal. She honored the transaction.

The night after the herd had left for Texas, she sat on the front porch with Leroy. She always felt comfortable discussing life matters with him.

"You know, Leroy, with the herd gone, the only thing to keep me from taking Cole and leaving the ranch is right out there." She didn't move, but her eyes remained fixed in the direction of Clint's grave.

Leroy didn't respond, as he sensed Katherine had more thinking aloud to do.

"Cole isn't cut out to be a rancher. I don't know what direction his life holds, but I want him to get out into the world and find his place," she continued.

"I knew Clint for less than a year, Katherine, but I got to know him pretty good. I know how strongly he felt about you, too. I don't think Clint would want you to stay here on his account. He's part of the earth now. Got a good burial, and lies next to his best friend. I'd bet he's pretty happy," Leroy advised.

"How old are boys when they begin college, Leroy?" asked Katherine.

"Usually between 17 and 20 years old, depending," Leroy answered.

"Leaving now or leaving later, won't make it any easier with Clint buried here," Katherine confusingly stated.

"We could take the money and just run a small herd, or maybe some other livestock, just enough to get ourselves by, not to drive to market," Leroy suggested, "maybe save some money for Cole's college."

"I'm feeling a bit unsettled in my thinking right now, Leroy," said Katherine, "let's see what tomorrow brings."

* * *

Tomorrow turned into almost three years. Katherine and the rest of the Bar-CJ had used the cattle money to buy some hogs and chickens. They also took to doing some farming, growing their own crops. The weather had cooperated, and followed suit according to the almanac each year, and they had been self-sustaining during their post-cattle years.

Cole was 16 and a half and growing more restless each day. He was a respectful young man, and he was very protective of his mother. Katherine was aging rapidly. Though she was just short of 39 year old, her tough years in Waterhole seemed to be catching up with her. She spent most of her time shuffling between the house and the porch. Leroy took to doing most of the cooking. Cole settled his restlessness by watching over his mother.

It was almost spring of 1889. Katherine's health began to grow worse with each passing day. After putting her to bed for the night one cold February evening, Cole, Bertram and Leroy sat around the fire, inside the house. It was too cold to sit outside on the porch.

"Cole," Leroy began to tell him, "I don't know how much time your ma has left. She's awfully sick."

Cole always found himself too choked up to talk about his mother's deteriorating health. He knew she was going, and he already felt an emptiness in his soul.

"I know this doesn't need saying, but Bertram and I consider you like a son to us. We'll always be here for you," Leroy told Cole.

Cole smiled and nodded. Age 16 was hard. Cole now stood 6'1" and weighed 180 pounds. He was the size of a man and could do the work of one, but on the inside, he still felt like a boy at times.

"Your ma and I have talked about your future many times over the past number of years," Leroy told him. "You know it is her dream for you to go to college, and as hard as you've taken to book learning the past three or four years, I'd say you're about ready."

"I won't leave the ranch as long as ma is here," Cole determinedly told Leroy with his head hunched over looking down.

"I know, son, I know," Leroy said.

"Wherever and whenever you decide to go," Leroy continued, "Bertram and I have decided to stay and keep the ranch going. There's no place else for us, and that way you'll know your pa, and ma, when the time comes, will be well looked after."

Again, Cole nodded, with his gaze continuing to be directed at the floor between his feet.

Katherine was buried on a bright, warm May morning. It had been the first clear, warm day of the season. She had passed in her sleep the night before. She was buried next to Clint. Over the years since Clint and Joshua had been laid to rest, Katherine had always kept the area around the grave in good repair. Now it would be Leroy and Bertram's turn to do so. Bertram dug a nice deep grave, while Leroy had built a nice coffin for her to rest in. He had been working on it, out of Cole's sight, for a couple of weeks.

After Katherine was in the ground, Leroy spoke words over her. When he finished, there was silence for a few moments. Then Bertram began to sing Amazing Grace. It was a song he learned as a boy, and sang many times over the burials of slaves on the plantation. Neither Cole nor Leroy had ever heard him sing before. He had a beautiful voice. Cole was deeply touched, and wept openly.

* * *

Over the next year, there was a lot of hard work on the Bar-CJ, but little of the conversation and playful teasing that had preceded Katherine's death. They all missed her terribly.

Leroy had sent away for information on different colleges. It was a long ride to the Colorado town to receive it, so he started obtaining the information right after Katherine had died. That gave him a good year to help Cole plan his college of choice. Leroy figured that with his father's Harvard legacy, Cole would have a good chance to be accepted anywhere he wanted to go. Leroy was right. He tried to convince Cole to go to Harvard, or another school in the East, but Cole was set on heading west. He chose St. Mary's College, a small, private school, just east of San Francisco, in California, for the fall of 1890, right about the time that Cole would turn 18.

With a year and a half until college would begin, Cole spent the time working hard on the ranch, and studying more than he ever had before. In his spare time, Cole practiced extensively with his father's old pistol. He was becoming quite proficient.

In August of 1890, Bertram and Leroy helped Cole load the wagon for a trip to Albuquerque in the New Mexico Territory. There Cole would catch the Atlantic & Pacific railroad for the trip to California.

They expected the wagon trip to be a week or more. As the wagon was loaded with Cole's personal necessities, including his father's pistol, and the picture of his mother that had dawned over the fireplace mantel, Leroy and Bertram could sense that Cole was experiencing some apprehension about leaving. He was excited to be going to St. Mary's, but he felt guilty for leaving behind the burial site of his parents. He had never really imagined not being with them; not being able to visit with them, even in the ground.

"How you feeling, son?" Leroy asked as the loading of the wagon was near complete.

Cole took a deep breath. He had added another inch and ten more pounds, now a full man size of 6'2" and 190 pounds. He was bigger than most, except for Bertram. Most people looked at Cole and saw a man, but Leroy knew Cole on the inside, and knew Cole's vulnerabilities. Presently, it was his difficulty in leaving the ranch. He was experiencing homesickness and he had not left yet.

"I know I'm supposed to go, Leroy," Cole began, "but it's hard. It's hard to leave ma and pa behind."

"I know it is, Cole, but let me make you this promise. Neither Bertram or I will ever sell this ranch. It's yours. We'll work it for you, and you may choose to live elsewhere during your lifetime, but this ranch will always be yours."

"It's yours and Bertram's, too, Leroy," Cole told him.

"And I hope to someday be buried here alongside your folks. I know Bertram feels the same way. So, I guess it's our ranch, too, in that regard. But Bertram and me see our job being to work the ranch, live our lives, and look forward to your return visits home," Leroy told him.

"I guess we ought to be goin'," Cole said.

"Let's climb aboard," responded Leroy, "you ready Bertram?" he asked.

"All set," Bertram replied as he climbed up into the wagon.

"Giddyup!" hollered Leroy, and the horses began moving forward.

As they passed the knoll where Clint and Katherine were buried, along with Joshua Rines, Cole felt a heavy heart, as if there was a rope connecting him to the graves. He had to force himself to look away.

"St. Mary's College, here comes your next bright scholar!" yelled Leroy, which brought a hearty laugh from Bertram and a chuckle from Cole.

For most of the trip's first day, Leroy kidded Bertram about his snoring, and Bertram returned by joking about Leroy's cooking. Both intended to keep Cole feeling at ease.

Their trip to Albuquerque was uneventful. They arrived right on time, late in the afternoon prior to Cole's departure the next day.

Leroy was the first to speak as they gathered the next morning at the train depot.

"We're sure going to miss you, son," he told Cole.

"Ah feels like mah own child's leavin'," Bertram added.

"I'm going to miss the two of you, too," Cole said, trying not to feel sad. "You're my family now. I appreciate all you've done for me, and ma and pa."

"Whatever you need, Cole, you know where to ask. We've got the money saved for your education, and by golly, we'll be sure it gets paid for. Whatever you need, you just let us know," Leroy finished with as he stepped forward and gave Cole his hand.

Cole grasped it firmly and maintained eye contact with Leroy. They smiled and nodded at one another. Cole did the same with Bertram.

"I don't know what else to say," Cole struggled to say.

"We know," said Leroy. "Time to get on the train."

Cole boarded and found his seat. He looked out the window at Leroy and Bertram, who stayed on the platform as the train began to head west. Once the train left the station, Cole continued his stare out the window, looking at nothing.

Leroy and Bertram did not move until the train was out of sight.

Part V
St. Mary's College, California, 1890

The train pulled into Oakland, California five days after leaving Albuquerque. Cole made some small talk with passengers, but whenever possible, he kept to himself. He did a lot of reflecting. Cole never had a vision for himself. As a boy, he had always expected to follow in his father's footsteps, and had never dreamed of a day when he would leave home. Though his folks had been gone for some time now, he suddenly missed them terribly. More so than anytime since their respective burials. He was missing Leroy and Bertram, too.

The conductor, a short, portly fellow with an unkempt mustache and a missing button on his vest, came through Cole's car.

"Oakland stop, son. Don't you get off here?" the conductor asked.

"Yep, this is me," Cole replied.

"First time in Oakland?" asked the conductor.

"First time in California," Cole answered.

"Well, good luck, college boy," the conductor smiled as he extended his hand to Cole.

"Thanks," Cole replied mirroring the smile he received. "Any idea how I find St. Mary's College?" Cole asked the conductor.

"In all the trips I've made through Oakland, I ain't never got off the train to know where anything is here," the conductor told him. "Ought to ask inside the depot," he advised.

"Thanks, again," Cole repeated as he picked up his satchel from beside his seat.

"The rest of your bags will be sitting outside," the conductor told Cole as he moved toward the door.

Cole stepped off the train and found his bags immediately. They were the only ones left unclaimed. With the satchel he had carried onboard, he totaled three bags. Inside, the train depot was busy. Small groups of people were milling around, either just having arrived and been met by familiar faces, or getting ready to leave on the next train and saying their goodbyes.

Cole made his way though the small, crowded room of people, more well-dressed than he was. They were all wearing city clothes, he thought to himself, as he stepped up to the ticket counter.

"Ticket, sir?" asked the man on the other side of the partition.

"No, thanks. I just got off the train. I'm looking for St. Mary's College. Know where I can find it?" Cole asked.

"Yes, sir. It's located at the corner of 30th and Broadway," the man began as he gave Cole instructions on the route to his new school.

"Would you like me to get you a carriage?" the man asked.

"Won't that cost money?" asked Cole.

"Well, yes sir," answered the man, confused by Cole's question.

"No thanks, I'll just walk," Cole decided.

Cole had never been in a big city. Nor had he seen so many people in one place before. After a couple of wrong turns and some revised directions from strangers on the street, it was two hours later that Cole found his way to St. Mary's College.

Though school would not start for a couple of weeks, Cole had been informed by telegraph that he could check in to his dormitory early. The check-in process went smoothly, and he carried his bags to his ground level room. As he opened the door to his room, he found another person putting away his belongings.

Waterhole

"Oh, sorry," Cole said, embarrassed at opening the wrong door.

"No, that's okay," said the student, "you must be Cole Herbert. I asked who my roommate was when I checked in." He extended his hand.

Cole accepted the handshake, but an inquisitive look showed on his face.

"Yeah, I know what you're thinking," said the student, "I look younger than you and the other freshmen. Well, actually I'm a sophomore, but I won't turn 15 until December," he told Cole. "Joseph Aloysius Corbett's the name, but people call me Joe." Joe Corbett was a better than average sized 15 year old. He stood a couple inches short of six feet, and weighed about 170 pounds.

"Cole Herbert," said the older roommate.

"Yeah, I know," smiled Joe.

Even though Cole was more than three years older than Joe, he felt his junior in terms of being a fish out of water. Joe was more at ease, Cole could tell, more comfortable in his new surroundings.

"Where you from?" asked Joe.

"Oklahoma Territory," answered Cole.

"You ever play base ball?" Joe kept the questions coming.

"Nope, I don't think so. What is it?" asked Cole.

"Why, it's just the greatest game ever invented!" replied an excited Joe.

"I guess I wasn't much for games in Oklahoma. Where you from?" Cole followed.

"Right across the water, over in San Francisco," Joe said. "You ever been to San Francisco?"

"First time in California," Cole told his roommate.

"Alright then, roomy, first chance we get, we're going to San Francisco for a first class meal, courtesy of my mother," Joe told Cole.

"I'd heard that 18 years old was about the time students entered college," mentioned Cole.

"Yeah, I guess so," confirmed Joe, "but I had what my mother calls *accelerated learning*. With my mother's help, I finished with all my studies a bit earlier than most. She was a school teacher, so I guess that helped."

"Reckon so," said Cole.

"You aren't very talkative, are you?" Joe inquired.

Cole shrugged his shoulders.

"That's okay, I guess I'll talk enough for the both of us," Joe said. "So, what's your family do in Oklahoma?"

"Have a ranch. It's just me and, well, I guess they're sort of my two uncles," Cole began. "My folks passed on, so the three of us handle it."

"How big is the ranch?" Joe continued.

"It's small, about 160 acres, but we don't have much livestock anymore. Kind of a combination between farming and ranching now," Cole explained. "We're pretty self sufficient. How about your folks, what do they do?"

"My grandfather made it big in the gold fields back in the late 40's-early 50's," said Joe, "we've been well off since then. My folks own a successful restaurant in San Francisco."

The only time Cole could remember eating in a restaurant was for his fourteenth birthday, in that Colorado town with his mother, Bertram and Leroy.

"Hey, you want me to teach you how to play base ball," asked Joe.

"Maybe later," Cole told him, "I need to head out and look for a job."

"A job?!" exclaimed Joe. "You're a college student, you'll be going to class and studying, and maybe when I teach you, you'll be playing base ball with me, too. How are you going to find time for a job?"

"Leroy and Bertram said they'd send whatever money I needed, but I don't want to be dependent on them. I gotta make my own way," Cole explained.

"Are Bertram and Leroy your uncles?" Joe wondered.

Cole smiled as he thought of the two of them.
"Yeah, they're the only family I got now," Cole told Joe.
"You ever been a waiter?" Joe asked
"A waiter?" responded Cole.
"Yeah, a waiter, you know, work in a restaurant, taking meal orders and serving patrons," Joe told him.
"Nope," said Cole.
'Well, I can get you a job in my folks restaurant, and I'm sure they'll give you hours so you can go to school and work," Joe promised.
"How would I get to San Francisco?" asked Cole.
"You take the ferry across the Bay. You can get there in a little over an hour. Their restaurant is right on the water," Joe told Cole.
"Thanks, Joe, but let me think about it. I was hoping to find something a little closer to school," Cole answered.
"Alright, but if you ever need the work, I can help," Joe acknowledged.
"Appreciate it," Cole replied.

Joe's parents had friends who owned a restaurant in Oakland. With Joe's recommendation, his parents put in a good word for Cole, resulting in Cole accepting a job only fifteen minutes from school. Cole's class schedule of biology, language, math, engineering and philosophy all ended by 2:00 p.m. daily, so he was able to work afternoons or evenings, depending on his study schedule. Cole really appreciated the flexibility that the restaurant gave him, as well as the $.10 per hour, plus tips.

Between his class and work schedule, and Joe's class and base ball schedule, the roommates saw little of each other for the first couple of months of school. Thanksgiving rolled around and Joe invited Cole to join his family for dinner. Had the restaurant not closed for the holiday, Cole would have likely worked, as he did every chance he got. This was Cole's first meeting with Joe's parents, although he had sent them a thank you note for helping him to get his job.

Cole enjoyed his evening at Joe's house, which also happened to be his first time in San Francisco. He had been too busy with school and work to make the trip earlier. It was a trip he looked forward to making again.

* * *

The young girl walked down Broadway, passing *The Clipper* restaurant. It was late and her carriage that was supposed to pick her up at 35th was waiting for her on the wrong street corner, as would later be determined. She walked down the long, dark street, reaching the corner of Broadway and 28th, just two blocks from Saint Mary's College.

Her long red hair had not been cut in six years, not since she was ten years old. Her locks were as beautiful as her green eyes, and her shapely figure. It was a crisp autumn evening. Winter was soon to arrive, but the young beauty would never see it. She was found two days later by a pair of students from Mills College, the girls' school, in the Oakland foothills. Her neck had been broken.

* * *

"You coming to see the game today?" Joe asked Cole.

"Gotta work," Cole told him, "but if the restaurant gets slow, I'll see if I can get out for a while," Cole offered. "I doubt you'll play anyhow," Cole kidded his roommate.

"Why you'd better not be late, or you'll miss me belting a home run!" boasted Joe with a smile.

"We'll see," Cole said, nodding his head up and down.

As Joe left the dormitory for his base ball game, Cole left for work. He was wearing his *The Clipper* shirt, and arrived early, as he always did. Two patrons were in the lobby area, talking about the murder of the young girl, four months earlier. No one had been arrested for the crime.

Waterhole

It had been a short winter. Spring weather arrived with March, which Joe philosophically defined as a good omen from the base ball gods.

Cole's schoolwork had gone well during his first year, but it did not come easy. His studious efforts produced slightly better than average marks from his professors. Joe received similar marks, but with much less effort. Most of his interest laid in his base ball pursuit.

Leroy had written Cole a letter, arriving in late February, wondering if Cole would be returning home for the summer. He had not yet made up his mind.

* * *

With only weeks to go before the end of the school term, Cole decided he would return to the ranch for the summer months. He told Joe of his decision, who was disappointed, wanting to show Cole the sights of San Francisco, which Cole had not visited since a Christmas dinner with Joe's family.

"You can't go home until you've watched at least one of my base ball games? Where's your old school spirit, anyways?" asked Joe.

Cole had informed the restaurant of his decision to go home during the summer, and they wished him well, offering him his job back when he returned in the fall.

"Okay," Cole moaned, "I'll come to tomorrow's game, but I probably won't like it," he teased. "I've got to go over to *The Clipper* to get my final pay. Be back in an hour or so," Cole said. "You'd better study for your final exams while I'm gone!" Cole scolded Joe.

It was early morning, and the restaurant would not yet be open, but Cole had made special arrangements to pick it up early so he could return and study for his final exams. Completing his fifteen minute walk from campus, he turned into the doorway of *The Clipper*, stumbling and falling forward, but catching himself by putting his hands on the door. He looked down beneath his feet. There she was. The girl was seventeen, blonde, and well dressed. Her neck had been snapped in half.

* * *

Final exams had ended for Cole and Joe, and they had agreed to room together again when school began in the fall. Joe was able to commandeer a horse and buggy to take Cole to the train station. It was a mid-June morning. The morning fog sat over the Oakland hills, as it often did this time of the year. Cole wore his coat over his best traveling clothes. His bags were boarded, and with satchel in hand, Cole bid goodbye to Joe, and wished him well with his base ball. Cole had been impressed with Joe's prowess for a game which he had never before seen played. Cole looked forward to seeing Joe play again the following year.

As he took his seat against the window facing the depot, he saw her for the first time. She had long dark hair, silky smooth, and wore a morning dress that fit her curvaceous figure like a glove. Her hands were covered by white gloves, but he knew instinctively that they were smooth and soft. He couldn't see the color of her eyes from his seat, but when she smiled, her pearly white teeth sparkled, and her eyes squinted in a way that Cole found attractive. He had never felt his heart jump like it did over seeing a girl. She looked about eighteen or nineteen, and appeared to be seeing another young female off at the station.

Suddenly the train began to move, and Cole felt a terrible pain in his stomach. Who was she? Having never experienced an attraction to a girl, Cole was tongue-tied, and he wasn't speaking to anyone. He didn't know what to do, so his indecision made the decision for him. As the train rolled past her position on the platform, Cole could only hope that he had not seen her for the last time.

* * *

Bertram and Leroy met Cole's Atlantic & Pacific train in Albuquerque and they talked almost non-stop all the way home. While Cole spoke, Leroy and Bertram continually exchanged glances at one another, astonished at Cole's rapid rate of speech. Cole caught a glimpse of one of these exchanged glances.

"What?" Cole asked

"Leroy chuckled, "In all the years I've known you, I ain't never heard you talk so gosh darn much!"

Bertram laughed, too, while nodding his concurrence.

Cole had told them about everything he saw and did during the school year, except for his brief visual encounter of the beautiful girl as he left the Oakland train station. Leroy had to tell Cole that his horse, Slinger, had to be put down. He was an old horse and had been a good one for Cole since he was six years old.

During his eight weeks home, Cole felt as though working on the ranch re-energized him. He didn't realize how mentally tired the school year had left him, but the physical ranch work made him feel as good as he had ever remembered feeling. He was excited to be home, and at the same time, excitedly looking forward to returning to school. The eight weeks seemed to fly by, and soon it was time for Cole to return to California.

As they pulled back into the Albuquerque train station in mid August, Leroy told Cole, "seems like we just picked you up from here yesterday."

"The summer sure went by fast. I never said, but the ranch looks great," Cole told Leroy and Bertram. "By the way, I'd sure like you to come out and visit me in California."

"Well, Ah knows fer sure we's be sittin' in da front row when ya graduate," Bertram informed Cole.

Cole smiled.

"Let's not rule anything out, but with the two of us gone from the ranch, we'd have to get someone to watch it for us while we was gone," Leroy surmised.

Cole acknowledged Leroy's point, but still wanted them to visit.

"Be sure to write us," Leroy told Cole as he readied to board the train, "especially about this girl that has you so jumpy."

Cole was astonished. His jaw dropped open as he stared blankly at Leroy.

"Only a pretty girl could make a fella your age act like you have all summer," Leroy told him.

Cole blushed, smiled, shook hands with Leroy and Bertram, then boarded the Atlantic & Pacific for Oakland. He was still blushing as the train pulled away from the platform, hand waving to his two family members.

* * *

Cole had sent a telegraph to Joe prior to leaving Albuquerque. Joe knew what train Cole would arrive on, and he was there, waiting on the platform when Cole arrived. Cole smiled as he saw Joe and extended his hand as they approached each other, but Joe reached out and gave him a quick, brotherly hug. Cole blushed again.

"Good to see you, roomy!" Joe practically shouted. "How was your summer?"

Cole smiled as he thought about the question.

"A summer of ranch work suited me just fine," he thoughtfully answered. "How was your summer of base ball?" Cole asked.

"I get better every day," Joe falsely bragged. "This year, I'm going to teach you how to play the game."

"We'll see," Cole said.

As they loaded Cole's bags and satchel into the buggy Joe had borrowed, Joe asked, "you remember those two girls who were murdered last school year, just outside of campus?"

Cole shook his head in acknowledgement.

"They found a third one this summer, this time on our campus. Turns out they all went to Mills College," Joe brought Cole current with the events.

"Have the police found any clues?" asked Cole.

"None yet, but they brought over the top detective from San Francisco to help with the case, a fellow named Isaiah W. Lees.

He's been San Francisco's top detective since back in the wild times of the 50s," Joe explained.

"My pa used to do some law work," Cole told Joe.

It was the first time Cole had told Joe anything about either of his parents. Joe could see that it was difficult for Cole to say that much, so he didn't press him for any more details.

"Well, I do believe that we have the same room as last year," Joe said, changing the subject.

"It'll do fine by me," Cole said.

"You going back to *The Clipper* to work this year?" asked Joe.

"Yep, said they'd hold my job for me 'til I got back to school," Cole answered. Leroy had given him some money before leaving the ranch, enough that Cole decided to put it in the bank this year.

"I'd like to stop by the Wells Fargo on the way to school, if you don't mind," Cole said.

"Be there in no time," Joe responded, as he gave a little twitch to the bridle reins.

After depositing his money with Wells Fargo, Cole climbed back into the buggy that Joe kept waiting in front of the bank. They arrived at school ten minutes later, where Cole unpacked his belongings, including his father's holstered pistol. It was the first time Joe had known that Cole had a gun.

"I'm not sure you're allowed to keep that pistol on campus," Joe cautioned.

Although Cole was a stickler for following rules, his attachment to the gun was stronger than his concurrence to the rule.

"Let's talk about it later," Joe said trying to lighten the mood, "school doesn't start for a week, and you don't have to start work until then, so I've got us a reservation at my parent's restaurant in San Francisco. Put on your Sunday best, and let's get going!"

Without question or comment, Cole complied and within ten minutes, they were bound for the ferry to San Francisco.

When the roommates arrived at Joe's family restaurant, *The Flying Fin*, Joe saw his father heading into his office, followed by a well dressed, older man. The older man was Isaiah W. Lees, the San Francisco police detective. After Detective Lees had left, Joe's father brought Joe and Cole current with their conversation.

"It seems that in addition to all three of the murdered girls being from Mills College, all three had also been recent patrons of our restaurant. Detective Lees was following the lead. I told him I didn't remember them, but I can barely remember your mama's name most days," said Joe's father, sarcastically.

For the first yearlong period, Cole did not grow. He remained a strong 6'2" and 190 pounds. He was bigger than most, and his appetite matched his size. Joe's father served them complimentary meals, and Cole ate two, one pound steaks, as well as two potatoes, vegetables and a loaf of bread. Joe tried to match his friend's appetite, but fell far short.

"I'd like to offer you more to eat," Joe's father told Cole, smiling, "but I've run out of food."

"Thanks, Mr. Corbett, but I've had enough," Cole replied, not realizing that he was being teased.

The boys spent the rest of the evening in San Francisco, seeing a show before taking a late ferry back to Oakland. The next morning, Joe asked Cole about his pistol.

"It was my father's," Cole began. "It's all I have left of him."

Cole spent the next half hour telling Joe all about his parents, and how Leroy and Bertram came to be like family to him. It was a long time for Cole to talk about anything, and he had never told the story to anyone. Joe had become like a brother to him, and he was comfortable opening up to him.

Joe was speechless while Cole told his story. He just shook his head.

"I'm very sorry," was all Joe could think to say after Cole was finished. Joe did not mention the pistol again.

After dinner that day, Joe told Cole he was going to the library. Cole decided to stay in their room and get to bed early, as classes would begin the following day, as would Cole's work schedule at *The Clipper*.

Waterhole

* * *

The following morning as Joe and Cole were getting ready to head to class, an acquaintance of Joe's came knocking on their door. He worked part time at *The Flying Fin*, which was how Joe knew him.

"Morning, William," Joe said to the student living down the hall.

"Joe, did you hear?" an out of breath William asked, "they found another dead girl," said William, answering his own question.

"Where?" Cole asked from behind Joe.

"Just outside the library, right here on campus. She had a deep scratch on her neck, like something had been pulled from it, and her neck was broken, just like the others."

"What was a girl doing on campus at night?" asked Cole about the all-boys school.

No one knew the answer to that question. Classes were cancelled for the day, delaying the beginning of the school year, and the library was off-limits while Isaiah W. Lees came to campus to investigate.

Joe went to practice his base ball that afternoon with some of the others on his team. Cole got ready to go to work. Before he left his dormitory room, he picked up some of the clothes that had fallen off of Joe's bed, onto the floor. As much as Cole liked Joe, his roommate was not a very tidy person. Cole picked up a shirt and a pair of pants off the floor and sat them on Joe's bed. He looked down and saw a necklace on the floor. Cole picked it up and looked at it. It was a girl's necklace. A simple chain with a small green pendant, surrounded by what may have been diamonds. The chain was broken. It appeared to be expensive looking. Cole was curious. He had not known Joe to have an interest in any particular girl. But he was running late for is first day of work, so he set the necklace on Joe's pants, and left for *The Clipper*.

* * *

School had started and Cole additionally filled his schedule with 30 hours of work at the restaurant. He enjoyed the work, and his classes as well, having decided to be an engineering major. Cole felt much more comfortable in Oakland during his second year. He was more apt to venture outside of his comfort zone, making new friends, although his time was mostly taken up with classes, studying time and work. While many of his friends and acquaintances went to San Francisco or ventured elsewhere during the weekends, Cole worked and studied. He wanted to make Leroy and Bertram proud of him.

It was his third Saturday night at *The Clipper*. Cole was waiting on a family of four, demonstrating his patience as the mother of the family couldn't make up her mind about her order. He glanced up while waiting for the overweight lady to contemplate between the mutton and the roast beef. There she was. The same girl he had seen last June as he boarded the Atlantic & Pacific for Albuquerque. She was just as beautiful as he had remembered. An olive colored complexion, with long, dark hair. She was fashionably dressed, and in the company of two other girls. All three appeared to be in their late teens. He wondered if they were college students. He had still not seen the color of her eyes.

"Young man . . . young man," the lady at the table called out to him. "I'd like the mutton, if you please," she told Cole.

"Ah, yes ma'am, right away," he answered with embarrassment at not being attentive to her order.

Cole retreated to the kitchen with the family's order. When he returned to the dining hall, he saw that the maitre d' had escorted the three young girls to his area. All of the sudden, Cole began to flush. He felt hot and was afraid he would begin to perspire. He stalled in approaching the young ladies table. Now, instead of wanting to meet the girl, he was afraid to. The maitre d' looked in his direction and motioned for him to take care of the table he was avoiding. He took a deep breath, and got his right foot to lead his left. With a few more steps, he was at the table.

"Evenin' ladies," Cole welcomed them, trying to sound sophisticated. "May I take your orders?"

He stood at the opposite side of the table from the dark haired beauty. She sat directly in his line of vision. He was now close enough to see her big, brown colored eyes sparkle when she smiled at him.

Two of the girls giggled as they looked up and saw him, but not the dark haired one. She just smiled. Cole smiled back.

"What is your name?" giggled one of the girls.

"Cole, Cole Herbert," he answered, redirecting his focus toward the one who asked him the question.

The two girl friends giggled again. He took their orders to the kitchen, then brought their table a pitcher of water and three glasses. He poured a glass for each girl. Cole continued to wait on his assigned tables throughout the evening, but taking every opportunity to look at the dark haired girl. When he did, he noticed that she was often looking back in his direction. This made him blush, but less so each time he noticed. There were many areas in life where Cole felt confident. His interactions with girls, however, was not one of them.

As the girls got up to leave, nearly two hours after sitting down, most of which was time spent gossiping and giggling, he heard one of them address the dark haired girl as Anna. The girls were nearly out of the dining hall, when Anna looked back one more time at Cole. She smiled. Once again Cole blushed, but he did manage to smile back.

"Anna," he said to himself, "and brown eyes."

* * *

Joe had noticed an unusual cheerfulness in Cole during the week following his Saturday night of work. He smiled more and even offered to have Joe teach him about base ball. Joe asked him if he was in need of seeing a doctor.

Though he had worked a couple of weeknights at *The Clipper*, he had not seen Anna again. Nor did he the following weekend.

Three more weeks went by without an appearance at the restaurant by Anna. The cheery disposition that Cole had been displaying was now replaced by a sullen one.

"What is going on with you?" Joe wanted to know. "You've been moodier than my mother just before my little sister was born."

Cole had not told Joe about Anna. He was embarrassed to even talk about her.

"Sorry," Cole said, "guess I just got a lot on my mind."

"If you ever need to talk," Joe offered, "I'm almost as good a listener as I am a talker."

Cole smiled and thanked Joe.

"Gotta get to work," said Cole. "See you later tonight."

"It's Saturday," said Joe, "I'll be up late if you want to talk."

Cole nodded as he walked out of the dormitory room.

* * *

It was another monotonous evening at *The Clipper*, which meant that Anna had not made an appearance. Cole went through the motions of his job responsibilities, then made the fifteen minute walk back to his room around 11:00 p.m. Joe was not in the room when he arrived. Cole had been back for about five minutes when William came from down the hall and knocked on the door. Cole answered.

"Hey, Cole, you heard?"

"Bout what?" Cole asked in return, half interested at best.

"Police found the fifth murdered girl earlier this evening. Another Mills College girl. This one put up a fight, and got a bit bloodied before her neck was broken," William informed Cole.

At a little past midnight, Joe still wasn't back. Cole decided to get some sleep and turned in for the night. The next morning he woke up to find Joe fast asleep on top of his bed, still wearing his clothes from the previous day. Cole got up quietly, not wanting to disturb Joe. While dressing, he looked over at Joe and noticed the blood on his shirt. Joe heard the rustling of Cole putting on his pants and opened his eyes.

"Morning, roomy," Joe said as his eyes fell shut again.

"Got in a little late I see," Cole commented.

"You didn't see nothin' cause you were snoring like a bear when I came in," Joe responded, still with his eyes closed.

"How'd you get that blood on your shirt?" Cole asked.

"Went for a walk, tripped and fell against a tree. Bloodied my nose some," Joe explained.

"That what kept you out late, a bloody nose?" asked Cole.

"Who are you, Detective Lees?" Joe asked mockingly, "no, I went to play billiards with some of the guys on the team, but I never found the place they described, so I eventually came back to the room."

"You hear about the murder?" Cole asked.

Joe paused before answering.

"Another girl?" he asked.

"Yep," said Cole.

"Where'd they find her?" Joe wondered.

"Don't know, William came by and told me last night. Said this one put up a fight. Got a bit bloodied," Cole told Joe.

"Sure hope they find this guy who's doing all the killings soon," said Joe.

Suddenly, Cole felt a cold sensation run through him. What if the most recent murder victim was Anna? He hadn't seen her for weeks. He thought for a minute, then went down to William's room and knocked.

William answered.

"Well," he greeted Cole, "never seen you visit before."

"William, what did the girl look like, the one who was murdered last night?" Cole wanted to know.

"She was pretty, like the rest of them," William told him.

"Do you know what she looked like, hair, eyes . . ." said Cole, searching for answers.

"Red hair, I believe she was a redhead," said William.

Cole was at once relieved. He thanked William, then went back to his room. He put on his coat to go out in the crisp, autumn, morning air. He didn't know what he was going to do, but he somehow wanted to find out about Anna. He didn't know her, but he was worried about her. He wanted time to think about how to find Anna.

* * *

It was late November. Thanksgiving day, and once again, Cole would join Joe's family for the holidays. This year, however, they were to have Thanksgiving dinner at *The Flying Fin*. The Corbett's made sure the best table in the house was available for them. Cole sat around the table with Mr. and Mrs. Corbett, Joe and his little sister. As they enjoyed a deliciously prepared turkey dinner, Cole saw Anna walk into the restaurant. She was with what appeared to be her two parents and two brothers. William was working the holiday, and quickly set upon waiting their table.

After she had been seated, and her family had placed their Thanksgiving dinner order, turkey and dressing, like everyone else in the restaurant, Anna scanned the room. When her eyes fixed on Cole, she seemed startled. Cole could tell by the expression on her face. She gathered herself and smiled at Cole. Cole smiled back. Joe took notice of Cole's expression, and glanced in the direction of his gaze.

"Somebody you know?" Joe asked.

"No," Cole responded, not realizing he was still smiling.

"Come on," Joe directed.

Cole suddenly snapped back into focus.

"Go where?" he asked Joe.

"Just follow me," he told Cole.

The two of them got up and headed across the room, but Joe took an exaggerated route towards Anna's table, so Cole could not catch on until it was too late. Joe stopped at Anna's table and introduced himself as the son of the owners of *The Flying Fin*.

Waterhole

Before he had a chance to introduce his friend, Cole, Anna spoke up.

"Cole Herbert, isn't it?" she asked.

Cole was astonished she remembered his name. Joe was impressed.

"Cole works at a restaurant I occasionally frequent when I'm at school," Anna explained to her parents. "I'm Anna Gilbert. These are my parents, and my younger brothers, Frank and Samuel."

"Pleased to meet you," said Joe, as he elbowed Cole.

"Yes, pleased to meet you," Cole mimicked.

Cole could see where Anna got her coloring. Her father was Anglo, and her mother appeared to be Mexican. Anna seemed to have inherited the best of both her parent's features. She was beautiful.

"Well, we didn't mean to interrupt your dinner, just wanted to introduce ourselves and welcome you to *The Flying Fin*," Joe told the party.

Anna looked at Cole.

"Are you part of the welcoming committee?" she asked, "because I didn't notice you welcoming anyone else who came in."

Cole and Joe looked at each other, searching for something to say and hoping the other one would come up with a response.

"We, ah," Cole began.

"We only welcome those who are here for their first time," Joe recovered, "the rest have been here before," he said with a sweeping arm motion around the room.

"Why thank you very much," Mrs. Gilbert said graciously.

Mr. Gilbert gave them a look that suggested it was time for the two of them to leave.

About this time, William returned with the Gilbert's dinner, giving a scowl look to his schoolmates.

"Enjoy your meal," Joe said as he prepared to leave.

"Yes, enjoy your meal," followed Cole.

They turned to return to their table.

"Goodbye, Cole," Anna said.

Without stopping, he turned and looked over his shoulder to see her give him a smile and a little wave with her hand. Cole smiled back, but before he could turn back around, he bumped into an occupied table, spilling the drinks of the entire party. Anna giggled softly, while Cole turned as red as the wine splattered across the tablecloth.

"Yep, roomy," Joe began, "you sure have a way with words. You are quite the orator," he continued to tease Cole.

Cole smiled, and bravely told Joe, "I'd like to see her again."

Joe smiled back at the bravado his roommate was demonstrating.

"Bravo, roomy," he said to Cole, "bravo."

* * *

Cole was working at *The Clipper* a couple of weeks after Thanksgiving. It was a cold, mid-December Saturday, and he was completing his shift. Just before 8:00 p.m., as he was saying his goodbyes to the staff, in walked Anna. She was by herself.

"Hi, Cole," she said with the prettiest smile he had ever seen.

"Hi, Anna," he replied.

He looked past her to see who else might be with her. She noticed his looking.

"I'm by myself," she told Cole, answering his unasked question.

His conversation had never carried past, 'hi, Anna,' so he wasn't sure what to say next.

"Hi, Anna," he repeated.

Amused, she smiled even more. "Hi, Cole."

"What are you doing here?" he asked.

"Well, I've been waiting for months for you to find me. Since you hadn't, I came to find you," she told him.

Cole was embarrassed to be the recipient of such attention, and he had no idea what to say. He continued to stand there, shuffling his feet and smiling.

"Would you like to go for a walk?" she asked him.

"Sure," was all he could find in his vocabulary to answer her.

The two of them walked for two hours that evening. Anna carried the conversation all evening, while Cole worked on mastering his 'yeps' and 'nopes' in response to her questions. He had never had a lengthy conversation with any girl before, nor had he ever had feelings for a girl. Anna realized that Cole was shy and uncomfortable, but she found it appealing.

Anna was a student at Mills College, in her second year, just like Cole. She was planning on becoming a teacher.

She was born six days before he was, in San Francisco. Her parents were hardworking, father working at the wharf, and mother taking care of the house and Anna and her brothers. Their family did not have extra money for Anna's college, so her uncle was paying for her education. He lived in Los Angeles.

It was a few minutes after 10:00 p.m. when Anna suggested she get back to her dormitory.

"I'm already out past curfew," she told Cole.

They were a couple of miles from Mills College, so Cole summoned a carriage to take them to her school. When they arrived, Cole escorted her to the entrance gate of the school.

"You'd better stop here," she told him. "I don't want to get in trouble. We're not allowed to have boys on campus after dark."

After defining mute by example all evening, Cole worked up the courage to ask Anna if he could see her again. She smiled and said yes. Then she turned and ran towards her dormitory.

Cole was giddy. He felt much better about himself than his performance that evening gave him a right to feel. He was practically skipping as he wandered back down the hill to where the carriage had left them. The carriage was gone. He decided to save his money and make the hour and a half walk back to Saint Mary's.

He, too, was late for curfew, but Cole was oblivious to time. He was caught being late and issued a demerit. It was his first since he arrived on campus the prior year. He didn't seem to mind, and even thanked the dormitory monitor, with a smile.

* * *

Cole woke the next morning, still feeling as if the world was suddenly perfect. He told Joe about his evening with Anna. Cole talked non-stop for fifteen minutes, without leaving out a single detail. Joe wondered if he had been this talkative with Anna. Cole shrugged in response to Joe's inquiry, not wanting to admit his conversational shortcomings, even though Joe was already aware of them.

Cole did not have to work Sunday. Though base ball games were not played on Sundays, Joe never missed an opportunity to practice. Sensing that Cole was in a good enough mood to agree to anything, he asked Cole if he wanted to learn the game. Cole agreed.

"Once you learn to play this game, your life will never be the same," Joe told him.

"After last night," Cole began, "my life will already never be the same."

Joe found some equipment for Cole to borrow. Cole thought the hats they wore were funny looking and refused to don one on his head, preferring to play hatless. Joe decided not to explain the rules of the game, and instead showed him how to grip the base ball, and how to throw it for distance, accuracy and velocity. What Joe saw surprised him.

"You've never played before?" Joe had to ask again.

"Never even held a base ball before," Cole responded.

Cole threw the base ball harder and farther than anyone on the Saint Mary's team, even Joe, who was the best player on the team.

"Cole, you've got to play this game. We need you," Joe pleaded. "Let's see how you hit the ball."

Joe pitched a few base balls to Cole. He swung and missed at the first four or five, then he began to wallop them hard and far.

"That's it," Joe declared, "you've got to come and meet the coach tomorrow. You may be the best player never to have played this game."

"Let me think on it some, Joe," Cole said. He didn't want to immediately reject Joe's proposal, but presently he wasn't interested in any thing except school, work, and Anna.

* * *

Due to their school schedules, Cole realized that he would not be able to see Anna until the following weekend. He did make the long walk over to Mills College on Monday, only to obtain the mailing address for the students at the school. That evening, he wrote her a letter. Cole was not much more of a writer than he was a conversationalist, but he wanted to let Anna know he was thinking of her and hoped to see her that weekend. He included his address in the letter.

It was the longest week Cole had experienced since he arrived at college. He found himself daydreaming in class and while he was studying. Joe had his conversation with the base ball coach about Cole, who was interested in meeting him. Cole was still uncommitted about pursuing the game.

It was Thursday night, just two days before Cole hoped to see Anna again, when there was a knock at their dormitory room door. Cole was sitting at his desk, studying, when Joe answered the door.

"Evening, boys," the man said as he removed his hat upon entry.

"Detective Lees," a startled Joe responded.

"Hoped I might have a talk with you boys," Lees requested.

"Sure, what can we do for you?" asked a curious Joe. Cole had remained silent since Isaiah W. Lees had entered the room.

"Well, you boys are aware of the murders that have occurred around your school," Lees began. "We're following all leads, and I wanted to ask you some questions."

Joe nodded at Detective Lees, who then turned towards Cole. Cole nodded, too.

"Here's what we know," Lees began. "All five girls were students at Mills College. They all had their necks broken. And all five had been patrons of *The Flying Fin* within a month or so of their murder." He looked at Joe as he stated his last fact.

Joe and Cole looked at each other. They had not realized that there were so many connections to the murders.

"The reason I'm here," Lees continued, "is because your parents own *The Flying Fin*, and I'd be interested in knowing if you knew any of the girls."

Detective Lees read off the names of the five victims. None of them rang a bell to either Cole or Joe. Neither of them knew of any girls at Mills College, except for Anna.

"I thank you for your time, boys. If you think of anything, I'd appreciate you letting me know through the police department, either here or in San Francisco. Though the murders occurred in Oakland, a couple of the girls are from San Francisco, and their parents carry political ties of significance," Lees concluded. "Good evening."

After Detective Lees had left, Joe turned to Cole and shrugged. Cole didn't know why he had not thought of it before, but hearing about the connection of all five victims to *The Flying Fin*, he thought of something William had said. That one of the girls had a scratch around her neck, as if a chain had been yanked from it. Joe had a necklace with a broken chain. The last victim had been bloodied putting up a fight. The following morning, Joe had blood on his clothes. A cold, eerie feeling flowed through Cole's veins as he thought about these facts. As Joe went back to lie on his bed to study, Cole looked at him, wondering, and at the same time, trying not to wonder. Not Joe.

* * *

Cole woke early on Saturday morning. He had requested the day off from *The Clipper* to spend the day with Anna. They took the ferry over to San Francisco so Anna could show him more of the city in which she was raised. It was now late December and the weather was cold. They bundled up in warm clothing. They spent most of the day in Golden Gate Park, picnicking and talking. Cole was already showing improvement as a conversationalist. As they changed from talking about one topic to another, Cole asked Anna if she knew any of the girls from Mills College who had been murdered. She had known four of the five, and one had lived across the hall from her last year in the dormitory. Anna told Cole how all the girls at Mills College were now quite shaken and nervous about leaving campus alone.

"Why is it that you came to see me last Saturday, in the evening, by yourself?" Cole asked.

"Actually, a friend of my father's had dropped off some clothes for me, and I asked him to escort me over to you. He was to wait for me until he saw that I would be with you. As we exited the restaurant together, I waved for him to go," Anna explained.

"I didn't see anyone, and I didn't see you wave," Cole told her.

"Of course not, silly, I didn't want to be made a spectacle of," she said coyly.

Many minutes more passed with the conversation continuing to ebb and flow into and out of different topics before Cole returned his attention to the murders, but he did not let on to Anna.

"Had you ever met Joe Corbett before that night he introduced us to your parents at *The Flying Fin?*" Cole wanted to know.

"No, that was the first time. He does seem like a really nice boy," Anna stated. "Does he have a girlfriend?" she wanted to know.

"No, why do you ask?" Cole questioned.

"A girl just likes to know who's available," she said demurely.

Cole didn't know how to respond. He felt as though Anna was his girl. At least he wanted her to be his. Anna noticed the pained look on his face and set him at ease.

"However, I am not interested for myself, but in the event that one of my classmates is ever in need of an escort, it's good to know who is available," she explained. "I do believe that I already have my escort."

Cole blushed, but less so than in past meetings with Anna. Anna blushed, too. As they sat side by side on a park bench, Anna reached down and placed her hand on top of Cole's. Though he was a bit chilled, his body temperature suddenly rose to a comfortable level. He looked at Anna and smiled. She smiled back. They did not speak during the moment.

* * *

Cole and Anna continued to see each other on weekends, but the relationship continued to border on platonic, not that its what either secretly wanted, but Cole was still too shy to move beyond being the recipient of Anna's hand.

Joe noticed a difference in Cole. Certainly his amorous feelings for Anna were pervasive, but he also seemed to be distancing himself from Joe. At first Joe felt as though Cole was so preoccupied with Anna that he was absentminded in spending time with his roommate. But then Joe decided there must be more to why Cole was acting differently towards him.

"The coach is still interested in talking to you," Joe told him one morning as they got ready for class.

"Thanks, Joe, but I just ain't interested," Cole concluded.

"What is it with you?" Joe asked in a terse tone of voice.

"What do you mean?" Cole said.

"You seem to be distancing yourself from me, avoiding me like I had smallpox," Joe told him. "Did I do something to get under your skin?"

"No, Joe, nothing's wrong. Guess I just got a lot on my mind," Cole said without looking at his roommate.

Not believing him, Joe walked out of the room without saying another word. Over the next few days, the two did not talk. Their relationship continued to grow more and more tense. Joe went home for Christmas to his folks' house in San Francisco. Unlike the year before, he did not invite Cole to join his family. Anna became aware of Cole being alone for Christmas and invited him over to her family's house for Christmas dinner.

"My uncle will be up from Los Angeles, so you could meet him," Anna was excited to tell Cole.

Cole gladly accepted her invitation. Anna spent the few days before Christmas at her parent's house. On Christmas morning, Cole woke in his dormitory room, dressed in his best clothes, and caught the ferry for San Francisco. Anna had given him her address, and directions. After the ferry landed in San Francisco, Cole bought some flowers from a street vendor. He brought them for Mrs. Gilbert. He had already decided that it would not be proper to bring a gift to Anna, even on Christmas day.

The holiday spent with the Gilberts' was wonderful for Cole. He thought of Joe only once, but let the thought pass quickly. Anna was pleased that Cole had come. Her only disappointment of the day was her missing uncle. She had so wanted Cole to meet her Uncle Bear, as she called him. Anna explained that she had thought her uncle had the stature of a bear when she was a young girl. He had sent a telegraph that he would not be able to make the trip, but wished everyone well.

* * *

The relationship between Cole and Joe continued to grow distant. They rarely spoke, and both tried to stay out of the room except to sleep. Joe was spending more time at home, in San Francisco, on weekends.

Neither of the roommates had spoken about why the tension existed. Although Joe was a verbose roommate, he wasn't one to discuss his feelings, and Cole was even farther removed from wanting to discuss his feelings than Joe. Besides, Cole still had trouble accepting his thoughts about Joe being involved in the Mills College girls' murders. If he was certain of it, would he approach Joe? Would he tell Detective Isaiah W. Lees? Cole did not want to consider the possibility, yet it made him very anxious to be around

Joe, who rightfully so, couldn't understand the distance that suddenly existed between them. The gap growing between them due to the lack of communication was being filled with anger.

The new year of 1892 had come and gone. Cold winds were now common on most mornings, and the temperatures required one's warmest clothing. It was late January, on a Saturday mid-afternoon when Detective Lees caught up with Cole at *The Clipper*. Cole was just finishing his shift. Since he had started seeing more of Anna, he had asked to cut back on his work hours, especially on Saturdays.

As Detective Lees entered the restaurant, Anna followed him in, though neither was aware of the other knowing Cole. Both made their way toward Cole, who wasn't sure who to direct his attention towards. Once Anna and Detective Lees realized that Cole was the object of both of their attention, they glanced curiously at each other.

Cole introduced Anna to Detective Lees.

"Nice to meet you, Miss Gilbert," Isaiah W. Lees told her, hat in hand.

"Please to meet you too, sir," Anna responded.

"Cole, I need to speak with you," Detective Lees said soberly.

"Yes, sir," Cole answered, "Anna, would you mind giving us a minute?"

"Actually, Cole, I'd like you to come with me across the Bay, to San Francisco. I need your help in answering some questions," the Detective told him.

Cole had looked forward to seeing Anna all week, and suddenly he felt an extreme sense of disappointment. He could see the same feelings expressed on Anna's face.

"Hopefully we can wrap things up by late afternoon, and have you back to see Miss Gilbert in time for supper," Lees said smiling.

"Anna's escort left once she got inside the restaurant," Cole told Detective Lees, knowing the routine Anna followed to ensure her safe travel to the restaurant.

Lees preferred to find an escort for Anna other than himself, as he was anxious to get back to San Francisco quickly. But he would not let Anna travel alone, if no other alternative was available. No one was able to offer an alternative, so Lees was resigned to make the trip to Mills College before traversing the Bay by ferry. As the three stepped outside of *The Clipper* and buttoned their coats, Lees took off in one direction to locate a carriage. Cole saw his dormitory acquaintance, William, a block away, walking towards the restaurant from the other direction.

"Thought I'd try and talk my way into a free meal," William said to Cole with a smile. "But my plan won't work if you're not," he kidded.

"Actually, William, I'm on my way to San Francisco, but I could use your assistance," Cole said to the young man to whom he had never grown close.

"What can I do for you?" he asked.

"I would consider it a personal favor if you would escort Anna back to Mills College for me," Cole said.

"I will gladly put my meal on hold in order to escort the lovely Anna back to school," William said, trying to sound dashing.

Anna expressed her delight in William's skill as an orator. Cole considered the favor to be similar to having a bad tooth pulled. Painful, but necessary.

Anna and William began their walk to Mills College. They had decided it would be a nice, although cold day, for a winter walk.

Detective Lees returned within five minutes of Anna and William heading off towards Mills College. He had the carriage driver wait as Cole climbed aboard.

"I found an escort for Anna," Cole told Lees, as the Detective wrinkled his eyebrows upon returning and not finding Anna present. "A dormitory mate of mine."

Without wasting time, Lees asked where Joe was.

"Probably in San Francisco, at his parents' house," was all Cole could think to tell him.

Lees could tell that something was on Cole's mind. Using silence, a method he had mastered over his long law enforcement career, Lees waited for Cole to speak next. The silence caused Cole to grow more anxious. It took a lot for Cole to feel uncomfortable, except when with Anna, though he was getting better in handling his feelings for her. But his thoughts about Joe weighed heavily on his mind.

"Why'd you ask about Joe?" Cole asked. "And what do you want to see me about?"

"I think there is something more to this connection between the girls and their having been patrons at *The Flying Fin* and attending Mills College. I don't know what it is, but I feel it. I thought maybe if I spent some time talking with you and Joe, maybe there would be something that would help me that you hadn't realized. Between his connection to *The Flying Fin* and you being his roommate . . . well, who knows?" Lees concluded.

Cole was practically perspiring now, and Lees could see it, but he maintained his strategy of silence, wanting for Cole to speak next. Cole sat next to Lees in the carriage, his chin tucked against his chest, looking down. He fiddled with his hands. All the while, Lees waited patiently.

"Detective Lees," Cole began, "what kind of person would kill all those girls?"

"Well," Lees contemplated before responding, "I expect it was a man of considerable strength. To kill with your bare hands like he's done." Lees' voice trailed off sensing that Cole had more to say.

"The fourth girl had a scratch around her neck, like a necklace had been pulled from around her neck," Cole began to recount the details he'd heard. He swallowed hard. "The next morning, I found a necklace with a broken chain. Can't say where just yet. After the fifth girl died, I heard she had put up a struggle and had been bloodied."

As he concluded with his recitation, Cole looked at Lees. The detective had a concerned expression on his face.

"What is it?" Cole asked.

"How do you know about the scratch and the bloodied girl?" Lees inquired.

"William told me," Cole answered.

"Who's William?" Lees wanted to know.

"He lives in our dormitory, why?" Cole continued to ask.

"Those details were never made public," Lees told Cole in a cautious, deliberate tone.

"Then how would he know?" As soon as the words left his mouth, a cold, eerie feeling swept over Cole. He looked at Lees.

"Only the killer would know those details," Lees suggested. "Where can I find this William?"

Lees saw the terrified look in Cole's eyes as the college student comprehended the question.

"He's the one escorting Anna back to school!" Cole said, his voice growing louder with each spoken word.

*   *   *

Lees directed the carriage driver to head to Mills College. His voice was stern and clear. During his long, distinguished career, he had learned not to let emotion interfere with his duties. Upon arrival at the college, Lees inquired about Anna's return to campus. A co-ed just outside of Anna's dormitory told Cole and Lees that Anna had not returned since leaving campus early that morning. Hearing that information sent ice through Cole's body. He did not like the feeling and did not know what to do next. Never more than at that very moment had Cole wished for his father to be present. Clint Herbert always knew what to do in a tense moment. Never a man was calmer while those around him were at a loss, not even Joshua Rines.

"Where would William take her?" Cole asked helplessly.

"At this time of day, he'd likely take her someplace remote, but a place she would be comfortable going," Lees answered. "What can you tell me about William?"

"Nothing, I don't really know him, other than to exchange greetings. I don't even know his last name. I do know he works for Joe's parents at *The Flying Fin*," Cole rambled. He now had a strong pain in his stomach. His degree of helplessness was growing by the minute, adding to his pain. Without thinking, or even realizing he had done so, Cole reached down and touched his right hip as if he was looking for something, but his pistol was not there.

"You say that William was to escort Anna back here to school, but we know she didn't arrive. She wasn't expecting to go anywhere else with him . . ." Lees couldn't finish his thought out loud. He needed Cole to remain calm and helpful. If he shared the possibilities of his fears for Anna, he would lose Cole's ability to be helpful altogether.

"We can't just sit here!" Cole anxiously stated. He was slightly bent over at the waist as he spoke, trying to cover his aching stomach.

"Cole, I want you to walk the perimeter of the school. It could be that they're somewhere on this campus, and it would be likely that it'd be outside. I'll extend the perimeter of the search beyond the campus. I have to think they'd be close." Lees had given Cole his directions. Not knowing much about either William or Anna, it seemed logical that, based on Cole's information, Anna wouldn't have agreed to go anywhere far, especially if she was expecting to meet Cole later in the day.

Cole jumped out of the carriage. Since Anna had not come in through the main gate to Mills College, Lees suggested that Cole begin by searching the road that paralleled the front gate. On foot, two people could casually walk by and not be seen if they were not being looked for. From the road, there were many foot accesses into school.

Cole started traveling west, and planned on taking a clockwise rotation through and around the perimeter of Mills College. Every female student that Cole saw was asked if she had seen Anna Gilbert. Not one had answered in the affirmative. Cole was running as he made his way around the perimeter of the school.

If no one had seen her, she likely couldn't have come this way, he began to rationalize. The running was helping to rid him of his ache, and seemed to be clearing his head some. Cole decided to cut through the campus, and continue his search on the other side. He got a lot of strange looks from the Mills' students he passed, or who viewed him running. It was not common to see a male on campus, much less one running. One student shrieked as Cole ran past her, startling her by approaching from behind.

As he reached the other side of campus, Cole stopped to take a breath and looked to his left, then to his right. He didn't see anyone. Since left would be towards the back end of the campus, he turned in that direction and began to run again. He figured it would be more remote back there. After running a couple of hundred yards, Cole heard some rustling in an area he had just passed, forty feet back. He stopped and turned around. Coming out of the bushes, brushing himself off was William. Cole had not given any thought about what he would say when he encountered William. He stood there, almost lightheaded as he watched William turn in the direction opposite from where he was standing. William had not seen Cole, even though he was standing in plain sight.

"Hey," was all Cole could muster. William turned around, surprised to hear a male voice. As his eyes found on Cole, he stumbled, losing his balance and falling. William quickly stood back up, but continued to backpeddle away from Cole.

"Where's Anna?" Cole sternly asked as he began to pick up his pace, moving in William's direction.

Still backpeddling, William answered, "who?"

Cole was suddenly filled with rage, immediately thinking the worst about a murderer who didn't even remember the name of the girl he was just with.

"Where is she, William?" Cole said in anger as he had closed to within 10 feet of William.

William turned and began to run. Cole broke into a sprint and made up the distance that separated them in no time at all. Cole tackled his prey. William struggled to get up, but Cole was much stronger, and easily held him down. Cole turned William over, face up, and as he did, he thought of Anna. Here he was chasing William, when he needed to find Anna. He became frightened again. Cole stood up, pulling William up with him. He began to walk back towards the area where William had appeared from the bushes. Without looking back at him, Cole kept a tight grip on William's shirt collar. William struggled to get away, but each time he did, Cole squeezed more tightly on the collar. As they arrived to the spot where Cole saw William appear, he stopped and turned.

"Take me to her," Cole demanded. William could see the menacing look in his eyes.

Searching for any hope of getting away, William responded, "I don't know what you're talking about."

Cole quickly slipped a hard punch into William's ribcage. His knees buckled as he received the blow. Cole pulled him back up straight.

"You take me to her now, or I'll kill you where you stand," Cole promised. His two-handed grip around William's shirt collar had reached the point of choking William. He was having trouble breathing. As he began to realize his fate of being captured, William made one last attempt at escape, kicking at Cole, then trying to land a punch to his jaw. Neither was effective, but it angered Cole, who drove his right hand through William's jaw. Immediately, William collapsed. Cole let go of his grip, turned and followed the path through the bushes to where William had come from. About forty feet inside the bush line, Cole found Anna. She was lying on the ground, motionless. Cole swallowed hard. He rushed towards her, gently lifting her up to his chest as he knelt beside her. She was breathing, but barely. Her throat was almost bloody, it was so red. Cole loosened the collar on her dress. The dress had been torn in numerous places, likely during a struggle. Cole picked Anna up into his arms and began to make his way back out of the bushes. He needed to get her to a doctor. As he appeared back in the view of the campus, Cole picked up his brisk walking pace towards the building closest to him. It was not Anna's

Waterhole

dormitory, but it was a dormitory, and it would have a bed. Cole reached the building and turned right to go up the stairs. As he did, he glanced back to where he had left William lying on the ground. The spot was empty. William was gone.

Cole set Anna down on a sofa in the parlor, then sent a Mills College student to summon the doctor as quickly as she could. She returned in twenty minutes with the doctor. A crowd of students began to crowd around Anna. Cole stood and in a respectfully yet demanding tone, asked the young ladies to move back. They all obliged him. The doctor examined Anna, and got her to sip water, even though she had not regained consciousness.

"How is she, Doc?" Cole asked.

"She's likely been through a terrible ordeal," the doctor began, "but she's a strong young lady. I expect she'll be fine in about a week."

Cole was relieved. The ache in his stomach had disappeared. Yet he felt a terrible burden of guilt for what took place. This pain was now situated in his heart. He had asked William to accompany Anna back to her school. He had sent her with a murderer. How would she ever forgive him? How could he ever forgive himself?

It was more than an hour before Anna began to regain her consciousness. Cole was seated at her side when she did. It was about that same time that Detective Isaiah W. Lees found Cole in the girls' dormitory. Cole did not see him approach.

"How's she doing?" Lees asked. Though somewhat startled, Cole didn't even look back over his shoulder. He knew to whom the voice belonged.

"Doc says she ought to be fine in about a week," Cole told him, without removing his gaze from Anna. "I found William," Cole said, "but he got away."

"No he didn't," Lees told him. "Found him coming off the campus during my perimeter search. I saw that he had taken a pretty good licking, and figured it was you. I arrested him, and had him carted off to jail before I came back to find you and Anna. Good work, young man."

Still without looking, Cole simply nodded. As he did, he reached down and softly, slowly stroked Anna's dark, silky hair. It was the first time he had ever touched her hair, and it made him feel at a loss of his faculties. It made him feel good. Anna smiled up at him, but did not try to talk. Cole placed his right index finger over Anna's lips and made a sshhh sound himself. He smiled back at her.

* * *

Cole spent most of his waking time the next week at Anna's bedside. When he wasn't with her, he was staying in a temporary shelter just outside the Mills College campus, arranged for him by Detective Lees. He was given special permission to remain on the Mills College campus after visiting hours. Nine days following her attempted murder, Cole walked Anna back to her own dormitory room. She was not yet ready to return to classes, but she had insisted on moving to her own room. Cole had not contacted anyone, either about his class schedule or his work schedule at *The Clipper*. He was sure that his job was lost, and that his professors would fail him in his classes for the term.

The twelfth day following Anna's attack, Cole made his way back to St. Mary's, at Anna's insistence. He walked into his dormitory room, head down, as it had been all the way from Mills College. When he closed the door to his room, he looked up and found Joe sitting on his bed. Without saying anything, Cole walked over and sat on his own bed. After a deep exhale, Cole looked up at Joe.

"Hi, roomy," Joe said with a gentle smile. "I heard about Anna."

Cole tried to smile back but couldn't.

"Joe," he began, and shook his head slowly, trying to find the words he was searching for, "I owe you an apology."

"No you don't," Joe told him.

"Yeah, I reckon I've been a pretty poor roommate for the past couple of months," Cole explained, "I even thought you may have been the killer."

"I know," Joe responded.

Cole's brow creased as he looked at Joe, wondering how he knew.

"Detective Lees stopped by a couple of days after Anna was hurt. He told me what had happened and what you had thought about my involvement. Sure made it easier to understand what you were going through."

"I'm sorry I didn't have more faith in you," said Cole.

"I guess there must have been some part of you that didn't believe I was the murderer, or you would have gone to the police much earlier," Joe reconciled. "The blood on my shirt happened just the way I told you. And the necklace you found was my mother's. She had asked me to take it to a jeweler friend of hers, here in Oakland. It needed a new chain."

"Guess so," Cole responded to the earlier part of Joe's statement. "I'm glad our relationship is intact, because I'm sure I'm out of a job and possibly out of school."

"Well, not exactly," Joe said with a smile. Cole looked at him with a confused expression. "After Lees came by, I went down to *The Clipper* and took over your shifts for you until you could get back to them. I also spoke to your professors. The job and school are still there for you."

An ever grateful Cole stood and walked towards Joe. He stuck out his hand. Joe stood and faced Cole. He grasped Cole's hand firmly, then pulled him closer. The two roommates hugged.

* * *

Three weeks after the attack, Cole and Anna were both back in school, along with Cole working at his old job. Lees had told Cole that William would likely get a life sentence in San Quentin for his murder spree. He had confessed to killing all five girls. According to Lees, William had met all five over a period of nearly two years, when they dined at *The Flying Fin*. All five had refuted his advances. He had met Anna at *The Flying Fin* last year when her family dined there during the holidays. He had tried to arrange to call on her, but Anna stated that she was already being courted, referring to Cole, although it had not happened as of that time.

The next few months flew by, and Cole and Anna spent increasingly more time together. Cole portrayed the ultimate gentlemen, having not yet kissed Anna. She would put her arm through his when they walked, but Cole's lack of experience with females left him continually nervous in situations when he and Anna were alone. Anna took the lead in most of their conversations. Surprisingly, as close as they were becoming, neither spoke at any length about their families. For Cole, it was still a difficult topic, especially for someone as closed as he was with his feelings.

June arrived and Cole dreaded the decision he had to make. With his second year of college ending, should he go back to Oklahoma for the summer to help Leroy and Bertram on the ranch, or should he stay in Oakland and continue his courtship with Anna?

Anna saw him struggle with his decision. It was two weeks before the end of the school year. Cole expressed his concern for going home and leaving Anna. She teased him gently, asking if he was afraid she wouldn't wait for him. Cole blushed, but also nodded his head with his affirmative answer. They had just returned from an evening at the circus. Cole had never before seen animal acts, and he thought the clowns were downright foolish. Anna explained that their act was all in fun, but Cole was not raised to find fun in foolish activities. Anna did not argue her point. She knew Cole was a good man, one who had been raised differently than she had been. Though neither was from families of money, her uncle provided for hers financially when needed.

Cole and Anna walked up the slight hill to the Mills College campus. Anna asked if he would stroll with her around the campus for a while. If it prolonged his time with Anna, Cole was obliging. As it had become routine, Anna placed her arm through Cole's. He felt proud to have such a beautiful lady walk beside him, arm in arm. They had walked silently for ten minutes before Anna spoke.

"You need to go home, Cole," she told him.

"Why do you say that?" he wondered, a bit hurt thinking she wanted to be away from him.

"Leroy and Bertram will need your help. And I will be here waiting for you to return," she answered with her beautiful smile.

Cole smiled back as he turned his head sideways to look at her. Anna stopped walking, and tugged slightly on Cole's arm, causing him to stop also. He turned to face her. As he did, Anna stepped closer to him. Cole felt the toes of her shoes touch his. She looked up at him and grasped both of his hands in hers. Cole felt his heart race and his breathing grow more shallow. Anna appeared to Cole to be calm and poised, just the opposite of how he was feeling.

"You go home," she repeated, "and while you're in Oklahoma, here is something to remember me by."

As she spoke, Anna slowly moved her face closer to Cole's. When she finished her sentence, Anna's lips touched Cole's softly. She kissed him. Anna felt Cole's hands stiffen, which caused her to smile as she held her kiss.

Two weeks later, Cole boarded the train with Anna waving goodbye from the platform. The train pulled away, and Cole immediately began to miss Anna. It would be a long summer. Just before they lost sight of each other, Anna blew him a kiss. Cole fell asleep that night in his boxcar, unable to remove his smile.

* * *

Cole had arranged with Leroy to buy a new horse in Albuquerque when the Atlantic & Pacific stopped there. Leroy arranged for the sale and wired a bank draft to the seller in advance. The chocolate-brown quarter horse, with the white mane was in the livery stable when Cole arrived. Cole would make the trip home to the Bar-CJ himself, saving Leroy and Bertram from making the trip to pick him up. Cole looked forward to the peacefulness he felt when riding alone.

Leroy was in the house cooking dinner when Cole arrived at the ranch. Bertram was in the barn tending to a sick calf that had been born in mid-spring, just two months earlier. Neither had heard Cole ride up. Since no one was in sight to greet him, Cole rode to the knoll where his parents were buried, alongside Joshua Rines. As his feelings for Anna grew deeper, he felt a new emptiness inside, knowing that his folks would never get to meet her. He sat atop his new horse as he looked down at the three grave markers. During the four day ride home, Cole had thought about names for his new horse, but none had come to his liking. The ride home on horseback had been a day quicker than the wagon ride, and he felt as though he could have easily knocked off another day if he had wanted to move at more than the leisurely pace he took.

Cole did not know how long he had been sitting on the knoll when Bertram came out of the barn, glanced in his direction and saw him.

"Cole!" he shouted, "Leroy, Cole's home!" he shouted again.

Leroy came quickly out to the front porch and gave a wave. Bertram joined Leroy on the porch as Cole covered the short distance to meet them.

"Howdy boys!" Cole chimed.

"Well listen to the college man," Leroy beckoned.

Cole climbed down and gave both a hug, catching the recipients a little off guard.

"It sure is good to see the both of you," Cole said.

"It's good ta have ya home, Cole," Bertram said smiling, as he gave him a playful punch on his shoulder. Cole smiled back as he received Bertram's gesture.

"Got a fine meal cooking in the kitchen," Leroy told Cole.

"I'm even hungry enough to eat anything you've made," Cole teased Leroy as Bertram laughed.

They all shared a fine time that evening, eating and catching each other up on what had been happening, both at school and on

Waterhole

the ranch. Everything except Anna. Cole felt unexpectedly nervous about bringing her into the conversation. He decided that bit of information could wait until later.

Cole was eager to get into his ranch clothes and get to work, the following morning, and each morning that followed. He felt a lot of satisfaction in ranch work, more than he ever had prior to leaving the ranch for college. Though Leroy and Bertram still did not take him for a lifelong rancher, they saw the glow in his face as he worked each day, tiring himself out, but always ending the day with a smile.

It was late-July when a rider approached the Bar-CJ as the evening sun was setting behind the bunkhouse. Cole was in the barn, helping Bertram catch a couple of chickens that had escaped their pen. Leroy was cleaning up the dinner dishes. The rider sat on his horse, not yet invited to climb down.

"Hello in the house," he shouted, "anybody here?"

Almost simultaneously, all three of the Bar-CJ partners appeared to the rider.

"Howdy," the rider said as he nodded in the direction of each of the three men. "I was looking for the Herbert place," he explained, still sitting on his pale-gold colored palomino. The question had been asked in Leroy's direction as he was the closest to the rider.

"No need to keep on looking," Leroy answered, "you found it."

The rider appeared unsure of himself upon hearing Leroy's answer.

"No sir, I mean the Herbert family from Dodge City, Kansas way," the rider further clarified.

"Same answer, boy, you found it," Leroy confirmed.

The rider looked at Leroy, then Bertram, not recognizing either. Cole was still a ways off, just outside the barn, and with the sun setting behind him, was hard to cast eyes on.

"Who might you be?" Leroy asked.

"I'm an old friend of Cole Herbert," the young man answered. "Name's Chad Henry."

The name was unfamiliar to both Leroy and Bertram. None of the Herbert's had ever mentioned Chad Henry to them. Chad had left Dodge City to go east and live with his aunt before the Herbert's had left Kansas. Neither Clint nor Katherine had ever reminisced that far back with Leroy or Bertram. Upon hearing the name, Cole squinted his eyes and peered at Chad, still sitting on his horse. He began to move in Chad's direction.

"Chad?" Cole asked as he kept on moving toward his old friend.

Chad paused for a moment to look in the direction of the voice.

"Cole?" he asked as both broke into a big smile. Cole began to run over towards Chad, who had climbed down from his horse and slipped around to the right side of the palomino to greet Cole.

Cole kept on walking, and gave a big bear hug to his old friend. It did Leroy and Bertram good to see Cole so happy about Chad's arrival.

"How'd you find us?" Cole asked once he let Chad out of his grasp.

"Well, after all these years, I finally had enough money to venture out on my own, so I caught the train for Kansas, bought me this here fine horse, asked a few questions in Dodge City, and here I am," Chad said with a grin.

"Sure is good to see you, Chad," Cole said.

"Good to see you too, Cole," Chad responded.

The two old friends sat outside on the porch. Leroy and Bertram joined them for a while before heading of to bed. Both now slept in the bunkhouse, leaving the main house to Cole when he was home. Leroy had rounded up some leftovers to feed Chad as they sat and talked.

The two kids, as Leroy called them, sat up most of the night, not getting to bed until an hour before dawn. Cole told Chad about all that had happened since they last saw each other. About Waterhole, about his folks and Joshua Rines, about meeting Leroy and Bertram, about Joe and college, and even about Anna. Chad told his story about his aunt taking him east, to Boston, when his mother had died. He was raised by a good lady, his aunt, but he never felt settled in the east. As soon as he was ready, he decided to head west and find Cole. When they finally retired, Chad slept in Cole's old room in the house, with Cole now occupying his parent's old room. Cole realized as he settled into bed for the first time in that room that his parents never had the opportunity to share it with each other. Clint had it before heading off to Waterhole, but he never returned to share it with Katherine. Fortunately, Cole was so tired that he didn't do much thinking of any kind once his head hit the pillow.

Cole had invited Chad to stay on at the ranch as long as he liked. Couldn't pay him to work, but the room and board was free. Chad said he'd never had a better deal. The two were inseparable the next five weeks. They did their share of ranch work, but they also spent time playing. They held shooting contests, Cole using his father's old pistol, Chad using a new model colt revolver. Though both boys would turn 20 years of age soon, they played as if they were ten years old. Leroy and Bertram chuckled in amazement at the transition they saw in Cole. He had never been one to *play*. He worked on the ranch, and while he had been happy, they never saw him giggle until Chad arrived.

"The way you two are acting," Leroy told Cole one evening as they sat down for dinner, "I don't know whether to send you back to college or to grade school."

Leroy's comments brought about the realization that Cole would be leaving within little more than a week for school. After some discussion over dinner the following night, it was decided that Chad would stay at the ranch, while Cole returned for his third year of schooling. They also agreed that Chad would make the trip to California in spring to spend time with Cole before returning to the ranch the following summer together.

On the first of September 1892, Chad and Cole rode out for Albuquerque together. Chad would bring back Cole's horse with him after seeing Cole off on the train.

"It's been great to see you, Chad," Cole told his friend as the conductor made an *all aboard* call to those standing around on the platform.

"I'll be out in the spring," Chad told him, "and I'm looking forward to meeting this girl, Anna, and swapping a few stories with her about her beau. I can tell her a few things."

"You do and you'll be walking home from California to Oklahoma with my boot across your backside every step of the way," Cole boasted.

Chad smiled and waved as Cole boarded the Atlantic & Pacific. The train pulled away, and Cole realized that life was good. He was leaving one best friend, and going to live the school year with another, Joe, while continuing to court Anna.

Cole had so much to think about that the trip west seemed faster than usual. He arrived back on Saint Mary's College campus on September 8th, only to find that Joe had not yet checked in. During the previous two years, Joe had always been the first to arrive. With school starting in a few days, Cole thought it odd, but also realized that Joe would show up game for anything once he did arrive. After unpacking, Cole went down to *The Clipper* to check in and arrange his work schedule for the coming school year.

* * *

"Did you see it!" Joe shouted upon entering their dormitory room two days later. It was 9:15 am, and school would begin the following day. This was his first appearance on campus.

"Hello to you too, roomy," Cole answered.

"Did you see it!" Joe repeated, waving a newspaper in front of Cole's face so quickly he couldn't focus on anything in it.

"See what?" Cole asked.

"The paper, the paper!" Joe hollered, "look!" He shoved the paper at Cole.

Cole began to look for something, but before he could find what it was that Joe was intending for him to see, Joe told him.

"My brother, James, he won the heavyweight boxing championship in New Orleans! He beat John L. Sullivan!" Joe said, still excitedly.

Cole saw the headline.

"Wow," Cole said. "I haven't ever seen a boxing match before, but if he's the champion of the world, he must be pretty good," Cole told him.

"Pretty good?!" Joe exclaimed, "why my brother, *Gentleman Jim* Corbett, just beat the great John L. Sullivan, you bet he's the best there is!"

Cole sat on his bed smiling at Joe, acknowledging his excitement as best he could.

"Oh, I wish I'd been there," Joe told Cole, shaking his head slowly.

Cole kept on smiling. Joe finally realized that in his giddiness, he had not said hello to Cole. Joe ran three steps and jumped on Cole, grabbing him in a headlock. Cole quickly stood up and lifted Joe off of him, then threw him across the room, onto his own bed.

"Wow, maybe you should be next in line to fight my brother," Joe said in response to Cole's strength.

"No thanks," Cole told him, "I'll stick with ranch work and school work."

"And working on Anna, too," Joe said, as he ran from the room with Cole chasing close behind.

Cole was eager to see Anna, but knew she would not be returning to school until that evening. She and her family had been the guests of her uncle in Los Angeles, and her school would not begin for another week. At 4:30 that afternoon, Cole made the long walk to Mills College. His anticipation in seeing Anna made the walk seem even longer than usual. When he arrived at the front gate, he was directed to the parlor of her dormitory, where he sat on a beige, tweed sofa. Anna had changed dormitory halls, opting to move into a bigger room, made available to upper class students. Knowing she would arrive anytime made his heart begin to beat faster, and his stomach do battle with butterflies. As Anna made her way down the staircase, Cole saw her and gulped loudly as he stood to greet her. She had grown even more beautiful since last spring. She reached the bottom of the stairs and made her way towards Cole. His boots felt nailed to the floor as he tried to move towards Anna. He managed to get three or four steps in her direction before they met. Cole glanced around to see who was watching, and as he did, Anna reached down and gently grasped both of his hands. Startled, Cole recovered nicely, looked at her and smiled. Her teeth sparkled back at him, and her big brown eyes danced as she looked at Cole.

"Hi, Anna," Cole said.

"My, you became quite the conversationalist over the summer, didn't you," she said smiling.

"Yep," Cole answered her sarcastically, but with a smile.

"Cole Herbert, I missed you so," she told him, almost in a scolding manner. He was pleased to hear it.

"I missed you too, Anna," he responded. They still were joined at the hands. "Care to go for dinner?" he asked.

"Why, I'd love to," she answered as she fluttered her long eyelashes at him.

As Cole turned to lead Anna outside, she set herself alongside of him, her arm firmly entrenched through his. Cole's chest puffed out a little bit more as they exited the dormitory. It would be a short walk to the restaurant, just three blocks from the campus.

While at dinner, Anna told Cole of William's trial that summer. He had been found guilty of murder, on all counts, and sentenced to life imprisonment in San Quentin.

* * *

Cole's third year at Saint Mary's was consistent with his last one. His time was spent with school, where he had declared himself an engineering major, working at *The Clipper* and courting Anna, along with the occasional instance of convincing Joe that he had no time to play base ball. Convincing Joe became even harder one unusually humid October afternoon. Cole had agreed to go and have a catch with Joe. Joe brought along a couple of base balls and, without Cole knowing, had arranged for the Saint Mary's base ball coach to observe their activity.

After throwing the ball around five or six times, Joe challenged Cole to a long throwing contest. Joe had the best arm on the team, and was able to cast his throw over 345 feet. Cole took his turn. He threw the ball just short of Joe's throw.

"Not bad, roomy," Joe said. "But you probably won't be able to follow this next toss unless you get a seat on the moon." Cole smiled at his roommate's bravado.

Joe unleashed a throw that exceeded his first throw by seven feet, landing at 352 feet away.

"Sometimes I amaze even myself," Joe turned and told Cole while smiling. "Want to feel my muscle?" he asked while flexing the bicep of his right arm. Cole couldn't contain his chuckle. Joe could always make him laugh.

"Now if you want to really get it out there, you've got to hop into your throw like I did," Joe told Cole. Cole nodded in deference to Joe's expertise.

Cole rotated his right arm around and around in a forward motion, just like he saw Joe do. He wasn't sure what good it did, but he wanted Joe to see he was paying attention and learning. Cole took a deep breath, added a short hop into his step and launched the spherical object. It went well past Joe's best throw, landing just over 400 feet away. As Joe and Cole ran to retrieve the ball, they were met by Joe's coach.

"Son, do you realize what you just did?" said the coach.

Cole did not know who he was speaking with, but shrugged his shoulders anyways. Joe introduced Cole to his coach.

"Back in 1872, a fella named John Hatfield threw a ball 400 feet, seven and one half inches. It's the longest throw ever made, and you nearly beat it!" the coach informed them both, as his voice grew more excited with each couple of words.

Both the coach and Joe gave their best sales pitch trying to convince Cole that he could be a great player. Cole relied upon his integrity by telling them that he wouldn't even think about their offer. He was not a ball player, and he didn't plan on becoming one.

"Well, at least I keep in good company," Joe said as he and Cole walked back to their dormitory room, leaving a disappointed base ball coach at the field. "My brother is the heavyweight boxing champion of the world, and my roommate nearly broke the world's long toss record."

It would be the last time that Cole went out to play base ball with Joe. Without saying, Joe understood that Cole did not want to have to continually defend his decision not to play. The unspoken, mutual appreciation between the roommates signified the strong bond of respect they had for each other.

Cole and Joe cleaned themselves up after returning from the ball field, then left for Mills College. Cole and Anna were introducing Joe to one of Anna's friends. Cole had never seen Joe so nervous before, but he knew how his roommate was feeling. Cole still experienced a case of nerves once in a while when he was expecting to see Anna.

* * *

Over the next few months, Cole and Anna introduced Joe to three different girl friends of Anna's. The third one finally seemed to be a match for Joe. Cole could tell because the nervousness he had displayed with the first two dissipated when he met the third girl, Louise. Joe's sense of humor returned and he and Louise began to see each other regularly, although Joe had admitted to Cole that he wasn't serious the way Cole was with Anna.

Cole spent Thanksgiving with Anna's family, who once again dined at *The Flying Fin* for dinner, the same place that Cole had first formally met Anna a year ago when he and Joe dined there. During Christmas, Anna's family traveled south to Los Angeles to spend the holidays with her uncle. Cole's relationship with Anna had grown strong enough that she considered asking if Cole could accompany her family south. They decided it would be best to wait on that kind of a trip, seeing as they had only been courting for one year. Instead, Cole went to San Francisco to celebrate with the Corbett family.

After a long, cold winter, spring arrived full of wind and rain. Joe was playing base ball as much as the weather permitted. It was April when Chad Henry arrived in Oakland on the Atlantic & Pacific. Cole was able to get him a job at *The Clipper*, which included a small room for him to stay in upstairs from the restaurant. Chad planned to stay until Cole finished school, then accompany him back to the ranch in Oklahoma. In no time, Cole, Chad and Joe became inseparable, except for when Cole was seeing Anna. Joe continued to see Louise and Chad had been introduced to Elizabeth, one of the girls Joe had not connected with in an earlier meeting. The six of them spent most of their free time together, visiting San Francisco, going to the beach, and picnicking in various parks, both in Oakland and San Francisco. While they were having fun together, Cole began to realize that all the group activities were interfering with his opportunities to spend time alone with Anna. He wasn't yet ready to make any changes to the group social life, but he continued to monitor his feelings.

In May, Anna invited Cole and the rest of their group to a party at her family's house. It was to honor her father's 50th birthday. Anna told Cole that it would be a formal affair, and that everyone must wear their best clothes. She was excited and looking forward to introducing Cole to her uncle, who would be visiting from Los Angeles to attend the celebration. The party would be on the last Saturday of May. Cole had been thinking about his future and he knew he wanted Anna to be a part of it. He wanted to marry her. Cole decided he would ask Anna's father during the party for her hand in marriage.

* * *

Cole, Joe and Chad went to Mills College on the night of the party to pick up the girls, minus Anna, who was already at her parent's house getting ready for the arrival of their guests. They took a carriage to pick up the ferry across the Bay. The three men had decided to stay the night at the Corbett's house, as the girls would be spending the night at the Gilbert's. Cole was nervous. Joe attributed it to his having to wear fine clothes. Neither Chad nor Joe knew that Cole was planning to ask for Anna's hand in marriage that evening.

The Gilbert's had a modestly decorated, yet spacious house in the Nob Hill area of San Francisco. They were expecting more than 75 guests. Family members would be arriving from all over California, along with many co-workers of Mr. Gilbert's from the wharf, and friends of the family and their children. The latter being the reason for Cole and companys' invite.

Cole was feeling more and more anxious about speaking with Mr. Gilbert. He started to second guess himself, and began to rationalize reasons for not approaching Anna's father that evening.

Anna had been busy helping her mother welcome guests and took her hostess duties seriously. She kept her eyes on Cole, however, and noticed that he appeared to be off by himself, wearing a sullen expression on his face. In passing Chad during one trip to the kitchen for more hors d'oeuvres, Anna asked Chad to see what Cole was thinking about. Chad excused himself from his date, who was humorously being entertained by Joe.

"How's that wall doing?" Chad asked his longtime friend after joining him across the large entertaining room.

"What?" Cole responded, not sure if he had heard Chad correctly.

"The wall, you've been holding it up since we got here," Chad told him. "Just wanted to know if it was doing all right. You need me to take a turn at it, so you can get something to eat?"

Cole smiled and shook his head as his chin dropped to his chest.

"To look at you, I'd think you was an old croaker," Chad told him.

"I'm feeling a bit like a coffee boiler," Cole told Chad, as their vocabulary seemed to automatically revert itself to their younger days in Dodge City.

Chad stood quietly, waiting to hear what Cole had to say. Cole took a deep breath and held it before letting it out.

"I was planning to ask Mr. Gilbert for Anna's hand tonight." There, he had said it aloud to someone.

Chad was dumbfounded.

"You was plannin' to do what?" Chad practically shouted, drawing a few looks from nearby guests. Cole blushed as he saw people beginning to look in his direction. Before Cole could answer Chad, Chad followed his own question.

"Well quit beatin' the devil around the stump and ask him," Chad said. "Does Anna know?"

"No, I haven't told her my plans. I thought it wouldn't be proper to ask her without speaking with her father first," Cole told Chad.

"What do you think he'll say? What do you think she'll say?" Chad asked in succession.

"I'm so balled up right now, I don't know what to think," Cole responded.

"Anna sent me over to talk to you and see what was bothering you. She said every time she's looked at you tonight, you've seemed dragged out," Chad told him.

As Chad and Cole continued their conversation, Chad noticed Mr. Gilbert go into his study with another man.

"Now looks to be as good a time as any," Chad mentioned as he nodded his head in the direction of the study. Cole looked at his childhood friend, eyes wide open.

"Here goes," he said as he took his first step towards the study. Chad gave him a friendly slap on the back as he passed by.

"Mr. Gilbert?" Chad said as he knocked on the partially opened door to the study.

"Cole, come on in," greeted Mr. Gilbert. "Cole, I'd like you to meet my brother, Charles Gilbert."

"Very nice to meet you sir, Anna has spoken of you kindly. How was your trip up from Los Angeles?"

Mr. Gilbert chuckled, "no Cole, you're thinking of my wife's brother. He's arriving later this evening. Charles lives up near Sonoma."

Being embarrassed by the first statement out of his mouth was not Cole's idea of a smooth opening to the conversation he was trying to have with Mr. Gilbert.

"Is there something I can help you with?" Mr. Gilbert asked.

"Yes sir, I'd like to have a moment with you if I may," Cole said as gentlemanly as he had planned.

"Sure," Mr. Gilbert said, "Charles, would you please excuse us?"

"Certainly," his brother replied as he nodded towards Cole and exited the room. Cole returned the nod.

As his brother exited the study, he closed the door behind him.

"Now Cole, what can I do for you?" asked Anna's father as he gestured for Cole to sit in the chair opposite his desk.

Cole tried to play the words through in his head before saying them aloud, but his thought process was causing a long delay, causing Mr. Gilbert to ask Cole once again, who was startled to suddenly realize he was causing Mr. Gilbert to wait.

"Well, sir," Cole began. "It's about Anna..."

"What about my Anna?" her father asked, sensing he knew why Cole had asked to speak with him.

Cole took another deep breath.

"Well, sir," he began again, "I love your daughter, sir, and I'd like for your permission to ask for her hand in marriage."

Cole waited. And waited. It seemed to him it had been fifteen minutes since he posed the question to Mr. Gilbert.

"My son," Mr. Gilbert began, "I have come to know you as an honorable young man. I know my daughter is very much in love with you." That was as much as Mr. Gilbert said. Without his knowing, Cole was being put on by Anna's father. He planned to give his permission to Cole, but not without making the young man sweat a little first. A father's prerogative, he concluded. Cole sat leaning forward, wringing his hands, with his forearms resting on his knees, waiting.

After Mr. Gilbert felt as though he had waited a sufficient amount of time, he gave his permission to Cole.

Cole exited the study, leaving a smiling Mr. Gilbert sitting at his desk.

Chad met Cole before he got five feet outside the study.

"Well? he asked Cole.

Cole did his best to feign disappointment, but he didn't fool Chad, who gave him a stiff, friendly punch on his right arm. Cole smiled as he rubbed his arm.

"So, when are you going to ask her?" Chad inquired.

"No hurry," Cole shrugged, trying to continue with his calm, aloof demeanor for Chad's sake.

"I'll go ask her for you," Chad said as he began to move away from Cole.

"No you don't!" Cole said as he grabbed for Chad's arm. Chad turned and smiled.

"Gotcha!" he told his nervous friend.

Cole and Chad continued to share the moment when Joe joined them.

"If base ball doesn't work out for me, I may take my act on vaudeville," he told his friends, "I had those girls mesmerized with my stories. What are you guys doing over here?"

"Cole here has a busy night planned," Chad said as he kept his gaze on Cole.

Joe noticed that Chad was not looking at him when he spoke.

"What's going on?" Joe asked, more curious than alarmed.

Chad remained quiet, choosing to give Cole the opportunity to share his news. Joe continued to alternately look at his pair of friends, his curiosity peaking.

"Well?!" Joe tried again.

"I'm going to ask Anna to marry me tonight," Cole sprung his news on Joe.

"Oh, is that all?" Joe said, "I thought there was something really interesting going on over here." After a brief pause to let his humor sink in, Joe threw a bear hug around his bigger roommate, and lifted him off the ground.

"It's about time," he told Cole.

The three young men continued to share Cole's plans among themselves, Chad and Joe trying to offer their advice, all of which Cole was profusely declining to accept.

"The last thing I need is advice from the likes of you two," he told them, resulting in a punch in each arm from the friends flanking him.

The three amigos found their way over to the punch bowl to celebrate Cole's good fortune. Chad and Joe considered asking Anna to be a mere formality. Getting Mr. Gilbert's permission was the hard part. Joe took the honors of filling their punch glasses.

"Here's to a good man, and an even better woman," he offered, raising his cup. Cole and Chad raised theirs to meet Joe's. Following a quiet clinking of the glasses, they all drank their punch.

Anna surprised Cole as she snuck up on him and squeezed his arm, almost causing him to drop his glass. Cole felt flushed as the eyes of Chad and Joe cast a hard gaze at him.

"We'd better see to our dates," Joe said. "I don't know about yours, Chad, but I'm sure Louise can't stand to be away from me this long." Joe pulled Chad by the arm as they left Cole and Anna alone at the punch bowl.

"I haven't had a chance to spend any time with you tonight," Anna told Cole, squeezing his arm gently with both hands. "Did you miss me?"

"I did," he said with a gulp. "I'd like to talk to you somewhere, maybe out front?"

The front of the house had a nice view towards the Bay. Cole thought it would be a romantic spot to ask Anna to marry him.

It was also away from the rest of the party, which took up all the rooms in the house.

"I'd like that, but first I want to introduce you to my Uncle Bear. He just arrived from Los Angeles," Anna excitedly told him, wanting to introduce him to her favorite uncle. She pulled him by the arm, leading him towards the far side of the entertainment room. When they arrived, Cole recognized Anna's mother, but the man speaking with her had his back towards Cole.

"Uncle Bear," Anna spoke proudly, "I'd like you to meet Cole." The man turned around to face Cole. "Cole, meet my uncle, Salvador Gregorio."

* * *

It was him. He was older, but strong and broad shouldered at 54 years old. Cole looked at him. His breathing began to quicken, and his muscles tightened, first across his back and in his stomach, then in his biceps. Without noticing, his hands began to flex in and out of fists. Sal Gregorio had no idea who Cole was, but it had been about eight years since he had seen Cole, who had grown from an adolescent into a strong young man.

"Nice to meet you, Cole," Gregorio said as he extended his right hand towards Cole.

Cole just stood there. His lips pursed tightly, eyes staring at Gregorio. Anna, her mother and Gregorio waited. Cole stepped forward slightly with his left foot, catching his heel on the corner of a throw rug, which caused him to slightly lose his balance. In the same motion, Cole followed with a right fist that brushed Gregorio's chin, knocking the sturdy man backwards against the wall, but he remained on his feet.

"Cole!" Anna shouted. Her mother remained motionless, frightened, not knowing how to react.

Joe and Chad, as well as most of the guests in the room, heard Anna scream and turned to look. They saw Cole standing there, fists still clenched, while Anna and her mother tended to Gregorio.

"You don't recognize me, but you'll remember me," Cole told him, frustrated that his stumble didn't allow his punch to land square on Gregorio's jaw.

"Cole, what are you talking about! This is my uncle ... apologize right now!" Anna continued to scream.

"This is the man who's responsible for killing my parents and who killed my father's best friend," Cole spoke in a slow, stern voice.

Joe and Chad had reached Cole's side to assess the situation. Gregorio stood upright and rubbed his jaw.

"Nice punch you have there, son," Gregorio said, trying to recognize who it was that had hit him. "But I'm afraid you have me mixed up with someone else."

"Waterhole, Arizona," was all Cole said.

Cole could tell by the sudden change in Gregorio's eyes that he remembered who Cole was, but he would not let on. Gregorio continued to feign ignorance.

"I'm sorry, Cole, is it, but you're obviously confusing me with someone else," Gregorio said.

"There's no confusion on my part," Cole answered, "and now that I've found you, I aim to kill you," Cole told him, not realizing what he had said until he heard the words come out of his mouth.

"Get out!" Anna screamed at Cole. "Get out of here, Cole!" she said again, beside herself with emotion.

"Let's go, Cole," Chad said quietly to his friend, as Joe placed a firm hand on Cole's right arm and gave a slight tug.

All eyes were on Cole, including Gregorio's, in whose eyes Cole understood that Gregorio knew exactly who he was. Neither said another word, but both maintained eye contact until Cole was out of the house, along with Chad and Joe.

Once they were outside, Cole broke Joe's hold of his arm and began to walk quickly away from the house.

Waterhole

"What the hell was that?!" Joe shouted at Cole as he followed him down the street.

Neither Joe nor Chad had overheard the introduction between Cole and Sal Gregorio, and they had not been able to ascertain Anna's uncle's name before leaving the house. All either friend had seen was an act completely out of character for Cole.

Joe waited for a response to his question, but none was coming. He and Chad exchanged glances. Chad shrugged his shoulders at Joe. At the end of the street, Cole stood and rested his hands against a hitching rail. Chad and Joe had been trailing by ten feet, and reached Cole in short time. They stood next to Cole, both on his left side, Chad closest, Joe on the outside. They stood there quietly. They had many questions, but saw that Cole wasn't about to speak until he was ready.

"The uncle of the girl I want to marry killed my parents," were the first words out of Cole's mouth. Joe and Chad looked with bewilderment at each other. Each of them had heard Cole's story about his parent's death, but only once. They had not yet caught on to what Cole was talking about.

"Anna's uncle is Salvador Gregorio," Cole said without emotion.

Hearing the man's name, Joe and Chad recognized it, and knew who he was. It also explained how Cole had reacted at the party. Neither, however, knew what to say.

* * *

"The boy must die," Gregorio announced to the three other men sitting around the table at his hotel room in San Francisco's Union Square area. Since he rode out of Waterhole eight years earlier, Sal Gregorio had continued to walk on the opposite side of the law, but he had maintained a lower presence, not wanting to risk drawing attention to himself as he did in Waterhole. Living in Los Angeles had allowed him to work among the large contingent also engaged in unlawfulness, including many who were in the law enforcement business.

"There's no statute of limitations for murder," Gregorio continued. "While it would be difficult for him to prove anything, I sensed in his eyes that he would not stop until he found justice. I think that his justice will come from a well-placed bullet."

Gregorio had been able to play the unwitting uncle at his sister's house. He had told the family that he had no idea why Cole had punched him, and made such outrageous accusations. While he rubbed his jaw, following Cole's departure, Gregorio wittingly told all within an earshot that he was often confused for many former Mexican banditos. "We all must look alike to the gringos," he mused.

In his hotel room the next evening, Gregorio plotted to complete his efforts to eliminate the Herbert family.

"My niece tells me that he is a student across the Bay at Saint Mary's College. He works at a restaurant called *The Clipper*. Most of his free time has been spent with my niece, but it appears that is likely to change," Gregorio smiled as he recounted the manner in which he obtained information from Anna, all the while expressing concern for her choice in a man to her. Anna and her family thought of Gregorio as the rich, loving uncle who paid her way through college. They were oblivious to the real Gregorio. His living in Los Angeles shielded him from his family knowing much about his daily activities.

"Here is what we will do," Gregorio told the hired help he found down near the wharf in San Francisco. He did not know of these men personally, but they came highly recommended from a mutual acquaintance.

* * *

"Anna says she won't see you any more, not unless you admit that you have mistaken her uncle for someone else, and apologize to her, her family, and Gregorio," Joe told Cole and Chad as he returned from Mills College three days following the incident. The three of them sat in Cole and Joe's dormitory room. Cole sat on his bed, feet spread with his hands on his knees. His chin rested on his chest as he looked at the floor.

"I don't know what to do," Cole told his two friends. "I love Anna, but I want to kill her uncle." Chad and Joe just listened. "By hook or crook, Sal Gregorio has got to be put away," Cole continued to speak, although Chad and Joe weren't sure if he was speaking to them, or just aloud to himself.

"Why don't you go to the law?" Chad asked. Cole just shook his head.

"And tell them what? There are no witnesses to my father's killing, nor Joshua Rines'. And my mother . . . what can I do to prove what he was responsible for doing?" Cole answered.

"Why don't I send my brother after him?" Joe suggested.

"Your brother is the heavyweight boxing champion, not a hired gun," Cole reasoned, "but thanks for the thought," Cole said, finishing with a smile. It was the first sign of humor he had shown since his encounter with Gregorio.

"Come on," said Chad, "it's nearly 6:30, let's go over to *The Clipper* and get us a nice big steak. You've been holed up in this room for more than two days," he said to Cole.

Cole was more unsure of himself than he had ever been. Some part of him wanted Anna, and another part wanted Gregorio dead. He was slowly coming to the realization that he would never be able to have both. He would have to choose.

"Let's go." It was Joe's turn to summon his heavy-hearted friend. He pulled at Cole's arm as Chad opened the door to their room. Cole stood and followed Joe out the door. Chad brought up the rear.

The three men made the fifteen minute walk last a bit longer, as they strolled at a slower pace in the unusually warm, late-spring evening. When they reached *The Clipper*, Joe opened the door, and after feigning good manners for his friends to enter first, Joe squeezed himself in through the restaurant door ahead of Chad and Cole. Chad caught the door that Joe had let go of and held it while Cole followed his jokester roommate in for dinner. They each ordered the biggest steak they could get, along with all the fixings, and two pieces each of warm apple pie. Chad and Joe did their best to keep Cole occupied with anything other than Anna and Sal Gregorio. They did a yeoman's job of it, as laughter filled the room throughout most of their dinner.

The sun had just set, leaving a reddish-orange horizon when Cole and company exited the restaurant just before 9:00. The waning moon was covered by low hanging clouds, leaving very little light in the evening sky. The temperature had dropped a good fifteen degrees during their dinner. Stepping outside the restaurant brought Cole back to his ever-occupying complexity: Anna and Gregorio.

Five minutes after leaving *The Clipper*, Joe picked up a rock, turned to Cole and tried to get a wager.

"A dollar says I can hit that tree over there with this rock."

Cole looked at the tree Joe pointed towards. It was about fifty yards away, and skinny, but with large, bushy branches.

"The trunk, not the branches," Cole said, settling on the rules.

Joe smile, nodded his head in agreement, then threw the rock. It struck the tree trunk dead center, ten feet off the ground. Joe turned and placed his hand out towards Cole, palm up. Cole smiled and flipped a silver dollar up in the air. Joe caught it on the way down. As the dollar coin landed in Joe's hand, he heard gunshots fired in rapid succession, maybe six, seven shots in all. He froze at the sound. It was loud and sudden. Chad threw his body to the ground, almost instinctively. Cole, too, lay on the ground. When the shots stopped, Chad got up slowly. He looked at Joe who was still frozen, his heart racing and his breathing short.

"You okay?" Chad said to Joe.

"Yeah," he responded with so much anxiety in his voice that he wouldn't have known if he had been hit.

"How 'bout you, Cole?" asked Chad.

Cole had not gotten up. Joe and Chad looked down at him and saw it. Blood beginning to soak the left side of his shirt, and another puddle forming on the ground under his right knee.

* * *

At 10:15 the next morning, Chad pounded on the front door. After waiting only a few seconds, he pounded again. Mr. Gilbert answered, displaying immediate annoyance at the manner in which Chad pounded on his door.

"Mr. Gilbert, I'm Chad Henry, a friend of Cole's," he introduced himself, although he had previously met Anna's father at the party.

I know who you are, young man," he replied. "What is it you want?"

"I'd like to see Anna, sir, it's important," Chad replied.

"She is not taking visitors," Mr. Gilbert said sternly.

"No disrespect, sir, but she'll want to hear what I've got to tell her," Chad persisted.

"No," Mr. Gilbert said emphatically.

"It's okay father," said a voice from out of Chad's sight, but he recognized it as Anna's. "Hi Chad" she greeted him. Skipping formalities, Chad jumped right to the point of his visit.

"Cole's been hurt bad," he told her. "He was shot last night. Don't know how he's doing or if he's going to make it."

Anna's anger towards Cole and his behavior towards her uncle dissipated immediately upon hearing Chad's news.

"What happened? Where is he?" Anna asked with concern as she stepped forward to be closer to Chad.

"We don't know for sure, but I'd like to know where your uncle was last night?" Chad inquired. Anna's anger returned.

"Not you too!" she hollered in the most un-ladylike voice Chad had ever heard from her. "My uncle was here, with us, all night long. He never left the house," Anna told Chad. As she finished her response to Chad, Gregorio showed up at the door.

Standing behind Anna, where she could not see him, Gregorio cast a steely glare at Chad, as if serving him a warning. Anna felt his presence and turned to look at him. His look immediately changed to one of concerned interest for Anna's friend. Chad noticed the difference. Not being sure what Gregorio had intended, but his look told Chad that he was involved in Cole's shooting.

"This ain't over," Chad told Gregorio, looking past Anna as if she wasn't even standing there.

"Son, you heard my niece. I was here all night. I do hope your friend recovers nicely, but I am slightly offended that you consider me a suspect in this affair," Gregorio told Chad.

"It ain't over," Chad repeated as he turned and left the Nob Hill area, and headed back for Oakland.

* * *

"He's lost a lot of blood," Chad heard the doctor tell Joe upon entering Cole's hospital room.

"What do you think, Doc," Joe asked, "is he going to make it?"

"He'll live," the doctor responded with a scowl, apparently upset over the informality of being called 'Doc.' "But it's going to take a long time. We were able to remove both bullets. The bullet in his side broke a couple of ribs, but would have caused worse damage if it had missed the ribs. It's the one that hit his knee that will cause him a long, slow recovery period. He will likely walk with a limp the rest of his life."

Cole lay in the bed unconscious from the anesthesia. Chad had sent a telegraph to Leroy and Bertram at the ranch to let them know what happened. Chad hired a rider from the telegraph office on the receiving end to ride out and deliver the telegraph immediately, wait for a reply, and send the reply to them at the hospital as quickly as possible. Chad expected they should hear a reply by the following day.

"What do you think he's going to do?" Joe asked Chad as he nodded towards their fallen friend.

"I saw Gregorio at Anna's house," Chad began to reply to the question indirectly. "I know Gregorio was involved, and he knows I know. If he tried to kill Cole once, he'll likely try again. I don't know what Cole will do."

The two friends sat quietly in the hospital room. Nearly two hours had passed since Chad returned from San Francisco. Joe had taken an involuntary nap for a good thirty minutes.

"Hey fellas," a voice said.

Joe, who was slumped in his chair but was now awake, and Chad both looked at Cole. His eyes were open and he was staring at the ceiling.

"Hey fellas," Cole repeated.

Both Chad and Joe stood and walked to the bedside. They were both on Cole's right side, Joe looking around Chad.

"What happened?" asked Cole.

"We think it was Gregorio who hired some men to kill you," Chad spoke.

Cole lay silently as he contemplated his situation. Uncomfortable with the silence, Joe spoke up.

"Chad thinks Gregorio may try again," said Joe, waiting to hear a response from Cole. Cole nodded his head slowly.

"He may, or maybe I'll take the play to him first," Cole pondered out loud. "Joe, you know where I keep my pistol. I'd like you to bring it to me."

Joe looked at Chad with a perilous expression. Chad responded to Cole's request.

"You think that's a good idea?" asked Chad. "It'll be a while before you can use it, according to the doctor. I've got mine in my room above *The Clipper*. I'll keep it with me. We won't leave you unguarded."

"I've never used a gun," spoke Joe.

Cole and Chad had never given any thought to Joe's lack of experience with firearms. Most boys who grew up in Kansas where they did had been introduced to guns at a young age.

"Don't worry, Joe," Cole said with a smile, "anybody tries to make another run at me, you can talk them to death about base ball."

* * *

It was a cold and foggy June evening as Sal Gregorio walked along the wharf with a moonless sky overhead. He stood and looked towards Alcatraz Island, waiting for his appointment to arrive. Gregorio had been involved in many acts involving killings during the past thirty years. He had learned not to meet in the same place with the same people. His hotel room had been used previously. This time it was the wharf, not a safe place to travel at night by oneself, but Gregorio did not fear going anywhere. He was armed and had demonstrated over the years that he had no hesitation in killing. His lack of caring for human life gave him the edge when it came to a confrontation.

Gregorio had waited ten minutes when the three men he met with in his hotel room showed.

"Hola, Senor Gregorio," the lead gringo said with a butchered Mexican accent.

"Cole Herbert lives," Gregorio said succinctly.

"For now," replied the gringo.

"I was told you were reliable men," Gregorio falsely praised, "but the job you were hired for was not completed to my satisfaction."

"We know where he is. We will finish the job tomorrow," said the second gringo.

Gregorio just smiled. The three hired guns smiled back. They were still wearing their smiles when Gregorio pulled a pistol from under his coat and quickly fired three shots. All three men dropped. Gregorio examined his work, recognizing that one was still breathing, he fired twice more into the man's body. Nobody left to talk about Cole Herbert.

"Shouldn't have taken five shots," he said aloud to himself. "Must be getting old."

* * *

It had been two weeks since Cole had been shot. He was becoming agitated more frequently as he anxiously waited to get released from the hospital. Chad and Joe sat in chairs outside the room, listening as the doctor promised Cole he could go home the following day. Chad had his pistol tucked inside his jacket. Joe noticed two strange men walking down the hallway towards Cole's room. He whispered Chad's name and nodded towards them. Chad turned his head quickly to look and at the same time put his hand inside his jacket. It was Leroy and Bertram.

As the doctor exited Cole's room, in walked the four people closest to Cole; Chad, Joe, Leroy and Bertram. Joe had been briefly introduced to Cole's family in the hallway.

"Who's watching the ranch," asked Cole, trying to lighten the moment.

"Hired a hand from a nearby ranch to watch things until we got back," Leroy told him.

"How's ya doin' Cole?" asked Bertram.

"Doc says I'll live. Time for me to get out of here," Cole responded.

"And do what?" asked Leroy. "Chad told us about Gregorio. Now is not the time. You need to rest and let time allow you to think more clearly about your decision."

Cole did not know what to say.

"Let's go home, Cole," said Leroy, "let's go home."

Part VI
Bar-CJ Ranch, Oklahoma Territory, 1893

Chad, Leroy and Bertram brought Cole home at the end of June. Everything Cole owned made the trip with them. Joe stayed in Oakland to graduate from St. Mary's, then headed east to begin a professional base ball career. Cole and Joe regretfully said their goodbyes to one another. They had developed a strong friendship. Joe felt uneasy about the timing of leaving for the east. A part of him wanted to be with Cole, to be there to help with whatever he needed. But Cole convinced him to pursue his base ball career, and promised to keep in touch.

By mid-August Cole's ribs had healed beyond the point of causing him pain, though he still felt the effects of the bullet. His knee, however, was extremely bothersome. He could not walk without a cane, and when he tried to put weight on his right leg, he would nearly collapse. He needed help getting on a horse, which caused him to be grouchy on the ranch. A ranch hand who couldn't ride wasn't worth much on a ranch in his mind. Leroy, Bertram and Chad tried daily to convince him that he needed to get well, then he would be able to pull his own weight.

Sitting on the front porch during the last afternoon in August, Cole watched as a rider approached the ranch in a gallop. Cole didn't recognize the man, but Leroy walked out on the porch as the man arrived.

"Howdy, Dennis," Leroy called out.

Waterhole

"Leroy," the rider replied, "have you heard about the land rush?"

"No, no we ain't. What are you goin' on about? What's this land rush?" Leroy replied.

"The government is opening up the Cherokee Strip part of the Oklahoma Territory to folks. It's going to be a race to stake a claim on the land. Thousands of people are expected to be part of it," the rider explained.

"Well, it won't be the first land grab in the territory. It's been done before. I guess I always reckoned more people would eventually settle out west. As long as they don't impede on the Bar-CJ, don't make no difference to us," Leroy said. "By the way, Dennis, this here's Cole Herbert. He owns the Bar-CJ."

"Part owner," Cole clarified, in reference to Leroy and Bertram. The rider tipped his hat at Cole.

"The Cherokee Strip is closer to us out here on the panhandle than the other land grabs were," reminded Dennis, who himself had a ranch about 75 miles east of the Bar-CJ, "keep a look out." With his parting words, he tipped his hat again and rode off.

* * *

Cole continued to rest his leg, but only when Leroy was looking. As much as he could, Cole would practice putting as much weight as he could bear on his right leg while walking in the house when Leroy was outside, tending to chores. The leg had really begun to atrophy. Its size was noticeably different to Cole, who did not let anyone else look at it. The healing process was slower than he had hoped. During one conversation with Bertram in late July, Bertram held up his left hand to show him his permanently scarred and partially disabled appendage. "Some injuries, de never fully heal," Bertram reminded Cole, who remembered the night Bertram suffered his crippling, helping to save Cole and his mother's life as they escaped from Waterhole.

Whenever his leg was not foremost on his mind, Cole found himself thinking about Anna. He missed her terribly, and had considered writing to her. One crisp August morning he picked up a quill pen and a bottle of ink, ready to put words to paper. No sooner did he sit down at his mother's old hickory desk in a corner of the living room when he thought of Gregorio. An icy chill ran down his spine and he dropped the pen quickly. He stood up and walked outside, supported by his cane. He saddled his horse and climbed up for the first time by himself since his injury. Cole rode out to the knoll where his parents were buried. He sat there until dark.

* * *

"I've got to leave for awhile," Cole spoke one mid-September morning during breakfast.

It was just light outside, the sun just beginning to crest over the horizon to the east. The sky was clear. Chad had gone out for an early morning ride.

Bertram was sitting opposite of Cole, and Leroy to his left, at the head of the table. Neither man spoke. They contemplated what Cole had said, exchanging glances as they did. An uncomfortable tension was building inside of Cole. It meant a lot to him to have Leroy and Bertram approve of his decisions, though he had decided his fate in this matter regardless of what they had to say. Still, he wanted to hear from them.

"Any place special?" Leroy asked.

"Waterhole," Cole replied.

Leroy and Bertram again exchanged glances, but this time with a mutual look of curiosity on their faces.

"Don't reckon der's much of a town left der now," Bertram said. "Yer pa and missah Joshua done cleared it out."

"I still gotta go," Cole tried to explain. "I've got a restlessness in me that I can't cure. I think a trip to Waterhole might help rid me of this haunting feeling I've had since I got home."

Waterhole

"What about your leg?" asked Leroy, "No train goes through Waterhole. Ain't no way to get there except by horse."

"I can ride," Cole answered, reaching down and feeling his right leg as he spoke. Both in his voice and in his mind, he knew the leg wasn't near full strength.

"When ya plannin' ta leave, Cole?" Bertram asked.

Before Cole could answer, Chad came bursting through the door to the house.

"You all better come," he told them, half out of breath.

"What's wrong?" Cole asked.

"Land grabbers," Chad replied, "the land rush for the Cherokee Strip started yesterday. Seems some folks think part of the Bar-CJ now belongs to them."

"How many are there?" Leroy wanted to know.

"About six, at least what I saw," said Chad, "and they're all wearing guns. Looks like they aim to start a ranch of their own."

"Did they say anything?" wondered Cole.

"I asked them what they was doing," Chad explained, "and they said they was claiming this land. Looks like they got in yesterday some time. I told them that this was the Bar-CJ, but the fella who seemed to be in charge told me, 'no more it ain't.' I saw a couple of the men put their hands on their guns, so I tipped my hat, turned and rode back here."

Without another word, Chad followed Cole's lead and they strapped on their pistols. Leroy loaded his Winchester, and Bertram stuffed extra shotgun shells into his shirt pockets, while grabbing his weapon. The four of them exited the house. Chad helped saddle Bertram's horse, while Bertram hooked up the buckboard for Leroy and Cole. Bertram and Chad flanked the buckboard while they rode out in the direction of their property line to the north. With the ranch house being near the southern property line, it took the four a good twenty minutes to reach their destination. Smoke from the morning fire was beginning to die down in the makeshift camp. As they approached the camp, Leroy told the rest to let him do the talking.

"Mornin', gents," Leroy said with a smiling face.

Leroy pulled back on the reins of the buckboard, stopping the horses on the perimeter of the camp, keeping a distance of 30 feet or so between the buckboard and the nearest land grabber. Chad and Bertram sat atop their horses, ten to fifteen feet from the buckboard. As he sat next to Leroy in the wagon, Cole felt an anger grow inside of him. He had decided on the ride out that these men would leave the Bar-CJ this morning, peacefully or otherwise.

Cole's restlessness was a building anger, one that started with seeing Sal Gregorio again, and finding out that he was Anna's uncle. Having Anna turn him away, on the night he had planned to propose to her, and Gregorio's attempt to kill him. His right leg was a constant reminder of all that had gone wrong for him, and his uncertainty with how to handle any of it. He was not thinking rationally. He was not thinking much at all. Anger was becoming his driving force, and he now was faced with a situation in which to let it all out. Cole did not let Leroy continue to do the talking.

"You've got thirty minutes to be off the Bar-CJ property," Cole stated bluntly, directing his stare at the man closest to him, who though he did not realize, was the leader of the group.

The man laughed at Cole's command. Cole climbed down out of the buckboard and walked steadily toward the laughing man. He did his best to disguise his wounded leg.

"Sonny boy, you better climb back up on that wagon while you still can," said the man.

Cole continued without hesitation. As he closed to within a couple of feet, the man saw the look in Cole's eyes, and his demeanor changed, though not in time. Cole stepped forward and dropped the man with a single punch to his jaw. He delivered his fist with such force that the man's jaw broke. He lay on the ground rolling back and forth on his back, clutching his jaw and groaning.

Though Cole's actions took place in the absence of the rest of the Bar-CJ men knowing of his intentions, each had drawn his gun as Cole delivered his blow.

Waterhole

"I won't say it again. This is the Bar-CJ ranch. I'll kill anyone not packed and gone. You now have about 25 minutes left to clear out," Cole said. He was anxious to pull his pistol, but for the first time since pulling away from the ranch, he thought rationally, deciding against killing anyone unprovoked. Behind him, he heard Leroy, Bertram and Chad all cock their weapons.

Within 15 minutes, the land grabbers were packed and nearly out of sight.

* * *

The ride back to the ranch house was quiet. No one had ever seen Cole show such anger, and they knew it had been touch and go whether or not he would have killed one of the land grabbers had they not obeyed him. Or been killed himself.

As Leroy eased the buckboard into the barn, he turned to Cole, who was sitting motionless, almost trance-like staring straight ahead, but looking at nothing.

"Was that some of the restlessness you was telling us about this morning at breakfast?" asked Leroy.

Cole just nodded.

"Somebody could have been killed back there, and it didn't have to be," Leroy suggested. "Might have been you. You keep going full steam like that, and someone will be hurt, even worse than that fella you dropped back there."

"I gotta get away for a while," Cole repeated his remarks made at the table earlier.

"Why Waterhole," asked Leroy.

"I can't figure it all out," Cole began to explain, "but it seems that everything bad that has happened in my life can be traced to Waterhole."

"Well, son," Leroy offered, "it ain't Waterhole so much as it is Sal Gregorio."

Cole thought for a moment. Leroy was right. Waterhole and Gregorio were connected, but it was Gregorio who was responsible for the fate of his parents, and for Cole losing the only girl he had ever loved. That quick realization seemed to help Cole focus on where to place his restless anger, on Gregorio, not Waterhole. Still, Cole wanted to see the place where his father had been shot, and where his mother had been held captive for seven years. He needed closure with that part of his life. Without it, he felt as though he could never move past the feelings he was now experiencing.

"You're right, Leroy," Cole told his longtime friend, "but I still got to go there for myself. I can't explain why."

"Some things don't need explainin'," Leroy suggested. "But your leg is still troublesome to you. Maybe you ought to wait 'til next spring."

"No, I got to go now," Cole said, his head shaking back and forth, slowly.

"You're your own man now, Cole," Leroy told him, "you make your own choices."

"I'll leave at first light tomorrow," said Cole.

Cole woke early the next morning and packed his saddlebags and his bedroll. The sun was not yet up, but Leroy had already risen and packed some food for the trip.

"This here sure looks like a lot of food," Cole commented. "I'll need a packhorse just to carry it all."

"It ain't all for you," said a voice from the door. Chad had just entered the house with his saddlebags in hand.

"Where you going?" asked Cole.

"With you," replied Chad, "I just want to make sure I get my share into my saddlebags. I know how you can eat."

Cole looked at Chad, then at Leroy. He took a deep breath, held it momentarily, then sighed. Bertram came through the door with a couple of rain slickers in hand.

"Leavin' dis late'n da year, could be yaw'll need dese," Bertram told the travelers as he handed them their slickers.

"Well, looks like I got no say in the matter," Cole spoke.

The other three all shook their heads and smiled.

"All right then, lets go partner," Cole told Chad.

Leroy and Bertram followed them out to the porch, and stood as the two young men tied down their bags and pulled themselves into their saddles.

"You two take care," Leroy told them.

"We will," Chad answered.

Then the two men who as kids had wanted to be deputies like the Masterson's and Wyatt Earp, like Joshua Rines and Clint Herbert, turned and headed their horses west. Leroy and Bertram watched until they were out of sight.

* * *

Cole and Chad reached Waterhole in nine days, during which time each of them unceremoniously acknowledged his 21st birthday. Their pace was neither quick, nor slow. It was a comfortable pace which allowed the two to practice their shooting prowess. They held shooting contests, just the two of them, just like Cole's father, Clint, had done with Joshua Rines. Cole was never fully aware of his father's shooting expertise, but he was becoming the spitting image of Clint in that regard. In fact, Cole and Chad resembled Clint and Joshua. The Herbert's were the more accurate, while their friends had the quicker draw.

Just getting away from the ranch seemed to help Cole relax. His leg was getting stronger each day, though he still walked with the cane and limped noticeably. When they arrived in Waterhole, Cole immediately noticed a difference in the town. It was run down. Most buildings had been boarded up. The hotel Cole and his parents had stayed in had burnt down. The telegraph office was gone, as was the general store. At first glance, only the saloon and the livery stable appeared to have any people moving around. The livery was next to the boarded up blacksmith shop, that had once been Bertram's. It was operated by an older, Hispanic man who had difficulty standing up erect. Cole and Chad left their horses at the livery, and headed for the saloon. Neither man drank anything stronger than the occasional beer, but a sarsaparilla was more to their liking.

The saloon was sparse with only three ragged looking men playing a game of poker at a table in the far corner. An old miner stood at the far end of the bar, nursing his whiskey bottle, and a portly bartender, who was as old as the miner, was slowly but deliberately cleaning the glassware with a rag, behind the bar.

Cole asked for a sarsaparilla for the two of them. The bartender laughed heartily.

"A sarsaparilla!" the bartender shouted once his laughter subdued.

Cole flipped two bits onto the bar, and waited. He did not answer back.

"Boy, we ain't got no sarsaparilla here! No buttermilk neither. If you looking for something soft, you might try sucking on your mother's tit!" the bartender crudely shouted for all in the bar to hear. The old miner at the end of the bar didn't pay much attention to the boisterous bartender, but the three men involved in the poker game, became interested, and joined in the laughter directed at Cole and Chad.

Chad turned and smiled at the poker players, noticing they weren't wearing side arms. He turned back towards the bartender, and as he did, lifted his pistol from its holster, sticking the end of the barrel against the bartender's nose. The laughter in the saloon ceased quickly.

"Maybe you'd like to suck on this," Chad asked the bartender as he shoved the barrel of his pistol a little firmer against the bartender's nose.

"A simple, negative response would have been sufficient to our request for sarsaparilla," Cole told the bartender in a calm, quiet voice, as he proceeded to walk around to the back of the bar. Cole picked up the shotgun from behind the bar, which was in arms length of the bartender. He popped open the barrels and removed the two shells, then snapped it closed again. Cole carried the empty weapon around to the customer side of the bar and set it down on a table. Chad withdrew his pistol from the bartender's nose, and as he did, the portly man let out a deep breath.

"You ain't got much of a sense of humor," the bartender told Chad and Cole, but this time spoke in a more respectful tone.

"We're young still, hopefully it'll come to us later in life," Cole explained.

"If you'd please, we'll take a beer," Chad asked kindly.

As the bartender poured two beers into clean glasses, the poker game resumed.

"Don't remember seeing you two around here before," the bartender said, trying to make friendly conversation.

"Never been here before," Chad responded.

The bartender nodded his head towards Cole, "what about you?" he asked.

"Been here once before," he said, "'bout eight years ago."

"Things were sure different back then," the bartender said as he shook his head and smiled.

"How so?" asked Cole.

"Man named Sal Gregorio ran the town and everyone in it, but there was plenty of action here in the bar. Had us girls, lots of customers, and plenty of money came through the doors, though most of it eventually became Gregorio's."

Without divulging what he knew, Cole asked, "what caused the town to die out?"

"A couple of guys came through here, 'bout eight years ago, maybe when you was here, and cleaned out the bad element," the bartender explained. "Gregorio killed one of 'em. Shot him in the back. The other was shot up pretty good, but rode out of town on his own. Never learned what became of him. I'll tell you though, them two was the best men I ever saw, both with courage and with a gun."

"You saw the fight?" Cole asked.

"Yep, I shooed out the backdoor when the first shots were fired, but I peeked in at the tail end. In time to see all Gregorio's men dead, and the two . . . I heard they was some sort of famous lawmen, but I ain't heard of them . . . still standing, but then Gregorio sneaked in through that door," he said pointing to the swinging doors that led to the street, "and shot one in the back. The other one raised his pistol, but Gregorio high tailed it out of here before he could get a shot off. Next morning, we found two more of his men, a couple of Indians, killed off behind the hotel. Waterhole ain't been the same since. Town has sort of died off slowly, a bit more each year than the last."

Chad just listened, expecting to take his cue from Cole. Cole was leaning on both forearms against the rail of the bar, staring at the mirror behind the bar, seeing his reflection looking back at him.

"Were you one of Gregorio's men?" Cole finally asked, breaking his silence.

"Nope, though I did pretend to be. Wasn't healthy to live in Waterhole in them days if you said no to Gregorio," the bartender explained. "The saloon was his, and I just ran it for him. He still took his special taxes out of my pay, just like he did to everyone who owned a mine outside of town, or who seemed to prosper in any sort of way. He was one mean cuss of a man. Never knew another like him."

Cole took a short swig of his beer, thanked the bartender and turned toward the door. Chad tipped his hat and followed his friend.

Once outside, a realization came to Chad.

"We ought to take that bartender back to San Francisco and have him tell Anna about her uncle."

"I don't think Gregorio can be arrested in San Francisco for his crimes committed here," Cole answered.

"No, but at least Anna would know the truth," Chad told his friend.

"I doubt that bartender would want to go all the way to San Francisco to tangle with Gregorio," Cole surmised.

"We could persuade him," Chad offered, tapping his holster lightly.

Somewhere during the trip to Waterhole, Cole gradually developed a peaceful feeling about his parent's demise. Somehow, returning to this town helped him close the empty feeling he had had since arriving back at the bar-CJ after being shot. For the first time, he could think of his parents with pleasant thoughts and not feel overwhelmed with grief over their early passing in life.

"No," Cole told Chad, "I don't need to bring the bartender back with me. It's been good for me to come back here. I've got to think about what comes next, but whatever it is, I can handle it without feeling burdened about my parent's death, or about dragging anyone else into this thing."

Cole and Chad were camped outside of town that night. Their time in Waterhole was short, but valuable to Cole. It helped him bring clarity to his situation, and to his reason for what would come next.

Cole sat silently, peering into the campfire, as if he hadn't heard Chad's question.

"That deep in thought," Chad assumed, looking at his friend, "you're either thinking about Anna or her uncle."

Cole continued to stare into the fire, but answered Chad's statement with a slow, ongoing nod of his head.

The following morning, the two young men saddled their horses and made the return trip to the Bar-CJ.

* * *

The next three years on the Bar-CJ weren't much different than they had always been, though Leroy was growing older, and Cole's leg wound left him with a permanent limp. Now 67 years of age, Leroy's duties had become restricted to the household chores. Cole and Chad, however, were growing restless. Leroy had asked Cole every few months about his interest in finishing his last year at Saint Mary's. Cole always responded by telling his wise old friend that he'd think about it.

Cole had exchanged letters with Joe a couple of times a year since they parted. Joe had begun playing professional base ball. He had just concluded his second year, this one with the Baltimore

Orioles after a year with the Washington Senators, when Cole received a letter from Joe in October 1896.

"Well, I'll be . . . ," Cole smiled broadly as he read Joe's letter at the dinner table one evening.

"What's Joe have ta say?" asked Bertram.

"He's getting married!" Cole proclaimed.

"That poor girl," teased Chad, "all he talks about is base ball!"

"We're all invited," Cole continued to read and share the important facts. "The wedding is scheduled for December 10th in San Francisco."

"Who'll watch the ranch if we all go?" wondered Chad.

"I'll get a couple of workers off the neighboring ranch," Leroy told the rest at the table. "We'll all go."

It had been three and a half years since Cole left San Francisco. Three and a half years since he had seen or heard from Anna. Cole's time spent thinking of Anna had lessened, but whenever he did, he felt the same strong feelings he always had. His thoughts of her actually caused him to feel a physical pain in his heart.

Leroy, Bertram and Chad all knew better than to bring her up, especially now, with a trip to San Francisco pending. They all knew how conflicted Cole was when he thought of Anna, because in doing so, he also had to think of Sal Gregorio.

The trip to San Francisco was becoming one of conflict for Cole also, as the date to leave for the west grew closer. He was thrilled to be going to see Joe and attend his wedding. But he couldn't think of San Francisco without thinking of Anna and Gregorio.

The Bar-CJ men decided to leave the Oklahoma Territory in time to arrive in San Francisco by the end of November. Leroy and Bertram had never spent much time in San Francisco and were looking forward to doing so. It would be their first vacation since gaining their ownership in the Bar-CJ.

Cole had no preconceived thoughts about an encounter with Gregorio, but he was not going to be caught unarmed in the big city. He holstered his pistol and packed it in his satchel. Chad knew to pack his weapon also. Bertram placed his shotgun, with a box of shells, in the bottom of his suitcase, and Leroy brought a rifle along, in plain sight for everyone to see. None of the men had discussed bringing their firearms.

"Might want to do some hunting on the way to Albuquerque," he told his traveling companions.

Ten days later, the four boarded the Atlantic & Pacific railroad car, bound west.

Part VII
San Francisco, California, November 1896

Cole wanted to see his old friends and employers at *The Clipper*, so they took the train into Oakland, rather than transferring to the Southern Pacific and get off in San Francisco. Leroy also wanted Cole to check in with Saint Mary's to determine his status for re-enrolling for his final year. Cole agreed to visit the campus administration office, but his heart was really not into returning to school.

The four men enjoyed a wonderful meal at *The Clipper*, which was on the house. Cole was embarrassed not to pay for their meal, but the owners insisted. They each had large slabs of prime rib, along with mashed potatoes and gravy, and large ears of corn on the cob.

It was after 9:30 on the evening of their arrival, November 29th, when they finished their meal and said their goodbyes to their hosts. Rather than cross the Bay at night, they took a couple of hotel rooms near the restaurant. San Francisco would have to wait until morning. Cole was looking forward to seeing Joe and his family. Joe's brother, James, was expected to be home. Cole had never met the reigning heavyweight boxing champion before.

At 7:00 the following morning, the Bar-CJ men stood at the Oakland pier, waiting for the first ferry of the day. The sun shone through a darkening sky, but the temperature definitely indicated a cold day lay ahead. They were not used to sleeping in, and had already found that city life seemed to start a bit later than they were accustomed to.

Waterhole

The first ferry departed Oakland at 8:00. Each man paid his five cents for the trip across the Bay. Bertram was a little apprehensive about crossing the large body of water, but when he saw the size of the boat, along with the number of people climbing aboard, he swallowed his fear, and followed Leroy up the plank.

A slight westward wind made standing out on the deck a cold experience, but a refreshing one at the same time. All four stood out on the deck, in the front of the ferry so they could see the approaching city landscape.

As the ferry landed in San Francisco, Cole and company remained on deck, watching the water lap up on the shore below them. The plank that passengers were using to exit the boat had become crowded and slow moving, during which time, Bertram and Chad brought everyone's belongings to the front of the ferry. Without giving much attention to the slow moving process of exiting the ferry, Leroy led the four of them down the plank. It had cleared out by the time Leroy reached the bottom of the plank. He was greeted there by five men, large men, one of whom was holding out a brown, bowler style hat.

Leroy nodded to the man as he passed him. He did not get more than a foot beyond the man when he felt a hand placed on his shoulder that was meant to stop him from proceeding. At the same time, one of the other five men at the bottom of the plank moved into the path Leroy was walking, preventing him from moving forward.

"That'll be ten cents," said the man with the bowler hat, whose hand was on Leroy's shoulder.

"Sorry mister, but we paid our fare when we boarded in Oakland," Leroy answered kindly.

"You paid to ride the ferry. We're collecting your landing tax," the man continued.

Chad had trailed Leroy down the plank, followed by Bertram, then Cole.

"What the hell is a landing tax," Chad asked.

"You got to pay to come to this City," another man spoke up, this one wearing a gray suit, about two sizes too small for his large frame.

"On whose authority and according to what city law?" asked Leroy.

Leroy's questions confused the tax collectors. It was meant to. Leroy did not believe there was any such tax due according to established city laws. A third man, who was smaller in stature than the other four, wearing a green colored suit and tie with a matching bowler spoke up.

"You gotta pay because we says you do," sneered the smaller man.

"Well, I guess like any law, if we break it, you gotta take us in," Leroy bluffed. "Better lead us to jail, cause we ain't got the money to pay."

Ferry passengers who did not pay the landing tax had never been taken to jail. On the rare occasion that a passenger did not have the money to pay, they were thrown into the Bay, sometimes after being roughed up a bit.

"Stop wasting our time," the man with the bowler in his hand said as he shook the coins around in his hat. "That'll be ten cents each, or a swim in the Bay."

By this time, Chad, Bertram and Cole were off the plank and on flat ground, as were all the tax collectors.

"It seems as though we've got a stalemate here, gents," Leroy told them, "you see, we ain't paying. In fact, we'd been considering charging San Francisco for the privilege of our company. Maybe you'd like to take care of paying us. I think ten cents a day would be fair, don't you think so, Bertram?"

"Sounds 'bout right," Bertram answered thoughtfully, putting his hand out as he answered. "We's plannin' on stayin a couple weeks if'n yaw'd like ta jes pay all at once."

The tax collectors had become confused and angry.

"Slim," the man holding his bowler addressed the larger one in the gray suit, "it appears that we need to show these gentlemen what happens to those who don't pay their taxes."

Waterhole

Slim took out a billy club from his back pocket and slapped it into the palm of his other hand. He took a step in Leroy's direction when Cole called out.

"Best you stop there," Cole told Slim and the rest. As they looked in his direction, Cole was pointing his Remington New Model Army .44 at Slim.

"I guess you'll just have to take my word for it, but I'm a pretty good shot with this eight inch barrel," Cole said aloud for everyone to hear.

"You're making a big mistake, mister," Slim told Cole, "I won't forget you."

"Nice to be remembered," Cole said, smiling.

During the conversation between Cole and Slim, Chad had reached into his satchel and pulled out his Colt pistol.

"Time to take a swim, boys," Leroy said. Slim and the others looked at each other.

"We ain't going in there," answered the man holding his bowler, pointing to the edge of the Bay.

Cole cocked the hammer on his pistol, Chad did the same. Neither spoke a word, deferring to Leroy to direct the conversation.

"Wrong answer," said Leroy. "Chad, see that small feather on the top of Slim's hat? Why don't you see if you can shoot it off from here?"

Slim put his hands out in front of him, as if they could stop a bullet.

"No, no, don't try it!" Slim pleaded. He began to move closer to the water. As he did, Chad began pointing his pistol at the other tax collectors. Each one began to walk toward the water's edge. They all stopped short at the edge of the pier, looking back to see if their orders had been rescinded. The water was shallow enough that even for any who couldn't swim, they were not going to be in any danger. Embarrassment would be enough, Leroy had figured.

"Go ahead, fellas," Leroy said.

Slim jumped first, followed by the other four almost simultaneously. The five men stood neck deep in the cold water of San Francisco Bay. The one holding the money in his bowler was able to keep his hat above water, not losing any taxes already collected.

"Been a pleasure," Leroy said as he tipped his hat at the men, "you make quite the welcoming committee."

"We'll be seeing you again," promised the small man in the green suit, his voice already quivering from the few moments he'd been submerged in the Bay.

* * *

Rather than find a carriage to take them, Cole led his party on foot to the Palace Hotel, at the corner of New Montgomery and Market Streets, a walk of less than a mile. Seven stories tall, it frightened Bertram a bit as he had never stayed in such a large or tall building. He requested that Leroy and Cole arrange for rooms as close to the ground as possible.

Chad and Bertram waited in the lobby for Cole and Leroy to return with their room keys.

"Sorry, Bertram," Leroy said with a straight face after arranging for their rooms, "all they had left was a room at the top of the hotel."

Bertram was stunned, not knowing what to say. After a brief pause, Leroy couldn't contain himself and broke out in laughter.

"Don't worry, big man, we're on the ground floor," he told his large friend.

Cole and Chad had one room, with Leroy and Bertram in the room right next door. As two bell hops helped with the bags, Leroy asked Cole when he planned to see Joe.

"Think I'll take a walk up his way later this afternoon," Cole answered. "We ought to unpack first, then get ourselves a big lunch in the dining hall."

"It's not yet ten o'clock," Leroy informed Cole, "dealing with tax collectors sure causes you to work up an appetite."

By the time the bags were unpacked and the four men had cleaned up, they reached the dining hall closer to 11:00. The dining hall was not yet re-opened from breakfast, but by 11:20, they were escorted to a table in a corner opposite where they entered.

"Anything familiar about those tax collectors?" Leroy asked Bertram once the waiter left the table with their lunch orders.

"Da last time Ah sees men collectin' taxes was in Waterhole," Bertram answered.

"I was thinking the same thing," Leroy added. "Mighty familiar that tax collectors always seem to show up where Sal Gregorio is or has been."

"I wonder which it is this time," Cole said, "*is* he here or *was* he here?"

"Could be we'll find out soon enough," Chad suggested.

* * *

Cole re-acquainted himself with directions to Joe's family's house, then set out on foot towards their home in the Telegraph Hill vicinity at three in the afternoon. He did not know if Joe would be home, but he expected someone would be and he looked forward to visiting with all of the Corbett family.

Carrying guns in the city limits was against the law, or so Cole had been informed, but he was determined to remain armed at all times while in San Francisco. Leroy and Bertram's conversation about Sal Gregorio and the tax collectors was too coincidental for his liking, and with the trouble they experienced at the ferry pier, he felt obliged to wear a makeshift shoulder holster and carry his pistol under his duster. With the eight inch barrel on his pistol, wearing it under his duster was considerably uncomfortable.

As he began his ascent up Telegraph Hill, a buggy pull up alongside him and stopped. A driver remained seated in the front of the buggy, while two men climbed out of the back. Cole recognized one of the men from the group of the five tax collectors he had encountered that morning. He was wearing what appeared to be a brand new suit.

"Good afternoon," said the man Cole did not recognize. "My name is Eli Bannister. I'm a member of the Board of Commissioners here in San Francisco."

"Afternoon," Cole returned the greeting, waiting to hear what came next.

"Sir, I want to apologize for the behavior of some of my men earlier this morning. I understand that they took it upon themselves to shake down the patrons of this morning's ferry from Oakland. I also understand that you and your party were able to put them in their place. I want to assure you that they have been dealt with severely, and that their behavior will not be repeated," Bannister explained.

"Does *dealt with severely* mean they all got new suits like this man is wearing?" Cole asked.

"No sir, I assure you that was not the case," Bannister replied.

"I'm kind of curious . . . how is it that you were able to find me so quickly in this big city?" Cole asked.

"Well sir, I make it my business to know what happens in this city, especially when it involves new visitors," Bannister told him.

"That doesn't really explain how you found me," Cole responded.

"A good City Commissioner has his resources," Bannister said, smiling, not giving a more direct answer.

"Good day to you, sir," Bannister said as he climbed back into the rear of the buggy along with the tax collector. In seconds the buggy and its three occupants were gone.

Cole stood there a few more minutes before resuming his trip to the Corbett's house. Eli Bannister had not asked him his name, nor where he was going, nor his reason for being in San Francisco. Cole quickly determined that the meeting was to allow Bannister

Waterhole

to size him up; to form an opinion about the prospect of any future trouble from Cole.

Who is this Eli Bannister? Cole thought to himself.

* * *

When he reached the Corbett's house, Cole knocked on the door. Mrs. Corbett opened it herself, and let out a joyful screech upon seeing who was standing on the other side.

"Why Cole Herbert!" she said as she stepped out onto the porch and gave him a big hug. She squeezed him like he was her own son.

"Why it's so good to see you! I expect you got Joe's letter, but you know the wedding is still more than a week away," she told him.

"Yes ma'am, I realize. I just wanted to get here early, spend a little time in the city," he rattled. "Is Joe at home? I'd sure like to see him."

"No Cole, he and his brother went downtown to settle on their suits for the wedding. They should return soon. Why don't you come in and visit until they get back. You'll join us for supper at the restaurant, of course," Mrs. Corbett invited.

"Yes ma'am, I'll visit for a while, but I must get back to the Palace Hotel for supper. You remember Chad? He's here with me, along with Leroy and Bertram. You've heard me speak of them I believe," Cole explained.

"I certainly have, and I should scold you for not letting me know you were coming, but you're all invited to dinner," Mrs. Corbett said shaking her finger at Cole, expressing mock anger.

"Thank you ma'am, we'd love to join you," Cole said smiling back.

"Now come in and visit. Joe's father is down at *The Flying Fin*, but he should also be home soon," she said finishing with the whereabouts of her family.

Cole had visited with Mrs. Corbett for almost an hour when he heard the front door open. In walked Joe, followed by his brother.

Though Cole had never met him, he'd seen his pictures and knew who Joe's brother was.

"Well I'll be!" Joe shouted. He ran and jumped at Cole, giving him a bear hug, jumping up and down. "You're here!"

Cole grinned broadly, "Yep, I'm here," he told Joe.

"Same old Cole, never could get him to shut up," Joe teased his former roommate.

"Hi Cole," Joe's brother said, offering his hand.

"Oh my, where's my manners," Joe said. "Cole, this here's my brother, Gentleman Jim Corbett, the heavyweight boxing champion of the world!"

"Jim would be fine," Joe's brother said smiling as he shook Cole's hand. "Sure glad I didn't have to fight you to win the title. You look a bit bigger and tougher than old John L. Sullivan," Jim told Cole, who stood an inch taller than the champ.

"Cole," Joe interrupted, "I want to ask you something. I'd like you to stand alongside Jim here when I get married. What do you say?"

"I'd be proud to, roomy," Cole answered. "By the way, you never told me in your letter who you're marrying!"

"Mary Crowley," Joe responded. "Met her back east when I was playing for the Orioles. Known her about seven months, but I knew right away that she was the one for me. She and her folks will arrive here in about a week, on the sixth. They live in the Baltimore area."

"Well I can't wait to make her acquaintance," Cole said warmly. "How'd you decide on having the wedding out here?"

"My pa has been ill. His heart seems to be bothering him some, so we thought it'd be best not to have him travel across the country," Joe told him.

"But I thought he was down at the restaurant?" Cole wondered.

"Oh he is," said Mrs. Corbett, "he won't stay away from there, but he doesn't do much work, just likes to see his patrons."

"Hey!" Joe exclaimed, trying to lighten the conversation, "Is Chad with you? How about Leroy and Bertram?"

"They're all here," Cole told him, "we're staying down at The Palace Hotel."

"Pretty fancy," said Joe.

"Well, Leroy said that since it's our first vacation since we've known each other, that we'd splurge while we're here," Cole explained.

"Come on," Joe said to Cole, "let's sit on the porch."

"Its cold outside," Mrs. Corbett tried to reason with her son.

"We'll be okay ma, just got some catching up to do," Joe told his mother.

The two former roommates sat on the porch for over an hour, alternately talking about the Bar-CJ ranch and base ball. After discussing these topics in their entirety, Cole asked Joe a question.

"Have you seen Anna?"

"Just once, about a month ago," Joe answered.

"Did she ask about me?" Cole asked.

After pausing, Joe answered by shaking his head side to side. There was more.

"She's married, Cole," Joe told his friend.

The news struck Cole like a lightening bolt. He had never considered that she could be married to someone else. Even though Cole had no reason to believe they'd be re-acquainted, not with Sal Gregorio standing between them, it hurt him deeply to discover that she had married.

"As I understand it," Joe explained, "she married some guy she met through that uncle of hers, Gregorio."

Cole sat speechless, hands on his knees.

Joe continued, "guys name is Eli Bannister."

* * *

Cole's demeanor was noticeably one of depression when he returned to his room at The Palace Hotel. Chad was quick to comment.

"I was expecting a different look from you after having seen Joe for the first time in a few years," Chad said. Cole got right to the point.

"Anna's married," he said in a flat, monotone voice. Chad chose not to respond right away, sensing that Cole would want to continue.

"Joe said he learned about a month ago that she was married to someone she met through Gregorio. Anyone connected to Gregorio can't be good for her. What's more, I met the guy on the way to Joe's house. He's some kind of City Commissioner, and he had one of the tax collectors we met this morning with him. His name is Eli Bannister," Cole said, spilling what he knew.

Chad didn't know what to say.

"Not much I can do about it. Anna showed years ago that she wanted no more to do with me," Cole tried to justify feigning lack of concern. "Hey, let's get ready for dinner," Cole continued, "we've been invited to dinner at *The Flying Fin* by Joe's mother."

"Another free meal, sounds good to me," Chad said cheerfully.

"I'll go let Leroy and Bertram know. I told Mrs. Corbett we'd be at the restaurant around 7:30," Cole said. "Joe and his brother will meet us there."

"His brother . . . you mean the boxing champion?" Chad asked.

"Gentleman Jim Corbett," Cole answered with a smile.

"I guess we'll be safe this evening," Chad said jokingly.

* * *

Their party was early when Cole led the foursome through the door of the restaurant. The Corbett brothers were already seated at the family table, however, as was Mrs. Corbett. Mr. Corbett was visiting with patrons across the room.

It took about five minutes for everyone to exchange pleasantries, most of which was Joe and Chad jokingly getting re-acquainted.

The large, round table in the corner of the dining room sat the eight friends. Dinner had been planned in advance, with a special menu prepared according to Mrs. Corbett. It was every bit as delicious as she had planned for. They were in the middle of dinner, when another large group of guests walked in the front door and were seated across the room at the only other table big enough for their party. Leading the group was Eli Bannister. He was joined by six other men.

"You know him?" Cole asked Joe, who was seated to his left.

"No, never seen him before," Joe responded.

"That's Bannister," Cole informed him.

Eli Bannister took the seat with his back to the corner of the restaurant so he had a view of everything and everyone else. Bannister was a good sized man, about six feet tall with broad, strong looking shoulders. His dark hair appeared freshly cut, and his suit looked as though it had never been worn before. Among the other six men in his party, Cole recognized five as being the tax collectors from that morning. The sixth man was an extremely large fellow, larger even than Bertram. Cole had never before met anyone bigger than Bertram.

Leroy noticed the tax collectors and motioned with his head to Cole, who without looking, nodded back to indicate he had seen them. Within a few more seconds, Bertram and Chad were aware of the new party in the restaurant. Joe leaned across the table and asked his father if he knew the men who had just come in. He did not.

"I don't believe that it's a coincidence that they're here," Cole said to Joe. "I think it's time to welcome them to *The Flying Fin*."

Impulsively, Cole stood up and walked toward the table seating Bannister's party. Joe and Chad began to stand with him, but Cole put up a hand to indicate they should remain seated. Cole was interested in being the hunter, but was not looking to cause trouble. He did not like the feeling of being the hunted, but he was also without his pistol.

"Bannister," Cole said welcomingly as he reached the far corner of the restaurant. "Boys," he continued as he looked around at the tax collectors, "looks like you cleaned up nicely this evening."

The tax collectors tried not to show any reaction, but Slim and the small one who was wearing a green suit that morning gave him a menacing look.

"Mr. Herbert, nice to see you again," said Bannister.

"You must have good resources, Bannister, I don't recall giving you my name earlier today," Cole replied.

Bannister shrugged his shoulders as he smiled.

"My men here bring me a wealth of knowledge," Bannister said as he opened his arms in a circular motion as if encompassing the men at his table.

"I see you're dining with the champ," Bannister said referring to Jim Corbett.

"He's asked me for a couple of tips for his next fight," Cole responded sarcastically. Bannister just smiled.

"I understand you know my wife," Bannister said, expecting Cole did not know whom he was speaking about.

"I expect I do," answered Cole.

Bannister frowned at Cole's response, as it took away the element of surprise he had in store for Cole.

"Please give Anna my best," Cole told Bannister as he readied to leave his table, "and enjoy your meal. They don't come any better in San Francisco."

Cole returned to his table and resumed eating his meal. No one pestered him about his conversation. That could wait. Cole wasn't sure of Bannister's intent in visiting *The Flying Fin*, but he felt as though he had somewhat deflated his adversary's plan by being the aggressor. In less than six hours, Cole had already labeled Eli Bannister as an adversary. He wasn't sure if it was because he was Anna's husband, because he was somehow connected to Gregorio, or because of his already apparent illegal activity in The City. But an adversary he had become.

Leroy and Bertram arranged for a carriage to take them back to The Palace Hotel once dinner had concluded, and they had thanked their hosts. Cole and Chad planned to stay a little longer to visit with Joe and his brother, Jim. Eli Bannister and his men stayed at their table long after their meal had finished. Bannister realized that Cole and Chad were in no hurry to leave, so he stood and led his party out of *The Flying Fin* at 10:15. As Bannister exited the door, a familiar face passed him, entering the restaurant. He was by himself, and looked older than Cole remembered, but it had been 18 years since he last saw him. He carried himself with distinction. Many heads turned and people whispered to one another as he came into the room. The visitor was greeted pleasantly by Mr. Corbett, though it was possible that the owner did not know who the man was, thought Cole.

"Chad, take a look," said Cole, nudging his friend with his elbow and directing Chad's eyes with the direction of his own.

"Well, I'll be," said Chad.

Cole got up and Chad quickly followed to the table where Mr. Corbett had seated the visitor.

"Good evening Marshall Earp," Cole welcomed.

"It's been a long time since I did any marshalling, young man," replied Wyatt Earp, "but thank you none-the-less."

"You likely don't recognize us, but we knew you back in Dodge City, though we were just young 'uns at the time," Cole told him.

"You're right about not recognizing you," Earp replied.

"This is Chad Henry," Cole introduced his friend, "and I'm Cole Herbert. My pa use to do some deputying with you," Cole told the former marshall.

Earp, who until now had not given his full attention to the young men, suddenly looked Cole square in the eye, stood and extended his hand.

"Cole, it is my pleasure to make your acquaintance after all these years. I never knew a better man that Clint Herbert," Earp said. "Please accept my belated sympathies for your father. I understand that both he and Joshua Rines met a similar fate somewhere in Arizona some years back."

"Yes sir, we went looking for my mother. She had been captured by some Comanche, and we tracked her down in Waterhole, Arizona. She had been held captive about seven years when we finally found her. Pa and Josh went up against more than a dozen men to free her. They killed all the men, but one. He back shot Josh, then ran out of town like a coward. Pa died from his wounds the next day." It ate at Cole to retell the story.

"Damn shame," Earp said, "I never knew the details until now."

"What brings you to town, Marshall?" asked Chad, sensing Cole's discomfort.

"I'm here to referee the boxing match between Tom Sharkey and Bob Fitzsimmons in a couple of days," Earp told them. "Decided to come to town a few days early and enjoy San Francisco with my wife. She was a little under the weather this evening so she dined in our hotel room."

"Why then I bet you know who that man is sitting right over there," Chad said pointing back to where Joe and Jim were sitting.

Earp looked up and immediately recognized Jim Corbett. He gave a respectful nod towards the champion, who returned the acknowledgement.

"You boys dine in good company, I see," Earp told them.

"Yes sir," said Cole, "his brother, Joe, and I were roommates in college and we're in town for his wedding."

"And your mother, how is she?" asked Earp.

"She passed on a few years back," Cole said. "Her life was shortened considerably from her experience as a captive in Waterhole."

"A terrible shame," Earp said softly. "She was a wonderful lady. Did you ever find the man who was responsible for all this?"

Chad looked at Cole without saying anything. He knew it was Cole's place to do the talking.

"His name's Sal Gregorio," Cole said, choosing not to go further into how he was his ex-fiancé's uncle.

"I know that name," Earp said. "I'm not a peace officer anymore, but I hear things. Down in Los Angeles, Gregorio is well known for his illegal activities."

"I do plan to kill him someday," Cole blurted out. Earp looked at him with a concerned expression.

"You certainly have every reason to do so, son," Earp began, "but be extremely careful. Gregorio is not a man to be taken lightly."

Cole and Chad made small talk with Wyatt Earp for a few more minutes before adjourning back to their table with the Corbett brothers. Chad was hoping that Cole took Earp's warning seriously. If a man like Wyatt Earp would be cautious of Sal Gregorio, certainly Cole should be also.

* * *

Once Cole and Chad returned to the hotel, they sat in Bertram and Leroy's room, discussing all that had happened that day.

"It was no accident that Bannister found me on the street or us at the restaurant," Cole concluded. "He made such a quick connection and must have recognized my name, the way he connected me to Anna."

"And the way he found you so quickly, he must have somebody spying for him, letting him know when strangers hit town," Chad added.

"But der be hundreds, maybe thousands of strangers in San Francisco. He can't knows 'bout everyone. Why us?" Bertram asked.

"My guess is that someone got out of the Bay right away this morning and followed us to the hotel. Either that or he's got someone in the hotel, maybe at the front desk, who lets him know of strangers. If Bannister knew where we were staying, he would not have difficulty finding out our names. Bannister likely made the connection to Anna once he heard your name," Leroy theorized. "I can't think of any other reasonable explanation," he added.

"What we don't know is who is calling the shots here?" Leroy suggested. "Is Gregorio behind the tax collecting and who knows what else that could be going on, or has Bannister learned well from Anna's uncle? Or is it someone else all together?"

"Well, it's still more than a week until Joe's wedding, so I expect we'll find out soon enough," Cole added.

"If'n missah Gregorio finds out dat we's here . . . dat Cole's here, we's be needin' ta be prepared," Bertram said what everyone was thinking.

"Alright, there seems to be lots of possibilities. Let's not get ahead of ourselves. We'll take precautions, not go out alone, but otherwise, there's not much we can do," said Chad.

It was getting late. Cole and Chad returned to their room and everyone retired for the evening.

* * *

"I met a friend of yours today," Eli Bannister told his wife that evening as he stood in the kitchen, watching her prepare some vegetables. "He asked me to give you his regards."

The Bannister's were living in Anna's parent's house. Her parents had decided to relocate to the Los Angeles area to be closer to her mother's family. Anna and Eli were given the house as a wedding gift.

"Oh, how nice. Who was that?" Anna asked. She did not look up from slicing fresh carrots she had bought earlier in the day.

"Cole Herbert," Bannister replied. "He's staying at The Palace Hotel."

Anna stopped slicing upon hearing Cole's name.

"How do you know about Cole?" she asked, "I've never spoken to you about him."

"Your uncle told me about him. It must have been about a year ago, just after we were married," Bannister replied. "It was a name he thought I should remember."

"Why did he say that?" Anna asked.

Bannister just shrugged his shoulders and smiled.

"You know your Uncle Bear," Bannister began, "he only wants what's best for his Anna."

Anna was very uncomfortable with her husband's response. For some time now she had noticed a pattern of incomplete answers from Bannister. He did not seem to be the person she thought she had married. It wasn't that she didn't love him, but that he was so mysterious about his daily activities in the important job her uncle had helped him to get. Anna's Uncle Bear did not have any formal position in the city government himself, but he seemed to be well connected, able to help get people he wanted into important positions. Why so secretive? she wondered about her husband.

* * *

The next few days were uneventful as far as it pertained to Sal Gregorio, Eli Bannister, or the tax collectors. Cole, Chad, Leroy and Bertram spent their days visiting different parts of the city and its surrounding areas. Bertram was especially taken with the Pacific Coast on the west side of San Francisco. The never-ending view of the ocean disappearing over the horizon was a bit scary to Bertram, who did not consider himself comfortable in water that went over his head.

The morning of December 4th, 1896, Cole was reading in *The San Francisco Call* a news report on the previous night's fight between Fitzsimmons and Sharkey. Apparently, referee Wyatt Earp disqualified Fitzsimmons due to hitting Sharkey with a low blow. The decision was quite controversial, according to the paper.

It was nearing 8:00 in the morning. Leroy and Bertram had long gone downstairs to the dining hall for breakfast. Cole and Chad were beginning to settle into city life by sleeping later in the morning. Leroy began to tease the younger men by telling them that a man who let the sun beat them out of bed might as well sleep the day away, as there wasn't enough of the day left at that point to be useful.

A knock at the door was answered by Chad. A bellhop had a telegraph for Cole.

"It's for you," Chad said, handing the paper to Cole, who was sitting in a chair.

Cole opened and read the telegraph in silence. He clutched it in his hand as a curious expression developed on his face. He looked up at Chad who was across the room, putting on his boots.

"It's from Anna," Cole told Chad.

"Anna!" said Chad.

"She wants to meet me in front of a printing shop, Pernau Brothers, on the corner of Kearny and Commercial Streets," Cole explained.

"Why would she want to meet with you, and why there?" asked Chad.

"I don't know," answered Cole, "I don't know what to make of it."

"You gonna go?" Chad wanted to know.

"I think I will," Cole said, sounding confused as he spoke.

"You want me to come with you?" asked Chad.

"No, I think I'll go alone. I'll see what she wants," Cole said. He put the telegraph down on the table next to his chair. Cole was already dressed, so he grabbed his duster and hat.

"Better take this too," Chad said, holding out Cole's holstered pistol.

Cole thought for a moment, then put his hand out and took the gun from Chad. He strapped on his shoulder holster before putting his duster over it. Cole walked out the front of The Palace Hotel, and hopped in a carriage that was one of four waiting out front for hotel guests seeking to get around the city. He gave the driver instructions, and the carriage began to move immediately.

Reaching the corner of Kearny and Commercial Streets was a short ride, but Cole was not familiar with the location and didn't take the time to ask for directions. He was there within ten minutes. The carriage stopped and Cole got out and tipped the driver, who didn't wait around. Following a quick snap of the reins, the carriage was gone. Cole stood at the corner, looking in all directions for Anna. There were a few people walking the streets that morning, but a cold wind was keeping many inside. Anna was no where in sight. Nearly twenty minutes passed, but still no Anna. Cole looked up and saw that he was in front of Pernau Brothers, the shop Anna mentioned in her telegraph. He decided to go inside to see if anyone knew of Anna. A bell that was attached to the door chimed as Cole opened it. Before he could close the door, he was grabbed from both sides. Cole quickly recognized the man on his left as one of the tax collectors. Before he could look to his right, he was hit from behind. His knees buckled and he slid to the floor, unconscious. The two tax collectors left Cole on the floor for a couple of minutes. When a buckboard pulled up out front, they lifted him off the floor, and carried Cole outside, loading him in the back of the buckboard. The third man inside, the one who hit him on the head, covered him with a tarp, then all three men jumped in the back of the buckboard, while two more sat up front. The buckboard drove off.

* * *

Shortly after Cole left the hotel, Chad joined Leroy and Bertram downstairs for breakfast and told them about the telegraph. Leroy immediately became suspicious.

"I don't understand. Just a note to meet her? After all these years, and with the bad blood sitting between them. Doesn't sound right to me," Leroy hypothesized.

By the time Chad arrived downstairs, Leroy and Bertram were having one last cup of coffee. They had long finished breakfast.

"You finish on up," Leroy instructed Chad, "then we ought to go have a look around for Cole."

With a plan made, Leroy and Bertram went upstairs to get ready to leave. Chad ate a quick breakfast consisting of biscuits and bacon. He took a few gulps of his lukewarm coffee, and was no more than five minutes behind them heading back upstairs. Chad put his pistol on under his duster, just like Cole had done. With hat in hand, he reached for the door. Before he could grab the knob, another knock was heard. It startled him for a second. Chad waited a moment, then opened the door.

"Hello, Chad," she said.

"Hello, Anna," Chad replied.

"I asked downstairs for your room number. I told them I was your sister here to visit. I hope you don't mind," Anna explained how she found the room.

"How did you know where we were staying?" asked Chad.

"Well, I heard my . . . ," she began before pausing.

"We know about your husband," Chad acknowledged.

"Eli mentioned that he ran into Cole. I also heard him talking with some men who work for him that you were staying at *The Palace Hotel*," Anna told Chad. "Chad, I never even told Eli about Cole. He says he found out about him from my uncle. Something doesn't seem right. I don't know that I can trust Eli anymore. I had to come and see Cole. Is he here?"

A strange look crossed Chad's face when he heard Anna's question.

"He went to meet you," Chad told her.

"What? Where did he go?" she said.

Both she and Chad now wore expressions of confusion. Chad went to the table across the room and picked up the telegraph Cole had received. He showed it to Anna. By this time, Leroy and Bertram were standing in the hallway, behind Anna. Both were armed, though carrying their weapons beneath their dusters. Startled, Anna turned around.

"Anna, this here is Leroy and Bertram," Chad introduced the rest of the Bar-CJ to her.

Upon hearing her name, both men knew who she was.

"I thought you were meeting Cole?" Leroy spoke up quickly.

"No," Anna answered, "Chad just showed me this telegraph, but it didn't come from me."

"We thought that might be the case," said Leroy, "we're on our way out to find Cole now. You ready?" Leroy asked Chad.

"Yep, let's get going," he replied.

Anna followed the three men downstairs as they walked directly to the nearest carriage. There was always one available outside of the hotel.

"I'd like to come with you," Anna spoke up.

"Don't know that that would be a good idea," Chad told her.

"Please, Chad," she pleaded.

"Might be that she could help us if Cole ain't where he's supposed to be," Leroy said. "Climb aboard ma'am."

Leroy directed the carriage driver to the corner of Kearny and Commercial Streets, the location where Cole was to meet Anna. When they arrived, the corner was now busy with people moving along the city streets, but no Cole. Chad went inside Pernau Brothers to see if Cole might be inside. He described Cole to the cashier and asked if he had seen Cole. The cashier replied that he hadn't. Chad turned to leave and join the rest waiting outside for him. As he reached the door, he noticed off to his right, behind a free standing barrel, was Cole's hat. Chad walked over and picked it up. He returned to the cashier with Cole's hat in his left hand. In his right hand was his colt revolver, hammer cocked.

"Didn't know printers sold hats like this? Chad asked, his voice ringing with sarcasm. The cashier remained silent, but the look on his face told Chad that he was frightened. Chad slowly pushed the barrel of his pistol forward, landing softly against the cashier's forehead, between his eyes.

"Likely I don't have to describe my friend to you again," Chad said, "and I don't like to have to ask more than once. Was he here?" The cashier took a big, audible gulp, then slowly nodded his head yes.

"Where is he now?" Chad continued.

"I don't know," replied the cashier, "three men came in here this morning and told me they would be waiting for a friend. They were mean looking guys. I've seen them bully others in the neighborhood, so I didn't protest. When your friend came in, they bushwhacked him and dragged him out to a wagon. They loaded him in and drove off. I don't know any more about it, mister."

"If you're wrong about any of those facts, I'll find out and I'll be back," Chad promised, giving the man one more chance to alter his story if need be.

"That's the truth, I swear," the cashier assured Chad, who quickly holstered his pistol and turned for the door.

He told the others the story the cashier had told him.

"What now?" Bertram wanted to know.

"Ma'am, I'm going to speak frankly to you," said Leroy as he faced Anna. "Your husband or your uncle, maybe both, is responsible for this. If you really want to help us get Cole back, tell us where they might have taken him."

Anna was confused and felt as though her head was spinning out of control. She couldn't understand how her husband or uncle could be involved in kidnapping Cole, just as she never believed that her uncle was responsible for the plight of Cole's parent's. None of this made any sense to her.

"Anna," Chad said, "we need your help. Could be they're not involved," he said in reference to Bannister and Gregorio, though he didn't really believe it, "but we need to check all possibilities, and right now, it's the best we got to go on."

Leroy could see how difficult this was for Anna, and he tried to balance allowing her time to think while describing to her the urgency of initiating their search.

"Let me ask you," Leroy began, "is Gregorio in the city? Have you seen him?"

"No, I haven't seen my uncle in a week or more, but he's spending most of his time living in San Francisco now," she responded.

"Does either he or your husband have a place, maybe out of the way, where they might meet with others?" Leroy pressed with another question.

Anna tried to slow down her thought process enough to think clearly.

"I've heard my husband talk about a warehouse down near The Presidio. One night at our house, he was meeting with some of his men, and when I brought them refreshments, I heard him mention this place that my uncle had let him use," Anna thoughtfully divulged.

"Do you know where it is?" asked Leroy.

"I'm not sure. I've never been there," she answered, "but I might be able to find it according to their description."

Leroy had required the carriage to wait for them. They all climbed aboard and told the driver to head for The Presidio, quickly.

* * *

The cold winds from earlier in the day had brought on a winter storm that arrived late in the morning. Cole could hear the rain hitting the building outside. He had regained his consciousness, but he had not yet opened his eyes. He could hear men around him, speaking, but he chose not do divulge his awakened state until he could better ascertain his surroundings. At present, he did not know where he was, not that it would be all that helpful for him to know, he concluded. He was lying on the floor with his hands tied behind his back, but his feet were free and his mouth was left without a gag in it.

"What we gonna do with him, Eli?" Cole heard a man ask.

"Nothing for the moment. Our instructions were to wait, so we'll wait," responded Bannister. Cole recognized his voice.

Cole could tell from the echo in the building that it was big, and likely, mostly empty. It was cold and damp inside. His duster and gun had been stripped from him. He estimated that he had been awake for about fifteen minutes when he heard a door open, and felt the light from outside reflect off his face. He continued to feign an unconscious state. He listened as the boot steps approached where he was laying on the floor. They stopped in front of him. Suddenly, Cole felt an immense pain as a boot was planted with a hard kick into his midsection. Caught of guard, Cole let out a grunt.

"Ah, it appears as though our visitor is now awake," said a voice all too familiar to Cole. It was Sal Gregorio.

Cole opened his eyes and tried to catch his breath that the kick had taken away from him.

"Welcome to my humble place of business, young Mr. Herbert," said a smiling Gregorio. "Consider my welcome to you an evening for the punch you landed on me a few years back."

"Now that we're even," coughed Cole, "I guess I can go now."

"Ah, but I never allow someone to just be even with me," Gregorio responded to Cole's wisecrack, "I must come out ahead. That is why we will now hang you."

Gregorio now had Cole's full attention.

"How are you going to explain my hanging, once Anna finds out I'm dead?" Cole tried to reason.

"A good question, Mr. Herbert. Although San Francisco is not the lawless town it was of years ago, there is still plenty of illegal activity to blame a hanging on. The wharf is full of cut throats, and then there are the Mexican bandits or the Chinamen, the possibilities are endless," Gregorio said.

"Let's do this the old-fashioned way, like in the gold fields," Gregorio directed. "Eli, put him on a horse," he told Bannister.

For the first time, Cole looked around the warehouse and saw the group of men. In addition to Gregorio and Bannister were the six tax collectors who had dined at *The Flying Fin*.

Bannister led a bay horse by the reins over to where Cole laid on the floor. Ironically, the horse looked very much like Cole's old horse, Slinger. Cole looked up and saw the open rafters about twelve feet above him. One of the tax collectors produced a rope; the hangman's noose was already in place. Gregorio nodded, and the tax collector threw the noose over a rafter, catching the noose as it came flying back down the other side.

"Help him up, boys," directed Bannister, who appeared to enjoy taking the lead in the proceedings, not realizing he would only do what Gregorio wanted to be done.

While one tax collector held the noose, and Bannister the horse, two other tax collectors picked up Cole by the arms. As he stood, Cole turned to his right and head butted the man in the nose, causing him to loosen his grip on Cole's arm. Cole jerked away, turned to his left and kneed the other man in the groin, allowing him to break free from both tax collectors. Cole began to run for the door, only as fast as his game right leg would allow, but put just twenty-five feet between him and Gregorio, when he felt a sharp, burning sensation in the back of his right thigh. Cole tumbled to the floor, unable to grab for his leg with his hands still tied behind his back. He rolled back and forth, in agony over being shot. He caught a glance of Gregorio and saw that he had been shot by Anna's uncle with his father's old pistol. Two other men who had not been injured by Cole, ran to him and picked him up from the floor. Cole did his best not to scream from the pain. They dragged Cole back to the horse, and placed him in its saddle.

"You're just as I remember your father," said Gregorio as Cole was being placed in the saddle, "you like to make things difficult."

Cole looked down at Gregorio who was standing to the horse's right, while Bannister stood, holding the noose, near its left flank. Cole looked down at Gregorio, despising the smiling face looking back up at him. Capable of nothing else, Cole leaned down and spit in Gregorio's face, causing Gregorio's smile to disappear. Gregorio wiped away the spit with his jacket sleeve, and looked back up at Cole, this time with a menacing look on his face.

"Put the noose around his neck," said a glaring Gregorio.

* * *

As their carriage approached The Presidio, Anna looked closely at the many warehouses and other buildings she saw. Nothing was looking familiar to her. They began a second trip around the perimeter of The Presidio, when Chad looked down a side street and saw a buckboard with a horse, sitting in front of an old, worn down looking building.

"Stop here," said Chad, forcefully but not too loud, not wanting to give away their presence. The carriage driver stopped.

"Look there," Chad said, pointing towards the buckboard. "Back at the print shop, the cashier said Cole was taken away in a wagon. Maybe he meant a smaller buckboard. And why would a buckboard be sitting out front with a horse?"

"Anybody be done would tend ta da horse properly," added Bertram.

Anna sat motionless.

"What is it, Anna?" Chad asked. She paused before answering.

"That's our buckboard," she said softly without taking her eyes off of it. Her eyes began to tear.

"You wait here," Leroy directed Anna as he climbed down from the carriage. "Stay put," he told the carriage driver.

Chad and Bertram climbed down as soon as they saw Leroy move. The three were a good couple of hundred feet away from the warehouse where the buckboard sat.

"What's we gonna do?" asked Bertram, suddenly realizing they had been so consumed with finding Cole, that they had not made a plan of what to do once they found him.

"If its Bannister, we can expect those tax collectors to likely be with him, and maybe Gregorio, too," said Leroy, "but I don't think we have time for a long, drawn out plan," he added as he pulled his rifle from beneath his duster. Bertram produced his shotgun, and Chad put his Colt revolver in his hand. "Chad and I will go through that door there," Leroy said pointing to the door next to where the buckboard sat. "Bertram, see if you can find another entrance around the far side. We go in ready to start shooting. Don't hesitate if it needs to be done."

As they reached the front corner of the building, Leroy pointed to the right, where he spotted another entrance and was directing Bertram to go. Bertram began to move quickly, but as quietly as a man of his size could. Leroy and Chad reached the other door a few seconds later.

Waterhole

"Ready?" Leroy whispered.

"Yeah, lets go find Cole," Chad answered.

Leroy opened the door slowly, hoping not to make any sound, but the old wooden slat would not cooperate. The door was nearly open when it let out a squeak. The squeak coincided with Bannister placing the noose around Cole's neck. When the door's noise attracted the attention of those inside the building, Gregorio gave the bay horse a hard slap on its right flank. It bolted suddenly, leaving Cole swinging from the rope. Chad was startled to see Cole swinging; he froze, not remembering what to do. Leroy fired the first shot, dropping one of the tax collectors instantly. After the first shot, Bertram entered from the side, and seeing Cole struggling, kicking his feet, he ran for him, drawing out his Bowie knife as he did. Cole's face was purple, and his eyes began to bulge as Bertram reached him. Cole hung low enough for Bertram, using all of his 6'4" frame to be able to reach up and cut the rope with one swipe.

Leroy and Chad's entrance had drawn the full attention of the men inside, allowing Bertram to reach Cole unnoticed. But as Cole slumped to the floor, two of the tax collectors turned and saw Bertram, each one had a pistol. Holding his shotgun with a single hand, he fired one barrel into the smaller tax collector who had worn the green suit, sending him flying backwards with a large hole in his stomach. He was killed instantly. Bertram reached down and cut the rope that had bound Cole's hands. Cole was beginning to cough as he did. For the first time, Bertram knew that Cole was alive.

As Bertram looked up, the big tax collector, the one who they had seen in the restaurant approached Bertram and Cole, gun drawn and pointed. He extended his arm and fired at Bertram, but the gun misfired, causing the man to drop it, his gun-hand burning.

The big tax collector continued to approach Bertram.

"Let's see how tough you are, black man," he said.

"No time fer dat now," Bertram responded and he emptied the last barrel from his shotgun into the big man's face. He fell over like a giant oak tree. Half of his face was gone.

Bannister had hid behind a crate when the shooting started. He was firing in the direction of Chad, but didn't appear to be an accurate shot, fortunately for Chad, who was slow to collect his senses after seeing Cole swinging from the rope.

Leroy dropped the tax collector named Slim, with a bullet in his left shoulder. It was a severe enough wound to render him useless in the fight.

Once Chad gathered his senses, he was able to drop two tax collectors with his Colt. Both of them fell dead. He had only used five shots. The last tax collector standing was the best shot of the bunch. He shot a round that grazed Chad's scalp. Chad staggered towards the door, then tumbled to the ground across the threshold, his Colt pistol flying from his hand out the door. He then turned on Bertram. The big man stood with two empty barrels in his shotgun. He flung the Bowie knife at the shooter, but missed badly. The tax collector took slow aim and placed his bullet in the middle of Bertram's chest. Bertram didn't move. The shooter fired again, and again. Bertram's knees began to buckle, but he remained on his feet. The fourth shot finally caused Bertram to fall, face down, dead.

Leroy was occupied with Bannister, each exchanging shots, neither finding his mark. Seeing Bertram fall, Leroy spent his final round firing at Bertram's killer, striking him in the side of his neck. Blood gushed from the fatal wound as the last tax collector fell.

Cole was beginning to gather his senses. He slowly raised his head, and saw Bertram lying next to him on the floor. Bertram's eyes were open, but Cole recognized immediately that his friend was dead. He looked around the warehouse and saw bodies strewn across the building, including Chad's on the far side. Cole's eyes began to blur, so he closed them momentarily, before opening them again. He saw that there were two men, one firing shots at the other. He recognized Leroy, and the one doing the shooting as Bannister. Leroy did not have cover, but Bannister was shielded by a large crate.

Cole continued to look around. Not far from where he lay, he saw his pistol lying on the floor. He crawled towards it, and reached it just as Bannister realized that Leroy was out of bullets and came out from behind his crate, pistol pointed at Leroy.

"Should have left town when you had the chance, old man," Bannister said confidently, thinking he was the only one left with ammunition.

"And miss out on the opportunity to see you taken down," Leroy said, "wouldn't have missed it."

"I'd say you will miss it, and besides, it ain't gonna happen," replied Bannister. He continued to walk towards Leroy, pointing his pistol as he walked.

Cole had risen to his feet and began to move slowly up from behind Bannister, his old army pistol pointed at Anna's husband. His right leg was dragging all the way, allowing Bannister to hear him approaching. Bannister turned and pointed his pistol at Cole, a fearful expression across his face. He fired once, but missed.

Cole was having difficulty keeping his balance, but was a superior marksman to Bannister. He fired once, striking Bannister in the heart. He fell over on his side and lay dead.

No sooner had Bannister hit the ground than Cole heard another shot. He looked up and saw Leroy fall to the ground. Standing behind Leroy, in the doorway, was Gregorio. He had shot Leroy in the back, just like he had Joshua Rines.

As soon as the shooting had started, Gregorio had slipped out of the warehouse, waiting to see the outcome of the fight. He decided it was time for him to join back in.

Only Cole and Gregorio were left standing in the warehouse. Gregorio kept his rifle pointed at Cole as he proceeded cautiously towards him.

"You Herbert's are hard to get rid of," Gregorio spoke.

"Not so hard when you back shoot us," Cole countered.

"Since this isn't Waterhole, I expect by now someone has summoned the police. It's time for me to go. Goodbye, Mr. Herbert," Gregorio said as he raised his rifle.

Cole heard a shot and simultaneously closed his eyes. His breath was coming quickly and shallow, but he was still standing. Cole opened his eyes and saw Gregorio face down on the floor. He looked up to see Anna standing in the doorway, tears running down her face as she dropped the pistol to the floor and fell to her knees, sobbing.

* * *

Gregorio had been right. When the police arrived, they found ten dead bodies, and a wounded Chad and Cole. Cole had not realized that Chad was still alive. The police saw that one of the dead men was a San Francisco Commissioner, and hauled Cole and Chad off to the city jail, injuries notwithstanding.

Anna was left to fend for herself. She quickly gathered her strength, sought out the carriage driver who had brought them to the warehouse, and directed him where to take her.

The following morning, into the jail walked Joe Corbett, in as bad a mood as if someone had just hit a home run off of him. He was followed by two men.

"I'm here to get Cole Herbert and Chad Henry. I want to see them now," ordered Joe.

The jailer looked at the two men accompanying Joe and did what he was told. The jailer led the three men to the cell where Cole and Chad were being held on murder charges. A doctor had been called upon the previous evening to tend to their wounds. Chad's head had been patched up, but the bullet still resided in Cole's leg.

Cole and Chad heard the men coming down the hallway outside their cell. Cole smiled when he heard Joe's voice in its dictatorial tone. The jailer stopped when they reached Cole and Chad. Joe stood before them, as did Wyatt Earp and Detective Isaiah W. Lees.

Anna had summoned Joe directly after leaving the warehouse to let him know what happened. Once they found out about the murder charges against his friends, Joe went for Detective Lees, while his brother, Jim, found Wyatt Earp.

"Open the cell," Joe ordered the jailer, who was becoming annoyed at taking orders from Joe. But the jailer had already received instructions that charges against the two had been dropped, and told them so as he opened the cell door.

"You boys okay?" asked Detective Lees.

"Yes sir, it sure is good to see you again," answered Cole.

"This is my friend, Chad Henry," Cole introduced the pair, "Chad, meet Detective Isaiah W. Lees."

The two nodded at each other kindly.

"I sure glad you two were in the city," Cole told the former marshal and his detective friend. "Facing murder charges wasn't a pleasant thought."

"I'm sorry to hear about Leroy and Bertram, Cole," Joe said solemnly. "They were good men."

Cole was quiet as he thought about losing his two old friends.

"The last family I had," Cole said softly. "Where are they now?"

"They're down at the city morgue," answered Earp.

"What are you going to do?" asked Chad.

"Take 'em home and bury them next to my folks and Joshua," Cole said matter-of-factly. "It's where they belong."

Cole and Chad were taken to Joe's house. All their belongings, as well as Leroy's and Bertram's, were collected from *The Palace Hotel*, and the bill paid for. Cole never learned by whom. A doctor was summoned to take the bullet out of Cole's leg, and the extraction was successful. Cole had been given so much chloroform that he didn't waken for three hours following the surgery, during which time Chad and Joe made the arrangements to transport Leroy and Bertram home on the train.

Cole and Chad had been three days at Joe's when they decided it was time to get Leroy and Bertram home the following day. The three friends had been sitting, sharing thoughts their last evening together, and all feeling guilty for what had happened; Cole for being captured, Chad for losing consciousness, and Joe for not having been there to help. Before they adjourned for the night, they agreed to accept what happened and not try to rationalize how it could have been different. It just was.

The next morning, Cole was downstairs before Chad. Joe was in the kitchen, helping Mrs. Corbett prepare breakfast.

"You'll make Mary a fine wife," Cole teased his old roommate. "I'm really sorry I haven't been able to meet her, and that we can't stay for the wedding," he said, his tone changing, "I know it's only a day away, but . . ."

"Don't think twice about it, Cole, I know . . . ," Joe told him. "Besides," he continued in an upbeat voice, "Mary and I will be out there to visit that Oklahoma ranch of yours soon enough, I promise."

Mrs. Corbett had left the kitchen to set the dining room table. Cole needed to know something.

"How's Anna?" Cole asked. It had been five days since the shooting. Both her husband and uncle were dead.

"I don't know," answered Joe. "After she came to get me, she disappeared. I don't know where she is. Detective Lees went to check on her at her house, but no one was there. He's looking out for her."

Mr. Corbett and Jim had loaded the carriage that would take them to the train. Leroy and Bertram had already been loaded aboard, earlier in the morning.

Following breakfast, Cole and Chad said their goodbyes to the Corbett's. It was particularly difficult for Cole to say goodbye to Joe. The two roommates looked at each other. Cole began to feel his throat swelling up. He couldn't talk. Tears began to well up in his eyes, as they did in Joe's. The two hugged each other. His right leg still a long ways from mended, Joe helped Cole aboard the carriage.

* * *

When Cole sat down in the train opposite of Chad, he felt as though his whole world was in a state of confusion. He had come to San Francisco for Joe's wedding and left with two dear friends dead. Other than the soon to be five family gravesites, Cole wondered what the Bar-CJ held for him anymore.

The train was less than half full as the conductor hollered, "all aboard!" from the platform. Chad was already fast asleep.

"Mind if I sit here?" asked a quiet voice.

Cole looked up. Standing in the aisle was Anna. She had the same uncertain look on her face that Cole was feeling.

Seeing Anna suddenly drained all of his energy yet made his heart jump at the same time. Cole put his hand out and Anna took it.

"Are you sure? This train's headed for Oklahoma," Cole asked.

A tear fell from Anna's eye into Cole's lap. He had his answer.

Epilogue

Though *Waterhole* is a work of fiction, numerous historical characters in the story lived at the time and in the location in which they appear throughout the book. Their roles in Waterhole are fictionalized.

Wyatt Earp and Bat & Ed Masterson did serve as peace officers in Dodge City, and Wyatt Earp was in San Francisco in December of 1896 to referee the Fitzsimmons-Sharkey heavyweight boxing match.

Joe Corbett did play baseball at St. Mary's College before playing professionally, and was the brother of heavyweight boxing champion, "Gentleman Jim" Corbett.

Isaiah W. Lees was a San Francisco police detective.

Throughout the story, base ball is written as two separate words, as it was in the time period in which *Waterhole* takes place. It wasn't until the beginning of the 20th century that baseball was commonly written as one word.